"If you've never read a Vivian Arend book you are missing out on one of the best contemporary authors writing today."
~ *Book Reading Gals*

"The bitter cold of Alberta, Canada, is made toasty warm by the super-sexy Coleman brothers of Six Pack Ranch."
~ *Publishers Weekly*

"Brilliant, raw, imaginative, irresistible!!"
~ *Avon Romance*

"This story will keep you reading from the first page to the last one. There is never a dull moment..."
~ *Landy Jimenez*

"I definitely recommend to fans of contemporaries with hot cowboys and strong family ties.."
~ *SmexyBooks*

"This was my first Vivian Arend story, and I know I want more! "
~ *Red Hot Plus Blue Reads*

"In this steamy new episode in the "Six Pack Ranch" series, Trevor is a true cowboy hero and will make any reader's heart beat a little faster as he and Becky discover what being a couple is all about."
~ *Library Journal Starred Review*

A RANCHER'S HEART

STONES OF HEART FALLS: BOOK 1

VIVIAN AREND

This is a work of fiction. Names, characters, places, and incidents either are the product of the author's imagination or are used fictitiously, and any resemblance to any persons, living or dead, business establishments, events, or locales is entirely coincidental.

A Rancher's Heart
Copyright © 2017 by Arend Publishing Inc.
ISBN: 9781976328268
Edited by Anne Scott
Cover Design © Sofie Hartley of Hart & Bailey Design Co.
Proofed by Lynda Ryba

1

October, Silver Stone ranch

*C*aleb Stone ran like hell.

He wasn't prone to moving at high speeds, and he sure didn't think jogging was a thing any red-blooded man did for entertainment, but at that moment, running wasn't about anything except survival. Caleb tucked in his chin, pumped his arms and drove his feet into the ground, sprinting full-out toward the nearest fence.

Two feet away he dove, thrusting his hands forward to propel himself through the metal railings.

He went down hard, body slamming into the dust and mud outside the pen.

The furious bull on his heels jerked to a stop inches from the fence, snorting a final warning. The beast glared between the rails as if daring Caleb to step back into *his* territory.

Check out the new bull, will you? Caleb could hear his brother Luke's request. Fine. The beast was checked, and it appeared he was wildly cranky and not too pleased with his new owners.

"Impressive bit of flying."

Caleb rolled to stare at the sky, ignoring the pain in his body. If he lay there for long enough, his annoying baby brother might find something better to do.

Unfortunately, good sense didn't come in large packages amongst his five younger siblings. Neither did the concept of showing a man mercy when he was down.

Dark brown eyes in a familiar, yet younger version of his own face stared back as Dustin leaned over, his amused smirk far too broad considering the kid was only nineteen, a full sixteen years Caleb's junior.

Caleb raised a brow, deliberately offering as little emotion as possible. As if he were lying on his backside because that was exactly where he meant to be. "Need something?"

Dustin shook his head before changing his mind and nodding. "Luke's looking for you. He's in the main barn."

Caleb got to his feet, clenching his teeth to keep from moaning as a sharp pain shot through his ribs. Nothing was broken—*that* sensation was familiar to him as well. He'd only banged and bumped himself this go-around, but no way he was going to give any of the young punks he worked with the satisfaction of knowing how much taking a tumble had begun to hurt.

He wasn't old. Thirty-five wasn't old, damn it.

"I'll be there in a minute." He checked his watch then eyed Dustin. "How come you're not working?"

Dustin grinned. "I am working. Luke's got me doing fence checks for the rest of the afternoon. You were kinda on the way to where I left the quad."

His little brother—the kid was as tall as Caleb but still had a few years of filling out to do—adjusted his hat then sauntered off, whistling. Moving slowly, but at least in the right direction.

Caleb recovered his own hat before heading the opposite way, picking up the reins from where he'd ground-tethered his horse. He swung a leg over her back and turned toward the barn.

Dustin wasn't a bad kid. For all Caleb's concerns about having to raise his siblings after his parents had died suddenly in a car crash, they'd all turned out pretty good. A little more reckless than Caleb appreciated. Like Walker, brother number three, who was currently on the circuit risking his fool neck.

Though, they were all fools. Ranching was a potshot—success subject to the whims of weather and the ever-changing price of livestock. There were no guarantees at the end of the day.

The only certain things were chores and bills.

Luke joined him as he entered the barn, his far too astute brother giving him a close once-over before grinning. "What'd you think of the new bull?"

Caleb held his expression in check. "Seemed sound enough."

Luke nodded. "I thought he was moving a little uneasy. Slightly lame on the foreside."

Not that Caleb had noticed, but then it was hard to judge a beast's gait while fleeing for your life in front of the working end of the horns rather than admiring from a safe distance.

"Keep an eye on it," he ordered. "What's up?"

Luke's easygoing smile faded. "I've been double-checking our feed supply, and depending on how hard a winter we get, things might get tight. We're running more head this year, and with the floods two springs ago, we lost a lot of ground."

Caleb let his brother talk him through what they had stockpiled, but he couldn't remember enough details from the previous year to give a firm answer off the top of his head. "All the records are in the office. I'll check them, but at this point there's not much we can do except hope for the best."

Luke nodded. "Just thought I should mention it."

The two of them paced through the main barn in companionable silence. The familiar posts and beams that formed their playground growing up was now a base that provided their adult living.

"The new nanny gets here today, right?"

The topic Caleb'd been trying hard not to obsess over—the upheaval in the household about to take place. While he was desperately happy there would be someone to help take care of Sasha and Emma, Caleb was damn sure this was the worst-great idea he'd ever agreed to.

Those little girls were his sunshine and light. Now nine and seven, it had been four years since he and their mother had divorced. Sasha had accepted the change with stoic resignation, but Emma had gone quieter than before. She'd never been a huge chatterbox, but now she rarely spoke, and never to strangers.

Still, they knew he loved them—he made sure of that each and every day. Hiring a full-time nanny was supposed to fill in the missing gaps and help keep everything in their worlds spinning right.

That made the coming awkwardness bearable, because Tamara—

Yeah, it was going to be awkward.

"Said she'd be here by evening."

Luke nodded. "You must be looking forward to having a woman around the place again."

Caleb held his tongue as he headed to the nearest horse and bent to check its hooves so he didn't have to look his brother in the face. Tamara Coleman, the soon-to-arrive nanny, was most definitely a woman to look forward to. Bold yet feminine, just the way he liked. Soft edges and bright spark, luscious and...and he adjusted position uncomfortably.

Didn't that just figure? The first woman to tempt him since

his wife had left, and she had to be the most hands-off prospect around.

He stuck to the facts. "It'll be good to have her here. The girls need a woman's touch in their lives. God knows I'm not the one to give it to them."

Luke snorted but he didn't move, waiting until Caleb had to put the hoof down or look like a fool.

The instant their eyes met Luke shook a finger at him. "You might not have a woman's touch, whatever the hell that means, but those girls love you. You're a damn good daddy to them, so don't go putting yourself down. It's not your fault you've had to be both mom and dad."

"I appreciate the good word, but the truth is a guy can only go so far raising a couple of little girls. And now that Ginny and Dare are gone—"

His sister and foster sister had done more than they ever should've since his wife left, but they'd both moved out earlier that fall. One to travel, one to set up her own home.

"You're doing the right thing getting a nanny in full time." Amusement danced in Luke's eyes. "I'm just saying your girls aren't the only ones who'd appreciate a woman's touch right about now."

Luke's comments were cutting him to the core. Caleb and Tamara's first meeting had been brief, but memorable. Mostly because he spent the nights *after* their encounter tangled up in lustful dreams. Long, dark brown hair, flashing eyes, curves that didn't quit. Curves that made him daydream about learning her so thoroughly he could move over her with his eyes closed.

Would Caleb appreciate the woman's touch right about now? *Fuck.*

Caleb ignored the answer he wasn't about to give. "This is not about having a woman in the house for anything other than being a nanny. Make that clear to anyone who says otherwise."

Although he was bull-shitting himself pretending the thought of Tamara being around wasn't enough to make his libido kick into overdrive. "I don't want her spooked off before we even give this a chance."

"You won't spook her—you're solid and predictable." Luke smacked him on the shoulder. "I'll make sure I remind the hands again, and I'm taken, so you'll just have to warn off Walker when he gets home. Oh, and Dusty."

"She's nearly thirty," Caleb drawled. "You really think she'd be interested in Dustin?"

"He may be young, but he's a Stone." Luke waggled his brows. "The ladies like us."

Caleb resisted rolling his eyes. "You're so full of shit."

Luke just grinned harder.

A quick check of his watch poked Caleb into action. "I need to get moving to finish before the girls are home from school."

His brother considered. "You know what? I'll take a break and meet the bus. I haven't seen the girls in a few days, and I'll be gone next week. Let me take care of them. Once you're done working, go grab a little freedom before you have to get your new employee all trained up."

New employee. *God.*

Caleb wasn't sure if it was a blessing or curse, but he nodded. "Spaghetti sauce is in the crockpot, so you don't need anything—"

Luke waved a hand. "I can figure it out," he said easily. "Ginny and Dare aren't the only ones who've spent time taking care of your kids."

An arrow of guilt shot straight through Caleb, the barbs on the shaft slicing hard.

Luke must've seen him cringe. "Hey, that wasn't a complaint. I'm damn glad to spend time as Uncle Luke. But you should go before I change my mind and make you do my chores in exchange."

Caleb slapped him on the shoulder in thanks.

He finished a couple tasks in the barn over the next hour before using that free time. He let his horse take her head as they wandered toward wherever, thoughts drifting until he realized they were headed to what had to be his favourite spot on the whole Silver Stone ranch.

Obviously, his horse felt the same way as she glided down to the pool at the base of Heart Falls.

The land in this small section was accessible from a road off the public highway, and it had been willed over to the community. The family had placed a bench far above the water for people to sit and enjoy the view. On warm summer nights teenagers used the trail to get to the rocks so they could jump into the cool depths, and they'd occasionally ask permission to float down the river that started there and passed through Silver Stone.

Caleb sat on Lacey's back and stared over the water, watching the sun glitter off the water's surface, like sunshine on morning dew. He took a deep breath of the fresh air, and the sound of the falls rolled through him and soothed the tension that had built up.

As head of Silver Stone ranch, he had to make the right decisions. If he screwed up, they could lose it all, but in that moment right there and then, it was if the land itself said *everything is going to be okay.*

God, he hoped it was true.

He closed his eyes and took another deep breath, soaking it in. Feeling calm settle into his soul, and it felt good.

Until it didn't.

An unwelcome sensation stole over him. He slid off his horse, dropping the reins to let her graze as he fought with himself.

How had Luke described him? Solid and predictable? *Fah.* Code words for old and boring. As if the only reason a woman would be willing to come and stay in his house was because he was *safe*.

Which wasn't all bad. Hell if he wanted Tamara, or anyone else to be scared of him, but—

He found himself grasping the bottom of his shirt, lifting it over his head as he toed off his boots and stripped. A full-out grin rose to his cheeks. The water would be icy cold. It was probably the last week of the year before snow fell in earnest, but to hell with logic.

Not known for his impulsive moves? Try this one on for size.

He stepped to the edge of the rocks and stared into the deep blue depths.

I bet Tamara would be daring enough to jump.

The mental tease sent another shot of lust through him along with the naked image of his soon-to-be but very-much-hands-off nanny...

Jeez, now he needed the ice water to cool the fire in his veins.

CONSIDERING voyeurism wasn't one of Tamara's kinks, she'd had more run-ins with nudity than the average woman. Even now as she sat minding her own business, she had to admit the surprise show was proving spectacular.

Shadows cast by the towering pines to the west were playing peekaboo with his face, and he was mostly in profile, but even if the man had been in full sun she was far enough away she wouldn't have been able to spot details like facial features. She had no idea who he was, which meant she didn't know if she should feel guilty for ogling him.

He could be a married man, or the Heart Falls Community Church pastor communing with nature—although if *that* was the local man of the cloth, she was about to have a religious experience.

Ignorance was one benefit of being new to town.

It was also a downfall as she'd have all sorts of *new* to contend with over the next days and weeks. She was mostly looking forward to it. After twenty-nine years in one spot, the idea of a fresh start appealed to her. She was going to miss her family, most of them, but a change had been needed.

Her mystery man was now naked from the waist up, his face hidden in shadows. Solid muscles flexed in his biceps and chest as he shoved his jeans and the rest to the ground. She wished her observation spot on the trail was a little closer to the pool, because while the view was lovely, it was too far away to offer details beyond generalities. Trim hips, strong thighs. Not an inch of fat on him.

She pushed her glasses into place and sighed happily.

Yes, this new beginning was going to work just fine if this was how they did things in Heart Falls.

The star of her floor show stepped to the edge of the rocks and paused long enough for Tamara to take a final, sweet mental snapshot. In appreciation of the human form, like anyone in the medical field would have—

As the man threw himself silently into the water, a bitter taste hit her tongue. She wasn't part of the medical community anymore.

Fired. Out of a job, and what's worse, her nursing certification had been revoked. One well-meant but slightly illegal decision years ago, and it was all over. Illegal, not immoral, she reminded herself. Even knowing the consequences, she'd do it again in a flash.

She watched her current mood-booster take strong strokes across the pool, headed toward the waterfall, as she considered what had really gotten her into the mess. Her impulsive nature, yes. And being too interested in other people's business. She didn't *think* she was a busybody, and she always meant well.

Only when *meaning well* went bad, it soured over everyone. Bottom-line, she needed to change her habits. And this was as good a time as any, considering Heart Falls was a clean slate, and all.

Tamara leaned against the rock behind her, hands resting on her knees. She'd been told about the lookout by her cousin's fiancée, Dare, who used to live in the area. The same friend who'd gotten her the job she was about to start.

The trip to Heart Falls passed quicker than expected, and it was too early to show up at the ranch. From what her friend had told her about the lookout, it had sounded like the perfect place to pause for a final *get her head on straight* opportunity.

I will change, she swore. No matter how tempted she was to act impulsively in the future, she needed to—

Down in the pool, the swimming man had lasted longer than Tamara expected. Hypothermia wasn't something to fool around with, and the water had to be bitterly cold.

He was headed for the rocks, and she breathed a sigh of relief as he placed a hand on an outcropping and pulled himself up.

Her sigh turned into a gasp, and she shot to her feet as the man fell backwards and disappeared beneath the surface. She hesitated for a couple of seconds before heading farther down the path, one eye on her footing and the other on the water surface.

He didn't come up.

By the time she got to the bottom of the trail, Tamara was full-out sprinting, racing around the perimeter of the pool to the rocks he'd originally jumped off. She peered into the water, but couldn't see anything.

Swear words echoed in her head as panic tried to take control.

There. Oh my God, *there*—the hazy shape of an arm.

Tamara shouted for help as loudly as she could as she stepped out of her runners. She dropped her glasses on top of them then took a deep breath, moving to the edge of the rocks.

No hesitation. She threw herself off.

Icy-cold water compressed her chest in a vise. Her face went numb, bare skin tingling as if she were being chewed on by millions of tiny fish with razor-sharp teeth. Panic hovered.

Had she been worried about hypothermia? Forget that— someone would cut their bodies from the ice years from now like preserved wooly mammoths.

She peered around quickly, grateful she'd landed close enough to her target to see him. She snatched at the nearby limb, wrapping her fingers around a thick, solid calf, ready to pull him to safety.

The foot shot out of her grasp straight toward her, connecting with her gut and hip hard enough all the air she'd been holding escaped in a sudden rush. An instant later, stars formed in front of her eyes.

Her only goal was to get to the surface as quickly as possible, but her arms wouldn't move. The only thing keeping her from dragging in a lungful of water was she'd been winded hard enough *nothing* seemed to work.

The stars were fading from bright white points to dark black holes before she summoned every remaining bit of strength, kicking frantically toward the shimmering surface of the water.

Her head broke free. She hauled in a breath through the pain. Gasping sounds echoed in her ears even as other noises registered. Someone else was coughing and sputtering.

Tamara twisted to the right to discover her missing man had made it to the surface. Thank God. She was grateful *and* cautious. Panicky stranger close by in the water? Not what she wanted to deal with when she could barely breathe herself.

She lay back and floated, keeping a watchful eye on the dark-haired blur. He was far enough away she could fend him off if he headed her way and tried to take her down.

It hurt to take a deep enough breath to speak. "You okay?" she forced out shakily.

A string of growled curses mixed with spitting and sputtering floated back to her.

Well, then.

Maybe he was embarrassed at having to be saved, but it was too cold to stay in the pool and deal with the jackass. She headed toward the shore where it would be an easy walk out of the water instead of a climb. No way was she attempting that rock face without her glasses.

"What the hell were you doing?" His question came from a few feet away as she stumbled to vertical, the water up to her waist.

Tamara turned to face him, hands rising to her hips. "Saving your ass? By the way, you're welcome."

"Hauling me under water when I don't expect it is saving my ass?" He took a step closer, his voice going even softer.

Screw this. Tamara retreated farther up the shore. "You're hypothermic enough to be delusional. You fell and didn't come up. You were stuck in the rocks, and I pulled you out."

She slowed her pace, squinting toward the ground to follow the smoothest path to keep from stumbling. Dammit, why didn't she wear contacts instead of glasses?

The grumpy bastard didn't respond, just stepped past her. That wasn't as much fun as it might've been considering she was nearsighted enough that once he'd moved more than a few paces ahead of her, his naked butt was nothing but a spectacular blur.

By the time she made it to the top of the rock, he had his jeans on and was jamming his feet into his boots. They still hadn't exchanged more than a dozen angry words.

Fine. She'd put on her glasses and take a good look at the guy so she'd know which ungrateful jerk to avoid in the future.

"Your shoes are over here," he grumbled, stepping toward the edge of the rocks.

"Be careful. My—"

She couldn't see it happen, but there was nothing wrong with her ears. Breaking glass had a distinctive sound.

He swore again. "Why the hell did you leave your glasses on the ground?"

That was the last straw. Tamara saw red.

All her resolutions to watch her temper, and all her great intentions to keep a new slate shiny clean here in Heart Falls, burned away under the weight of *instant pissed-off*.

"You ever say thank you for anything? Also, you ever consider that when things go wrong, maybe it's *not* someone else's fault?" As she spoke she stepped toward him, anger shoving away the cold. She snatched the tangled remains of her glasses from his fingers, and took one final step so she was close enough to look him in the face as she delivered her closing retort. "Maybe it's *you*."

His dark eyes burned as he stared back, square jaw set in stone. A trickle of water ran from his hair down his cheek, catching on the rough stubble on his chin. Straight nose, far too sensual lips for a man. It was a familiar face, and not one she could possibly avoid in the future.

Because it was him. Caleb Stone, *him*.

AKA, her new boss.

Fuck my life.

2

*I*t seemed some things—like acting far too impulsively and putting her foot in it—would never change.

Still, she didn't think she was in the wrong, but there was no use fighting a battle she had no way of winning. She needed this job, and if that meant groveling, she would swallow her damn pride and do it.

Tamara released a harsh puff of air and prepared to cut out her spleen.

"I wasn't drowning."

His words were a lot softer than she'd expected, and a totally different direction than the "don't bother to unpack your bags because I wouldn't trust you with my children if you were the last woman on earth" retort that she'd have understood.

She stood in shocked silence.

"There's a cave near the base of those rocks," he said, his voice still rumbly but no longer gravel-pit harsh. "Sometimes an air pocket forms in there, and I was checking it out. I had my head above water and was breathing the whole time. Sorry I scared you."

Huh.

"Okay." She curled her fingers around the skeleton of her broken glasses, and fought to keep a shiver from taking her apart. The physical reminder gave the needed distraction to head the conversation into solid, manageable topics. "You need to get dressed and warmed up. It's far too cold to be out here half-naked."

"Agreed. We'd better both get home as quick as we can." He caught her by the wrist and took the broken glasses from her fingers. "But I don't think you can drive without these. Can you?"

Tamara shook her head. "I have spares in my luggage, so don't wor—"

"You're not hiking the trail blind." Caleb folded his arms over his chest.

"I'll be fine," Tamara insisted.

He grunted, then turned and walked away so quickly Tamara was left once again in a foggy blur. She peered around until she found her runners, soft curses escaping as she alternated between stubbing her toes and stepping on sharp-edged rocks.

Once her feet were protected, Tamara put her head down to pick a path best she could, but every third step another stone tilted, threatening to leave her with a sprained ankle, or worse.

Suddenly he was back, solid legs forming a wall in front of her.

"Maybe there's something to that hypothermia thing." He'd pulled on his shirt. "Fortunately, my ride can take an extra, and she doesn't care if you can see or not. Come on, I'll give you a hand."

She expected him to offer a literal hand to hang on to as they crossed to where he had his horse tethered.

Caleb had other ideas. A gasp escaped her as he scooped her up in a firm hold.

"I can walk," she insisted even as her arms flew instinctively to curl around his neck.

"Too slow. It's cold."

Which effectively shut her up. She spent the next few minutes cuddled against an increasingly warm torso, heat rising between them as she tried to find an angle to hold her head that didn't leave her staring straight into his face.

It was better in some ways when he lifted her into the saddle, and in one smooth motion, mounted behind her because then she couldn't see him.

But she could feel him. Rock-solid thighs and all the rest, with her body nestled right up against his. Impossible to ignore exactly how much contact was made while riding double.

He wrapped an arm around her waist, holding the reins confidently in the other hand. Landscape passed as nothing more than fuzzy masses of shades of green. She squinted to try to make out landmarks, but it was nothing but a collection of ranch-shaped blurred objects.

His fingers were spread across her belly, body moving in an easy rhythm as his horse carried them along.

With nothing much to see, it was either stay silent or come up with something to discuss. For a few moments she managed to keep her mouth shut. Only the silence made it too easy for her to focus on the rub of their bodies. They were both wet, and yet they could have been straight out of a sauna with the heat generating between them. The horse's gait created a seductive rhythm that made her feel every moment of her past months of chastity.

Tamara attempted to change position to open space between them, but all it did was rub her hips against his, and a low growl escaped him.

She froze.

He seemed to do a lot of that. The growling business. She didn't want to think too hard about what it did to her insides.

She'd opened her mouth to ask some inane question when he beat her to it. "Your truck and trailer. Are they at the lookout?"

"Truck's at the top of the hill. Trailer's at the weigh station."

"My sister told you about the falls, did she?"

Finally, something distracting. Tamara linked her fingers over the saddle horn and held on with a death grip, trying once again to ease their bodies apart the slightest bit. "Dare told me it was pretty, and I figured I had time to check it out before joining you. Is there a reason it's called Heart Falls? Or is it just named after the town?"

Caleb hesitated before answering. "If you stand on the rocks where I broke your glasses, the waterfall is the center and the lagoon curves apart into two rounds of a heart."

Tamara resisted making a comment about the anatomical incorrectness of calling anything heart-shaped. That kind of humour was usually lost on the nonmedical community. "Sounds a lot more romantic than what most of old-timers would have picked to name a gathering place."

The horse sidestepped, and Caleb tightened his grip, pushing a touch too hard where he'd kicked her.

A gasp of pain escaped before she could stop it.

"What's wrong?" he demanded.

"Just a bit of a bruise."

He didn't say anything more at the time, which was fine by her, and she took the opportunity to change the subject. "Since I'm here early, I don't mind getting started right away."

"I don't think you'll be doing much of anything until we find you some glasses," he pointed out. "We'll get your truck. I can grab your horse trailer while I'm at it, if you'd like."

"Would you? I hate to leave Stormy longer than necessary."

Guilt hit Tamara hard. "I didn't mean to make extra work for you."

"It's not a big deal. I'm the one who broke your glasses."

She sighed. "I'm the one who tried to save you when you didn't need rescuing. Par for the course, I'm afraid to say."

An unexpected chuckle escaped him. "Oh? You go jumping into swimming holes all the time?"

"More like jumping to conclusions, and yeah, I do a fair bit of that." She didn't mention how she'd vowed to change, because her tiger stripes were still firmly in place. "I'm sorry I messed up your quiet relaxation."

"You meant well," he returned easily.

Which made it worse, since that was *exactly* what she needed to change.

He kept talking, his voice stroking her as they rocked together far too smoothly. "We'll get you home and I'll show you your room. There's a shower in there, and you can get warmed up. Before you're done, I'll be back with your stuff. You can meet the girls during supper, but I don't expect you to officially start until tomorrow. We'll take it as it comes."

They were closing in on civilization, the broad shapes of barns and outbuildings becoming visible even with her terrible eyesight. "Thank you."

He grumbled for a moment. "You heard Emma doesn't like to talk, right? She's not mute, just quiet."

"Dare told me. I can handle that."

"I don't want her fixed, or anything. So we're clear—"

God. "Who the hell did you have for a nanny before?" Tamara demanded. "Or did one of her teachers spout this bullshit?"

Caleb sounded relieved and annoyed at the same time as he answered, "One of the babysitters wouldn't let her eat until she asked for every item out loud. Sasha came to the barns to get me, pissed off as a wet cat."

Tamara liked Sasha already. "Good for her. *Fixed.*" She turned the word into a curse. "Don't worry about me. I want to help, and I'm not into torturing children."

He made a low sound that didn't say much while saying a whole lot. "I didn't think you were. My sister thinks the world of you, and that carries a lot of weight. But the girls have gone through a ton of changes in the last couple of months. I don't expect them to be thrilled you're here at first. Let's give it time. Hopefully it'll work out."

He eased back. The horse responded instantly and came to a stop.

Tamara swung her leg over and prepared to jump.

Somehow Caleb dismounted first, his strong hands wrapping around her waist as he lifted her from the saddle and placed her on the ground as if she were a child.

She wasn't sure why his casual touch was so disappointing. Him ignoring the awkwardness between them was what she needed. This was a job position she was starting, and the last thing she wanted was for him to treat her like a potential date.

He caught her by the hand to guide her forward. "Three steps up to a landing, then the door."

"I'm not that blind," she said, but she didn't drag her hand away because she couldn't see *that* well, and the last thing she wanted was to fall flat on her face before even making it through the door.

Tamara didn't say a word about the fact they were both still wet—it was his house and if he didn't mind her dripping on the floor that was okay by her.

She'd clean up when she figured out where the mop was.

Caleb led her down a hallway—yellow walls reflecting the

bright light pouring in the windows—and opened the last door. "This is yours. Bathroom's the door on the right, and you've got lots of closet space. The girls are in the two rooms to our left. I'll show you the rest of the house later." He backed up, those dark eyes moving out of her line of vision. "I'll let you figure it out from here."

He was gone before she could say another word, leaving her to find her way through a blur of walls and furniture into the spacious master bath.

The shower felt amazing. Tamara stood directly under the pressure with it running as hot as she could for as long as she could bear.

That had gone well...

Not.

So much for her good intentions. But maybe this was a better thing—if Caleb's expectations were rock-bottom, the only direction she could go was up.

It took some time, but once she'd finished and wrapped herself in an enormous towel, she was feeling mostly human. She leaned close to the mirror, wiping away the fog to peer at her face and drag her fingers through her hair. Until her stuff arrived there wasn't much more she could do.

She pushed open the door and glanced into her new home.

A dark-haired little girl sat on her bed.

Tamara slid forward, trying not to look too creepy as she moved into close enough proximity to check out the kid's face. "Hi."

No answer.

Okay. No talking, which according to Tamara's sources meant this should be Emma. Daughter number two.

"Do you know if your daddy brought my truck to the house yet?"

Her lopsided ponytail swung as she shook her head. Then

she stared at Tamara intently, her lips turned down, a distressed look in her eyes.

Tamara took the chair across from Emma. "Is your sister around as well?"

The little girl's mouth opened for a second before she nodded.

"Okay, that's good. Your daddy said I'm not starting work as your nanny until tomorrow but I did want to meet you, and, here you are." She held out a hand to Emma. "I'm Tamara. I'm very glad to make your acquaintance."

Emma stared at her fingers suspiciously before catching them and giving them a quick shake.

"Your Auntie Dare told me you weren't fond of talking, especially to strangers. Your choice, but since I'm new here, I'll probably need to ask a bunch of questions. I hope even if you don't feel like answering with words, you can help me in other ways."

The little girl's mouth opened in surprise before she slammed it shut again.

Tamara paused.

Hmmm. Something was up. This did not appear to be a little girl who for whatever reason did not use verbal communication. More like a little girl who was trying to *pretend* she didn't talk.

Tamara hid her smile. "Hey, I think I hear noise outside." She got up and peered out the window. "Look at that. They brought my truck and there's my horse. Can I ask a favour, *Sasha*? I'd appreciate if you could grab the bags I left on the passenger seat."

Sasha sat motionless for a moment before demanding, "How'd you know I wasn't Emma?"

"I think the more important question is, why were you pretending to be her?"

Brown eyes narrowed evilly before Sasha turned all

sweetness and light, bestowing a chilling smile on Tamara. "She's my sister, and I don't like people being mean to her."

"So you were checking out the new nanny to see if I was a meanie?"

Sasha nodded.

Tamara dipped her chin in approval. "Good for you."

Sasha gave her an unreadable look.

"We can discuss this more later, but I do need you to get me those bags. I can't walk out there in nothing but a towel. One of those girl things, right? You know about that."

Sasha's feet hit the floor. She marched forward, opened the door without another word and slipped out, all the while keeping an intense watch on Tamara.

Oh, yeah, this was going to be interesting.

3

By the time Caleb got back from grabbing Tamara's truck, he was chilled to the bone.

Strangely, he didn't mind. The wet jeans clinging to his thighs had been enough to counteract the images he had to keep under control. The ride back to the ranch with Tamara nestled in his arms had been a unique form of hell. Why had he listened to his sister Dare in the first place and hired the dangerous creature?

Right. Because the girls needed a woman around.

For some reason Dustin was hanging out in the yard instead of by the bunkhouse where he'd moved after graduation last June. Caleb got his attention, tossing him the keys to Tamara's truck. "Park the trailer by the barn then get her horse settled, will you?"

Dustin looked over Caleb's wet clothes with amusement but for once made the right choice and didn't ask any questions.

Caleb grabbed the couple of bags off Tamara's passenger seat and carried them into the house, bumping into Sasha in the hallway.

"I can take those to the nanny, Daddy," she offered sweetly.

"Thanks, pumpkin."

She wrinkled her nose when he stooped to give her a kiss, then he escaped to his bathroom.

He turned on the taps, and hot water gushed out instantly. Tamara must have finished her shower—

And dammit if those forbidden images didn't come crashing back. It had been bad enough having her rub against him the entire ride home. He didn't need to add thoughts of naked skin under hot, steamy water. It was hard to stop them, though, all things considered.

After his wife left, Caleb had pretty much given up on love. He didn't need a woman in his life for romantic reasons. Luke could be the dreamer, and Dustin could sweet-talk and romance every young woman in town and the next three counties over if he wanted. Walker could use that cowboy charm of his while out on the rodeo circuit.

When it came down to it, what Caleb wished for most was someone to warm his bed at night. Blunt, but true. Screw the romantic bullshit, he'd like some sex. It was the one thing he hadn't enjoyed in a long time, and he damn well missed it.

But that was not a safe path to wander down when the woman entering his home was so hands-off he needed to consider her his personal kryptonite.

Moments later he was dressed and hurrying to join his family.

He took two steps into the room then pulled to a stop.

Luke sat with Emma beside him at the kitchen island. As usual, the sight of his youngest daughter hit Caleb with the impact of a kick in the gut. A miniature cameo of his ex-wife, except Emma was sweetness and joy. Also, currently frustrated— her blonde curls wiggled as she squirmed on the spot, homework book open in front of her as Luke pointed to something on the page.

Emma glanced up. Her blue eyes shone and her face

brightened with a smile like only she could give, and love melted his heart.

"Hey, button."

She eagerly abandoned her task, slipping off her stool and hurrying to envelop him in a hug.

He took a moment to enjoy being squeezed by teeny arms before pressing a kiss to her forehead. He rose to his feet to deal with the other unexpected person in the room. "Neat trick, Walker. Last we heard you were miles away. You grow wings overnight?"

Walker marched forward from the side counter where he'd been making a salad, hand outstretched to grasp Caleb's. "Got in my truck when the last event was done, and the wheels just carried me home."

He shook Caleb's hand, the smile on his square-jawed face not quite as wide as Luke's. A shadow lingered in his dark eyes Caleb didn't remember seeing before, but before he could ask more questions, Walker turned back to his task, speaking over his shoulder. "Luke says he has no problem with me being a slacker for the next couple of months, so I figure this is as good a place as any to hang my hat."

"Fine by me. You can slack all that Luke lets you," Caleb said evenly in return.

They both knew that meant never. Luke might be the fun brother, but he still demanded people get the job done.

Caleb glanced at the table then back at his daughter who was making faces at her homework. "Emma, I was going to tell you to put an extra plate out for the new nanny—she'll be joining us for supper, but it looks as if you already set the table for one more than we need."

She pushed away her homework, holding up fingers and counting off without naming names out loud. It was clear she was listing people, and Caleb silently joined in.

Emma, Sasha, him. Luke, Walker, Tamara...and one more.

Ahh. "Dustin is going to be here tonight, is he?"

Emma nodded exaggeratedly, her chin dipping all the way up and down, pleasure returning a smile to her expression.

Of course Dustin was going to join them, because if there was anything the younger Stone boys liked more than tormenting their biggest brother, it was satisfying their curiosity.

No wonder the kid had been hanging out close to the house. "I'm going to send him a bill if he keeps this up."

Luke ruffled Emma's curls as he stood, heading to the counter to drain the enormous pot of pasta that had been boiling on the stove. "It's great he still loves doing things with us. Got to appreciate that—some kids his age can't wait to get as far away from home as possible. That he only moved into the bunkhouse because he wanted to be more grown up is a good thing."

"He gets meals with the bunkhouse. Living completely on his own would require he cook for himself at least part time." Still, Caleb was smiling as he joined them at the island, slipping an arm around Emma's shoulders. "You like to spoil your Uncle Dustin, don't you, little girl?"

Emma leaned against him, her hair tickling his nose as she held up two fingers, her expression going sad.

He squeezed her, knowing there was no way she'd speak in the crowded room. Thankfully, he was able to figure out what she was referring to. "I know we're two less than before. I miss the girls as well. But Auntie Dare will come and visit when she can, and she'll bring your new cousin Joey with her. And we're supposed to Skype with Auntie Ginny next weekend. That'll be fun, right?"

Emma nodded before sighing heavily and adding another word to her homework page.

It wasn't math that got his little girl's goat, it was language.

They had to coax the words from her, whether it was her fingers or her mouth doing the talking.

Daughter number one rushed into the room like a whirlwind. Ignoring everyone else, Sasha climbed up Emma's stool and stuck her lips next to her sister's ear to speak rapidly, soft enough no one else could hear.

"Hello to you too, Sasha," Walker said with a chuckle.

She waved at him without interrupting her secret sharing. The longer she muttered, the wider Emma's eyes grew.

Footsteps sounded again, and Caleb braced himself before turning, only to discover Dustin marching into the room. "That was quick."

Dustin tossed a set of keys in the air and caught them with one hand, grinning widely as he glanced around the room at his brothers. "She's got a nice truck."

That's what he said.

Caleb mentally kicked himself for turning every damn comment about Tamara into something sexual. "You settled her horse already?"

"Yep." The next second Dustin shifted on his feet uneasily, looking just as uncomfortable as the girls did when Caleb caught them in a lie. "Okay, I didn't settle him. Ashton was there, and he said he didn't mind, so I parked her trailer and brought the truck up to the house. I didn't want to be late for dinner."

Luke pushed past Caleb to place a huge pot of spaghetti on the table, speaking softly as he went. "Because he wants to check out the nanny. Told you so."

Lord Almighty, wasn't that exactly what Caleb needed.

He chose to focus on the fact that Dustin had been *somewhat* useful. "Don't pass off your chores to our foreman, but thanks for parking the trailer."

"No prob." Dustin gave Walker a friendly shove on the shoulder in greeting before dropping into a chair and tipping back to balance it on two legs as he watched everyone else in the kitchen work.

Walker leaned past him to place a basket of garlic bread on the table, and Dustin snatched a piece as it went by.

The girls left the island and headed to their seats. Dustin fell into teasing them, his speech garbled as he spoke around the bread he was inhaling.

"I'm curious too," Walker admitted, speaking in Caleb's ear soft enough the girls couldn't overhear. "About the nanny. Colour me shocked to find you'll be hosting a woman in the house."

His expression was hard to read, somewhere between concerned and teasing.

"Behave," Caleb warned. The last thing he needed was for the girls to think there was anything to this nanny business except someone coming to help on a strictly work-type basis.

A squeal escaped Emma as Dustin poked her. Sasha retaliated, and while they were just playing, the volume rose louder than anyone was supposed to be in the house. "Girls. Dustin—do I have to remind you to use your inside voices?"

Dustin shoved a huge chunk of bread into his mouth before answering, obviously amused as his words came out muffled. "We got man'ers."

"Bad ones."

His family. Rambunctious and borderline wild, but he loved them—when he didn't want to kill them.

Tamara rounded the corner just as Dustin made a rude face, cheeks puffed out like a squirrel storing nuts for the winter.

It was childish, but Caleb couldn't help but feel for the first time that day something had gone his direction.

It hadn't been difficult to find the kitchen. Tamara let her ears lead her toward the noise even as she straightened her spine and mentally prepared herself.

Didn't matter that she'd spent years dealing with life-and-death situations, and had even given presentations in front of large groups on various topics during her nursing career. This was different. She was meeting the people she would be living with twenty-four/seven, and *they* were family. She was the newcomer. She had to fit in, which meant being on her best behaviour.

If she knew how to pull that off.

Two steps into the room she paused. This section of the house held an open-design room, with the dining room to the right and the kitchen laid out to the left in an L along two walls. A large island sat conveniently in front of the cooking workspace, a row of tall stools tucked under the overhang.

She noticed all that in an instant, kind of as a backdrop to the main event which were the faces turning her way. She ignored the male bodies and focused on the two little girls sitting next to each other at the table, motionless as they eyed her.

Sasha's expression was guarded as she leaned protectively toward a curly-haired blonde angel of a girl who had to be her little sister. Emma looked confused and worried, teeth digging into her lower lip as she chewed on it, her clear blue eyes examining Tamara intently.

Something inside Tamara settled with an abrupt click. *This* was why she was here—for these girls. And no matter that she would never admit how scared she was at having left her comfort zone and being a bit of a fish out of water, putting the job in perspective made it a lot simpler.

Taking care of the people who couldn't defend themselves was right up Tamara's alley. Making sure these kids were safe and happy she could do.

Which is why after offering them a smile, she glanced toward the four men in the room with more confidence. "I hope that delicious smell means I can convince someone to feed me."

The teenager sitting beside the girls jerked his chair to vertical so fast he nearly tipped over. A younger mirror image to Caleb, he chewed around an enormous chunk of food, cheeks flushing red as he raised a hand to cover his mouth.

Tamara took pity on him and looked the opposite direction.

She met Caleb's gaze just in time to see him wiping away a bit of a smirk. His balanced stoic expression returned, and his amusement vanished as if it had never been there.

He dipped his chin politely.

Before he could speak, another tall man with unruly red-tinged hair stepped forward, hand outstretched in greeting. "Food *and* water, if you can imagine. Hi, I'm Luke. Nice to meet you."

His smile was full-out welcoming, a twinkle of mischief in his brown eyes as she gave his hand a firm shake. "Nice to meet you too. Tamara Coleman."

Luke jerked a thumb over his shoulder toward the tallest of the lot who was leaning against the counter, arms folded over his chest. "That one is Walker. He's just back from time on the circuit, so I don't know how civilized he is at the moment."

"I don't know why you think you're funny," Walker muttered. "I really don't." His pitch-black hair and brows with his decidedly less friendly expression combined to make him look a lot more dangerous than the exuberant Luke.

Butterflies flipped for a moment in Tamara's stomach before she stepped forward and offered her hand in spite of Walker's non-welcoming body language.

He shook her hand briefly before moving to the sink to fill a pitcher with water.

"You know Caleb," Luke continued in his self-appointed role of Master of Ceremonies. "And that one over there is Dusty.

Don't worry, contrary to appearances you won't need to nanny him as well."

Poor Dusty's face was flaming red, and while Tamara understood teasing was part of being a family, she felt sorry for the kid.

She walked over and extended her hand same as she had to Walker. "While I don't have any big brothers, I have a bunch of older cousins, so trust me. I understand what a royal pain they are at times."

His lips twitched and a little of the tension slipped from him. "*Three* older brothers and *two* older sisters—pain and me are well acquainted. And it's Dustin, if you don't mind."

"Dustin it is."

Tamara turned to greet the final member of the family, dropping to her knees to put her head on level with Emma's. "I met your sister, which means you are Emma. I'm looking forward to getting to know you better."

She waited to see what kind of a response she got. She wasn't about to put the little girl on the spot by offering a handshake and potentially having it shut down.

Emma tipped her head and looked Tamara over, a little frown creasing her forehead before she lifted her hand and ran a finger along the edge of Tamara's glasses.

"Like them? Back when I worked in the hospital I had to wear certain clothes because of a dress code, and sometimes that felt pretty boring. I started collecting all sorts of glasses that were *not* boring. These are one of my favourite. Wearing them makes me feel like I'm having a summer day, even in the middle of winter."

They were sheer fun. Bright yellow frames with a row of miniature blue birds perched along the top.

Emma pulled her hand back but she was smiling a little.

"You have more than one pair of glasses?" Sasha sounded

amazed. "Auntie Ginny wears glasses, but she only has one pair. Oh, and sometimes she has sunglasses, and sometimes she doesn't wear them at all."

"I have to wear my glasses," Tamara told her seriously. "Otherwise everything is just a big blur."

"Emma and I don't need to wear glasses—"

"How about we get everybody seated," Caleb interrupted. "That way we can see food on our plates a little quicker."

Instead of the typical rectangular farm-style table, the dining area of the open floor plan held an enormous circular one laid with cutlery and glasses. Enough seats for a dozen people were arranged around it, the wooden chairs mismatched yet sturdy, and the result was surprisingly homey.

After a bit of shuffling, Tamara found herself seated in the chair Dustin had abandoned, only half of the big table being utilized. Caleb sat three spots down on the other side of Emma, and Tamara watched with interest as he set to scooping pasta, sauce and salad on the plates stacked in front of him.

As he finished the first plate he passed it to Emma, who carefully passed it to Sasha.

When Sasha laid the plate in front of herself and picked up her fork Caleb coughed sternly. "You have someone sitting beside you tonight," he reminded her.

It was on the tip of Tamara's tongue to pipe up that she didn't mind waiting, but this was his house and she wanted to know what she was getting into. How did they do things in the Stone family, and was she going to fit in...

No. If she was honest *that* wasn't the question. The question was—would she approve?

She accepted the plate from Sasha. "Thank you. It looks good."

"That's Auntie Ginny's chair." A sullen, childish reprimand.

"Sasha." A warning sounded in Caleb's tone. "Auntie

Ginny's in France. I don't think we need to leave the chair empty for her. Be nice."

Sasha looked back at her plate, but she was quiet for only seconds before turning back to Tamara speaking politely, but pointedly.

"It will be a good supper because Uncle Luke makes the *best* garlic bread. Daddy makes the *best* spaghetti sauce. Uncle Walker makes the *best* salad. Uncle Dusty..." She glanced across the table at where Dustin was waiting patiently for his plate to arrive. "Uncle Dusty..."

"Uncle Dusty is the best supper-eater ever," Luke drawled, catching hold of Dustin's elbow as it jerked toward him.

Dustin grinned at his niece. "How about Uncle Dustin serves up the best bowls of ice cream for dessert?"

Sasha looked up at Tamara with a bit of attitude. "Do *you* know how to cook?"

"I can make toast," Tamara said.

The little girl's eyes widened. "Is that all?"

"Maybe a few more things. But toast is my specialty."

Sasha looked back at her plate. So quietly there was no way Caleb could hear, she muttered, "We're going to starve."

Tamara fought to keep from laughing.

Caleb was efficient as he served dinner, and they all had full plates in quick order. No one touched their food, though, until Caleb put the serving spoon down, the final plate resting in front of himself.

Tamara waited in case the Stones had some other family tradition. But the instant Caleb picked up his fork, it was obvious that was the ready-to-go signal.

Tamara had no objection. Between the drive and the unexpected dip in cold water, she was hungry enough to do justice to the steaming hot food.

"Any idea how long you'll be sticking around?" Dustin asked Walker.

"Until the new year. I need a bit of a break, so I may as well spend my time with you."

Caleb eyed his brother. "Did you take a tumble you need to recover from we don't know about?"

Walker paused with his fork halfway to his mouth. "Do I look as if I took a beating? Don't worry about me. You're the one I saw limping as you walked into the room."

Shoulders lifting in a gentle shrug, Caleb focused back on his plate. "Wouldn't be the first time you were black and blue and didn't say a word."

"On a different note, did you girls figure out what you're wearing for Halloween, yet?" Luke asked. "It's just over a week away."

"I want to be an astronaut, and Emma wants to be a cat. We get to wear our costumes to school all day, and my teacher, Ms. Miller, says she's going to dress up like Mrs. McGonagall. I think *all* of the teachers should dress up, but Kelli says some of them take themselves far too seriously to let their hair down and have fun."

"Kelli said that?" Luke asked, a smirk twisting his lips as he glanced across the table at Tamara to explain. "Kelli's one of the ranch hands."

Sasha rolled on. "Kelli said she's going to dress up as a cowgirl, but I don't think that's a very good costume because that's how she dresses all the time."

"Ahh. *Cowgirl.* Now that makes sense." Tamara made eye contact with Emma. "You know, that's pretty much what my sister has been for every Halloween as far back as I can remember."

Emma leaned across her plate, wonder in her eyes as she

checked out Tamara closer. She bumped her shoulder against Sasha.

"Emma wants to know if you have a Halloween costume," Sasha claimed before staring pleadingly across the table at Caleb. "Can you take us trick-or-treating this year, Daddy? Can you, please?"

In the split second before everyone's attention turned to Caleb, Tamara swore she saw frustration on Emma's face. She wondered how often Sasha spoke for her little sister and got it wrong.

Caleb lifted a brow. "Don't I always take you?"

"Yes, but I just thought maybe..." Sasha glanced at Tamara suspiciously.

"Ahh." Caleb refilled his water glass thoughtfully before he answered Sasha's unspoken question. "Some of the things you used to do with me, or Ginny, or Dare, you might do with Tamara. That's what she's here for—so you don't miss out on fun stuff if I get too busy. But I'll always be there for the most important events."

Conversation twisted to new topics after that, like Dustin asking Walker for advice on his truck, and Sasha telling her Uncle Luke a long story about one of the ranch dogs who went by the auspicious name of Demon.

Tamara joined in at moments, but for the most part she listened and watched, trying to learn the rhythm of this new family. They had a kinship and a deep sense of love amongst them, but there was a missing piece as well.

Growing up on the Whiskey Creek ranch, it had been her and her two sisters with her dad for as long as she could remember. She loved her sisters, and she and her dad tolerated each other, but that same sense of something missing had sent Tamara from working the land to get her nursing degree. Working with her hands to help heal people had been a way to be accepted and appreciated for her skills, and the longer she sat at the table, the more certain she was that *this* was where she needed to be.

Settling in at Silver Stone ranch wasn't going to be completely comfortable. She was pretty sure she and Caleb were going to butt heads more than a few times, but there was something that felt right about being here.

When the meal was over and they'd finished clearing the dishes, Tamara didn't fight when Caleb all but dismissed her.

"The girls and Dustin can do the dishes tonight," he insisted, ignoring their groans. He looked Dustin in the eye. "Part of being a family—cook or wash, right?"

His youngest brother sighed heavily, but he hauled a stool into place in front of the sink and plopped Emma up on it with the ease of a well-known routine. "Come on, kiddo. You wash, I'll dry, and Sasha can put things away. Then you can show me what you got planned for your costume."

Moments later, Tamara took a second look around the room and discovered she was alone. Caleb, Walker and Luke had all vanished.

She wandered back through the house examining the homey touches here and there, some older than others. Gingham fabric curtains framed the tall living room windows that faced to the east, the same frilly material topping the glass window of an exit door to the side of the kitchen, but the fabric was faded by the sun. In contrast, there were bright new cushions on the couches and easy chairs.

The pictures on the walls were the same, some old, some new, along with the knickknacks displayed on shelves and bookcases. Each shot and item a bit of memory on display, all pointing to events and details she knew nothing about.

It was strange to be so...ignorant. Uninformed. Tamara wasn't sure she liked not knowing things.

She ran a finger over the edge of a gilded frame. Two families next to each other, a family of four and a family of seven. They stood under a tree, with a lake shining in the background. Caleb was clearly recognizable even though he was years younger. The smile on his face far more innocent and lighthearted than she'd seen so far.

Everything around Tamara held secrets—clues to this family she'd dropped into the midst of. There was so much she didn't know. Not just about them, but herself. Would Heart Falls be a long stop on the new journey she'd begun, or a short one?

All she knew for certain was she couldn't go back, which meant the future was wide open and very, very unclear.

4

*C*aleb strode into the kitchen after doing early chores and came to a complete and utter stop. Considering it was barely six a.m., the last thing he'd expected was to be greeted by the scent of fresh biscuits and hot coffee.

He didn't usually start making breakfast for the girls until after seven, and the hour break he took between chores and when they crawled out of bed was when he caught up on as much paperwork as he could stomach.

Now not only did the kitchen smell like a bit of heaven, the view was damn good too. His gaze shot like a homing beacon to land on Tamara's ass.

In his defense, she *was* bent over, pulling a pan from the oven, but it was wrong how he couldn't seem to look away. Sweet curves wiggled at him temptingly, and he stepped behind the island to put something solid between her and his rising erection.

She stood and twisted on the spot, lowering the pan to a couple of hot pads she'd placed beforehand before smiling enthusiastically. "Morning. I made coffee. You'll have to let me know how you like it."

He was pretty sure he would like *anything* she was willing to give him. Beyond the obvious.

Dammit, dirty daydreams meant Caleb was having a hard time remembering how to talk. "What're you doing?"

Other than making every hormone in his body percolate past high. Sexy, half-naked woman in his kitchen, cooking breakfast and making him coffee? It was far too tempting to let his imagination go wild.

Tamara frowned. "Something wrong?"

Something had to be wrong. Otherwise he would simply have grabbed a cup of coffee and gone on with his day, right? Because the instant his cock eased up control enough to let his brain function the tiniest bit, he realized she was doing what he'd hired her to do.

Nannies cooked and made breakfast, and that's all she'd done.

"Caleb?"

He'd been standing far too long without answering which just compounded the problem. "You need to put some clothes on."

The words came out in a rush. The instant they escaped, he wished he could take them back because number one, he sure the hell didn't mind the way she was dressed, with her long limbs under what was a perfectly decent knee-length robe.

Number two, what had been a happy expression on her face slammed closed into something far more guarded.

He waited for her to call him on his bullshit.

She didn't fight, though. Her chin rose, but her response was soft and meek. "Okay."

Nothing more as she turned to the oven and clicked off the power.

That was not what Caleb expected. He had an apology on the tip of his tongue before he noticed that instead of taking the shortest route from the kitchen possible, she'd stepped counterclockwise. A move that would needlessly march her past him.

He leaned against the island, resting his hands on the surface as he waited to see what was up.

He should have been a lot more worried than curious, because unlike most women who would turn their back as they passed a man, Tamara faced him. In the brief second as she moved through the narrow space between the island and kitchen chairs, her soft breasts slid across his chest. Her hip brushed his groin, and the whole attack sent his cock into full alert.

She stepped toward the hallway, the swells of her butt cheeks twitching against the silky fabric of her green robe, and he was mesmerized. Unable to look away.

A half step before she vanished down the hall, the robe slipped from her shoulders giving him a split-second, tantalizing tease of naked back and a pale blue, barely-there nightie.

Caleb moved slowly in deference to his unruly erection, stepping to the refrigerator. He jerked open the freezer door and stood there with cold air pouring down as he prayed for strength.

Stupid ass.

He closed the door and went to get a coffee, pacing the room uncomfortably. Would she come back, or had he already scared her away?

But not even five minutes later, when he'd barely settled on the stool by the island, she moved past him briskly, her rigid back to him as she poured herself a cup. A light-blue T-shirt tucked into jeans covered her curves, and when she twisted toward him, he jerked his gaze upward to make sure he was gazing into her eyes and not anywhere else.

Apologizing was the right thing, but God, it was awkward. "I'm sorry. My comment earlier was out of line."

She dropped a spoonful of sugar into her cup then stirred

vigorously, staring at the surface. "I'm sorry for overreacting." She lifted her gaze to his. "It probably doesn't seem like it considering I keep doing stupid things, but I really want this job to work."

Him as well.

It suddenly struck him— "What happened to your job at the hospital? You were a nurse. Why did you want to become a nanny?"

She sank her teeth into her bottom lip for a second, and he was damn near shocked. She wasn't the type to hesitate.

When she spoke it wasn't with her usual flair. "Dare never told you?"

Caleb shook his head. "She's my sister. I trust her. She says you're the one for the job, and I believe her, God help me."

Amusement lightened her expression as a snicker escaped. "Thanks for the vote of confidence. You really think you need heavenly intervention with me working for you?"

He needed it to stop dreaming about decidedly non-heavenly pursuits. Like her lips, soft and delicious. And those damn glasses she wore—he'd never realized he had a thing for glasses, but obviously, he did. The ones she had on today were black-rimmed with tipped-up outside edges. The way she peered at him through them made the dirty thoughts rise, along with his cock.

Which wasn't completely surprising because it had been a hell of a long time since the thing had gotten attention from anything other than his hand...

...and this was a direction he needed to avoid heading in the future.

Tamara spoke in a rush, probably taking his silence as judgment. "I didn't do anything terrible, but I was hoping to keep small-town gossip from starting before I'd been here twenty-four hours."

If she'd been sent by anyone other than his sister, that wouldn't have been nearly enough. "Dare wouldn't let you come within two inches of my little girls if she didn't know everything, and still trust you. I don't suppose I need details."

She visibly relaxed.

"Dare knows?" he asked, just to be sure.

Tamara nodded. "We sat down and talked before I came out. I hope you don't mind, but she also gave me all the details about your family. I mean, the part about how your parents and hers were best friends, and how after the accident you made sure that she got to stay at Silver Stone, fostering her as a sister."

The stupid, tragic accident that had taken his parents, Dare's, and her little sister in one moment. Caleb took a deep breath, the pain still sharp after all these years. "She'd lost enough. I figured she didn't need to lose all of us as well."

"Still, she thinks a lot of you, taking her on when you already had Ginny and Dustin to look after. Making sure that you all got to stay together as a family."

"It was the right thing to do." Caleb met her eyes. "Dare was a good kid who'd been dealt a shitty hand for a sixteen-year-old. I'm glad it worked for her to live with us. And I had help. Luke was twenty, and Walker nearly eighteen."

Tamara spoke softly. "It was a kind thing, that's all I'm saying. I'm sure being in familiar surroundings helped a lot."

"I think routine and familiarity was good for us all back then." There'd been times he'd wondered at the people who jumped from place to place all their lives. "There's something special about living in one place your entire life, but it's also a strange sort of burden."

She was nodding slowly, fingers brushing the handle of her coffee mug in slow circles. "I went away to go to school, but other than that, I've lived in Rocky Mountain House. It feels strange to realize the next time I go to town I won't see familiar faces at the grocery store." Her lips twitched. "It also means I won't be hit on by Samuel Tate. Can't say I'm going to miss that part."

Caleb hesitated in the middle of stealing a not-so-hot-anymore biscuit off the cooling rack. "He an old beau of yours?"

"He's an old something, but normally the words on either side of *old* would be *dirty* and *man*. He's mostly harmless, but a local hazard I don't mind leaving behind."

"I'm sure someone in Heart Falls will be just as annoying."

Her half smile slipped into full bloom. "Well, now, you do have a sense of humour."

"Never said I didn't. Just don't feel the need to poke and tease as much as Luke does."

With a firm dip of her head, Tamara pulled over a notepad she'd had ready on the island counter. "I went over the email you sent, but your list of what you wanted me to do on a daily basis was a little bare-bones. I thought I should double-check what you want me to focus on here for the next while." She glanced around the room. "You mentioned a calendar last night, but I don't see one."

"It's in the office."

She made a few notes on her paper. "If you don't mind, I'll set one up out here that we can all see. That will make it easier for me as I get into a routine. Probably make it easier for the girls as well."

Caleb brushed crumbs from his fingers, wondering if he could snag another biscuit or if that would be pushing it. "Smart idea. Go ahead and get what you need. We have an account at Independent Grocers that you can charge stuff to. Just get them to phone me for approval the first time."

Her eyes widened for a second before she brought it under control. "Now that's something I haven't heard in a long time. They let you keep a running tab at the grocery store?"

"I know Rocky Mountain House is small, but I have a feeling Heart Falls is even smaller. We've got some things we still do with a nod and a handshake."

"I kind of figured that when my total job interview and acceptance letter was something to the effect of you saying, *Fine, show up on Tuesday.*"

Caleb shrugged. "Didn't see the need to discuss it. You wanted to be here, and the girls need a nanny.

"List of jobs?" she reminded him.

He rotated a finger in the air. "Keep this place from burning to the ground or being condemned. That's all. Your to-do list is whatever that takes. When you cook, make enough for six, and if there's leftovers we'll eat them for lunch the next day if my brothers don't show up at midnight to demolish them. They aren't usually here. Walker and Luke both have spaces in the bunkhouse, and Dustin moved out there the instant he finished high school. They eat with the hands most of the time, and yes, we have a cook, but his name isn't Cookie."

"You crazy break-with-traditionalists. What is it?"

"Jalaj Patel, but he asked the crew to call him JP. He's Indian. We're the only ranch in the area that serves dahl as often as beans."

Tamara grinned before glancing at her watch. "You ready for breakfast? Or do you want to wait and eat with the girls?"

He rose to his feet along with her, a little uncomfortable as she reached into the fridge and pulled out a container of eggs. "You don't have to do that."

She stopped, laying the food on the counter so her fists could settle on her hips. "Caleb Stone, you hired me to do a job, so let me do it. You want to eat now or later?"

He ignored the twitch of pleasure that struck to see her standing her ground. "I'll wait."

"What time will the girls be ready for breakfast, usually?"

"Seven fifteen. Bus picks them up at seven forty-five and drops them off at three thirty."

She nodded decisively then basically shooed him from the

kitchen. "Go do whatever. I'll have breakfast at your usual time. If you can be here today, that will help ease us into the routine."

He picked up his coffee cup and went to the pot to top it up. "I intended to eat with the girls. You being here doesn't change that."

He added a shot of cream to his coffee before lifting his mug in the air in a salute. No choice but to go and face his office and the paperwork he hated.

"Caleb," she interrupted before he left the room. "How do you like it?"

Sheer willpower kept him from stumbling. "Excuse me?"

Tamara gestured toward his hand. "The coffee. Is it the way you like?"

Oh. Coffee, not sex. "I like it stronger."

She nodded. "More kick in the pants. Got it, boss." Then she turned to the fridge and started going through it, moving on with her day.

Caleb forced himself to move on with his, sliding down the hall to his office with that strange sense that more than just an additional person had entered the house.

She was a force of nature.

Tamara used the next forty-five minutes to finish exploring the kitchen, doing inventory on supplies and starting a shopping list. Cooking for the family wasn't enough to scare her. She'd spent enough time during her university days taking turns on the chore with her roommates, and later making large batches of stuff to exchange with her friends. Not to mention cooking for the horde of her extended family when they got together.

She could make more than toast, although the menu would

get a little repetitious after a while, but that wasn't her biggest challenge.

She had half an hour each morning to figure out more about the little girls, then an entire day to go through before they were home. The empty hours loomed.

Luckily, she still had this morning to distract her. She went with what was simple. There was a plethora of cereal in the cupboard, plenty of bread and eggs. She set the table with a few choices including juice and cut fruit and the biscuits cooling on the counter.

Then she sat down with a fresh cup of coffee from a new pot —Caleb was right, she'd made the first batch far too weak—and planned out her day, pretending having open spaces was a complete treat.

Ten minutes later she looked down at her chore list and laughed. What a bunch of baloney—she could hear her cousins cursing her shitty attitude.

So *what* if she was going to be home all day instead of turning up for a shift at the hospital? She had a ton of work to keep the house running efficiently, and ignoring that fact was insulting to everyone who worked at home.

She closed her notepad with a smack just as Caleb returned to the room.

He glanced at the table, hesitating before clearing his throat. "It looks good, but we usually eat breakfast at the island. It might be better—"

Tamara held up a hand. "You're right. I'm not looking to mess with their routine. It's enough of a change for me to be here."

"I should have warned you." His shoulders relaxed in relief, and he helped her grab the plates and move them to the island. "If we've got more than four for breakfast, we do eat at the table. It's just that usually it's only me and the girls, and when Ginny is here, she joins in at the side."

"Which side?" Tamara asked, thinking back to yesterday's faux pas when she sat in Ginny's spot.

Caleb's thoughts must've gone there as well. He pointed to the far end of the island. "There."

Tamara placed her plate on the opposite end of the counter, moving to adjust the stools. "Then I'll sit over here. It's a small enough change."

Caleb took his cup and went for another refill, sniffing the new stronger batch she'd made with appreciation before settling onto the stool next to where she intended to sit.

There was no time to feel awkward because an instant later Sasha and Emma rushed into the room. They tossed their backpacks on the dining room table before they turned and stopped dead, examining Tamara.

That ever-present suspicion was strong in Sasha's eyes, as if Tamara was going to sprout horns and grab a pitchfork at any moment.

Caleb seemed oblivious. He slid off his stool and opened his arms. "I thought you two were hibernating for the winter."

They scooted in for a hug before climbing on what had to be their usual stools.

"Anybody want a fried egg, and if yes, how do you want them?" She pointed at Caleb. "And unless you change your mind all the time, I should be able to get it right after you've told me once."

Caleb reached for a biscuit and the jam. "Sunny side up, if you can."

"Emma and I want ours cooked all the way through, not yucky like Daddy's."

Tamara glanced at Emma but she was reaching for a bowl and the cereal, so Tamara went with it. "Sunny side up, and two not yucky, otherwise known as over-hard. Got it."

She put the food together, including one for herself, then

joined them. Other than watching Emma make longing eyes at Caleb and her plates, the rest of breakfast went off without a hitch.

It was the calm before the storm, followed by the mad rush of brushing teeth, gathering school supplies and forgotten homework, then she and Caleb walked the girls to the front road just in time for the yellow bus to appear on the main highway.

"You have to put the shelter up soon, Daddy. It's going to start snowing, and we need our castle to hide in," Sasha informed him.

"I'll put it on the to-do list." He ruffled Emma's curls and gave Sasha's ponytail a tug before kissing them both and sending them on the bus.

The bus driver eyed Tamara curiously before glancing at Caleb. "Going to have snow before the week's out," he warned, an echo of Sasha's words. "Better make sure the girls are bundled up tight."

Caleb mostly grunted in response. He gestured to Tamara. "Dan, this is Tamara, the girls' nanny. She'll be the one meeting the bus most days. She's okay."

"See you this afternoon." Dan glanced back into the bus before closing the doors and heading into town.

A moment later, Caleb took his leave as well. "If you need me, my cell number is on the fridge. You don't have to worry about lunch. I'll eat with the crew since it's Walker's first day back."

He tipped his hat then strode across the grass toward the barns without another word.

Tamara watched him go, giving in to the urge to admire the view.

It was a truth that had to be admitted—the man looked good coming or going.

5

$\mathcal{T}$amara went back to the house and did up the breakfast dishes before exploring the house more thoroughly.

The second door off the kitchen led into a conveniently located laundry room, two hampers full of dirty wash waiting. She got a load going then checked out the downstairs play area before wandering back through the living room. All the pictures she admired the night before were slightly familiar now, which meant she could look closer. Some of Caleb and his brothers and sister when they were growing up. A few with a couple who had to be his mom and dad.

Lots of Sasha and Emma when they were young.

The house was cozy, but well lived in, and most definitely not clean to the corners.

It was tidy, though, and comfortable, and Tamara couldn't find very much to complain about. She added a few things to her chore chart, along with a few questions for Caleb.

She poked her head into the girls' rooms, just to get the lay of the land. Sasha's room was a bit of a bear pit, clothing strewn everywhere—it looked as if she'd tried on three or four outfits before getting dressed, like some miniature fashion diva.

Emma's room was tiny, with a smaller-than-normal bed and dresser. Her closet was open, and the toys were arranged in neat rows on the shelves, as far from the mess in her sister's room as imaginable.

The hall bathroom that the girls shared was somewhere between messy and neat, and Tamara smiled as their unique personalities began to stand out.

That's all there was on that side of the house, and she crossed the living space to the wing that extended to the west. Another bathroom—this one filled with the scent of Caleb's soap, woodsy and sharp in her nostrils.

The next door opened on an office. She supposed there was a desk somewhere under all the paper and rubbish. A filing cabinet in the corner had a couple doors that couldn't close because of the paperwork sticking out of the top. There might've been a credenza, and a number of chairs, but mostly piles of paper and an astonishing collection of dirty coffee cups.

Obviously Caleb spent time in here. How he found anything, though, she had no idea.

She collected the cups without disturbing anything, pulling the door shut with difficulty. Then she hesitated.

"Ahh, fuck it." She gave in to the devil of curiosity, pushing open the final door and peeking inside.

Unlike the previous room, this one was neat as a pin. Bed made as crisp as if he'd been in the military, the entire room was spartan. A dresser as small as Emma's was topped with a picture of the girls, their arms wrapped around each other, bright faces beaming with a field of wildflowers behind them.

It was the only decoration in the room.

The only other thing in the room was a bed, bigger than a

single, but nowhere near large enough for a man the size of Caleb.

She closed the door and backed away without peeking any further, feeling somewhat guilty that, for whatever reason, he'd given her the master suite, including his king-size bed.

Another thing to include on the list of topics to be discussed.

Tamara worked until lunch then decided it was time to explore the rest of her environment. May as well check to see how her horse was settling in. She pulled on a pair of boots and a warm coat, dropping a hat on her head.

She glanced in the mirror by the back door and all but froze.

A week ago she'd been garbed from head to toe in nursing scrubs. Today she looked more like her older sister than ever, Karen's cowgirl gear as much a part of her as breathing.

It felt—strange. Tamara hadn't dressed like this on a regular basis for over ten years. She still put in her time and helped out with the Whiskey Creek ranch when necessary, but it hadn't been her life, the ranch business. And yet now, it was, in a way.

She'd missed it. More than she wanted to admit.

She strolled outside, saying hello to the couple of dogs who rushed to greet her before guiding her toward the main barn. There were at least a dozen trucks parked near a long, low building to the south that she suspected must be the bunkhouse.

To the north was a lake, and she found herself intrigued. That was one thing that was different from the territory where she'd grown up. Tamara stopped and pivoted in a slow circle, looking over the land. The mountains were much closer here, sheer and dangerous, the craggy peaks already painted with white, and the cold wind that blew toward her warned Dan's prediction was right.

It was nearly Halloween. She could count on one hand the number of times there hadn't been snow by that point growing up.

Past the ranch house was a small cottage she assumed was Dare's, and she wondered if one of the boys would move into it. Just like her cousins did at home, constantly rotating houses so that everyone was as comfortable as possible.

Her gaze drifted over more outbuildings then danced back to the lake, the shining surface tempting Tamara forward. Not that she needed another dip in icy water, but it was pretty, and she promised herself a chance to walk along the bank, maybe with the girls, that evening.

Now she headed toward the barn, stepping cautiously as she entered to make sure she wasn't interrupting.

The sweet smell of hay struck her like a memory, and she closed her eyes and leaned against the nearest wall, using her other senses to experience the moment. Animals moved slowly, the sound of creaking boards. Somewhere someone was dragging a rake, the scratching sound far more soothing than nails on a blackboard but just as distinctive.

Yeah, she'd missed this a hell of a lot.

"I didn't hear anything about the Stones hiring another woman hand, so you must be the nanny."

Tamara snapped her eyes open to come face-to-face with dark brown eyes set in a very young face. The woman wore her brown hair in two tight braids, her cheeks tanned from the sun. She was short, at least six inches shorter than Tamara, who was modestly tall for a woman at five foot eight.

"I am. Tamara Coleman."

The woman shoved a hand forward and shook Tamara's with a grip worthy of a man twice her size. "Kelli James." She looked Tamara up and down once before wrinkling her nose. "Those clothes look brand-new. When Ashton said you'd brought a horse, I was hoping you'd actually know which was the working end of a shovel."

Tamara let out a snort of amusement. "The clothes are new,

but trust me, I know shit when I see it. I can clean it up or dish it out along with the best of them."

The irritation in Kelli's expression vanished between one breath and the next. "Good. I couldn't take another prissy princess in here, prancing around like some high-strung filly. You want me to show you where we stashed your horse? Ashton found a spot where you can access her without getting in the way of the ranch operations."

"That would be great." She eyed the other woman, then made a judgment call of her own. Kelli seemed the type to appreciate plain speaking, "You don't look old enough to work here during the day. You playing hooky?"

Kelli gave her a dirty look. "Twenty-six, thanks so much."

"Bullshit. Dustin looks older than you."

"Ha. The kid turned nineteen a few weeks ago and figured that meant he was old enough to ask me for a date." She glanced at Tamara. "He'll probably ask you too."

"Even though I'm so old?" Tamara teased.

"Now who's slinging the bull?" They stopped beside a stall, and Stormy came forward, sticking his nose over the gate to bump Tamara affectionately as Kelli came around the side. "He's a pretty creature."

"Stormy is a sweetheart and exactly what I need when I ride." Tamara brushed her hands on her jeans. "You're right. All my gear *is* new. I've been working a job off the ranch for long enough it's been important to have a trustworthy ride for the few days I did get to ride. My sister Karen knows horses, and she picked Stormy out for me a number of years ago."

"She picked well." Kelli ran a hand over Stormy's nose, petting him affectionately before sneaking a carrot from her pocket and feeding it to him. She turned back to Tamara. "I'll show you where we put your saddle and the rest of your gear, then if you want, I can take you on a little tour."

"I don't want to keep you from your work," Tamara protested, wondering how quickly she could get in more trouble with Caleb, stealing away his workers.

Kelli waved off her protest. "I'm not working right now. I just like to hang around the place. Acting tour guide gives me an excuse."

Within a few minutes it was clear Kelli wasn't exaggerating—she loved Silver Stone, and she knew all its history, and everyone who'd worked there, and all the animals.

"That one is Cherry Blossom. Ashton figures the last owners were either fat and lazy, or mean and lazy because the horse gets damn skittish when you try to put more than a blanket on her back." Kelli folded her arms and rested them on the cross post outside the arena where an older man with silver in his hair was walking a horse in circles. "She's going to be a great ride. I look forward to getting up on her." She glanced at Tamara before gesturing to herself with a hand. "Me with all my massiveness works well as a starter package for the jittery horses."

"You're not scared?" Tamara knew the answer, but she was interested to see how Kelli would respond because the other woman was turning out to be an absolute crackup.

Sure enough, Kelli made a rude noise before shining a wide grin Tamara's direction. "Hell, it's fun to get up on big things that buck."

She winked, and Tamara outright laughed. "We're going to get along well, you and I."

Kelli punched her good-naturedly in the arm then gestured toward the gate. "Want to meet Ashton?"

Tamara glanced at her watch. "I'd better save it for the next time. I got a few things to do before the bus arrives, and I should do a little more unpacking."

"Tomorrow, then," Kelli said. "If you think you can get away for a couple of hours, I'll make sure I'm free to take you on a longer tour. We can ride—I'll take you to Heart Falls."

No use in mentioning she'd already seen them, up close and personal like. "I'd like that."

Kelli walked with her toward the parking lot. "You moving into the cottage, or Ginny's room?"

Oh. That explained why Caleb wasn't in the master bedroom. "Not the cottage—I need to be in the house to help with the girls. I'm right next to them."

She stopped and waited because Kelli was no longer at her side but frozen in position a few steps back, her jaw hanging open. "Ginny's room is in the basement. Seriously? You're in the *master?*"

Dammit all, that means she *had* kicked Caleb out of his room. "I guess Caleb must've given it up so I could have a private bathroom."

In a strangely unlike-her gesture, Kelli looked everywhere but at Tamara as if she were considering hard before speaking, her face contorted with pain before her obvious attempt at maintaining control failed. "Caleb sleeps next to his office. And Ginny refused to move into the master bedroom because she said the lingering scent of brimstone kept her awake."

Okaaaay. It seemed there was a whole lot more baggage tied up in this situation than Tamara had expected. "I don't know that I want you to explain any of that to me."

"Which is code for you're curious as get out, but you're going to be polite and not go asking for all the dirt your first day on the job?"

"Pretty much," Tamara admitted.

"You're right. We're going to get along just fine," Kelli said with a grin, patting Tamara on the shoulder as she left her at the edge of the parking area. "Those kids deserve a hell of a lot better than they got when it came to their mama, but Caleb is a mighty sweet daddy. That's all the gossip you'll get from me for now."

Which was more than enough. "I'll see you after lunch tomorrow?"

"If no one's eating at the house, come join me and I'll introduce you to JP. Then we can ride for a while."

Tamara spent the next hour and a half getting everything ready for the evening. She wasn't a fancy cook, but she knew how to make tasty enough meals that would stick to the ribs and should still interest the girls.

Speaking of which—she made a batch of cookies. No reason she shouldn't sweeten the pot at the start of the *getting to know you* business. Especially since she intended on rocking the boat a lot sooner than they probably expected.

Dan grinned at her as he opened the bus door, the dogs who'd found their way over to sit with Tamara barking excitedly as they waited for Sasha and Emma to descend. "Hello, new nanny Tamara. Welcome to Heart Falls. You have a good day?"

"Yes, thank you," she responded simply. "Have a great afternoon."

Sasha stormed past, Emma taking the steps more cautiously.

Tamara turned her attention to Emma. "Your backpack looks absolutely full. Would you like me to help carry it?"

Emma was shrugging out of the straps when Sasha came barreling back.

"Come *on*, Em. I need to show you something." She caught her sister by the hand and dragged her forward.

Emma glanced over her shoulder at Tamara, but she didn't tell Sasha to stop.

Tamara walked behind them as they stopped running not even ten paces away from her, Sasha speaking at high speed again. Everything about the situation made Tamara twitch, and she debated if her gut reaction was going to get her in trouble.

Probably, but who was she kidding? She could set all the goals for self-improvement she wanted, but right here and right now, she had to stick to her first instincts. She wasn't going to let *anyone* push around the kids who were her responsibility.

Not even each other.

The girls disappeared into their rooms, backpacks abandoned in the hallway. Tamara picked the bags up and carried them into the kitchen, dropping them on the island. Then she leaned against the counter and waited.

Sure enough it wasn't long before they both came storming into the room, the same way she and her two sisters, Karen and Lisa, used to after getting off the school bus, starving.

"Okay, guys." Tamara brushed her hands as if preparing for action. "We don't have a real calendar yet, so I put up a piece of paper on the fridge. We'll write down anything that comes home from school that we need to worry about. If you want to empty your backpacks we can make sure that we've got anything new—"

"Daddy has a calendar," Sasha interrupted.

"He does," Tamara agreed. "And it's got everything he needs for all the Silver Stone things, and I'm sure it's got a whole bunch of your school stuff until now, but this is one of my jobs. Like your daddy said, I'm here to make sure you don't miss anything fun because it's *not* up on the calendar."

Instead of reaching for her backpack, Sasha folded her arms over her chest.

So. The battle was engaged.

Tamara turned to Emma. "If you empty your—"

"Emma doesn't want to empty her bag either."

Tamara raised a brow. "I wasn't asking you."

Sasha's voice rose in volume. "Emma doesn't talk. I talk for her, and she doesn't want to empty her backpack. And she doesn't want you to write anything on the calendar, and she *doesn't* want a nanny. Neither of us do."

"Well. Thank you very much for sharing your opinion. Now you need to wait your turn because I'm talking to Emma." Tamara turned her back on Sasha and focused on the little blonde-haired darling who was chewing madly on her lower lip. Where Sasha had gone louder, Tamara spoke with quiet authority.

"You're very smart little girl, and if you don't want to talk out loud, I figure that's your business. But that means when somebody asks you a question, or you want to tell another person something, you have to use the smarts you have up here"— Tamara tapped a finger against her forehead—"and make it clear what you'd like. You can write a note. You can draw a picture. You can act it out, but I'll warn you I have never been good at charades, so that one might take a long time."

Emma folded her arms over her chest, lower lip sticking out in a frustration, and for a split second she and Sasha looked like mirrored statues. Stubborn, not very happy statues.

"Emma doesn't like being bossed around—"

Tamara snapped a hand toward Sasha. "Please don't interrupt. Your sister and I are having a conversation."

Sasha's jaw dropped in shock, giving Tamara just enough time to pick up where she left off, looking Emma in the eye. "Your sister is lovely, but she's not you. If you *want* her to answer for you, tell her that. Poke her, throw something at her, use sign language. I don't care how, but when I'm around she's not allowed to simply talk *for* you unless you tell her she can."

Sasha bristled. "I know what she wants."

"You just interrupted again," Tamara pointed out. "But fine. Let's talk about that. I'm sure you do know what Emma wants— sometimes. Maybe even most of the time." Tamara eyed Emma and crossed her fingers, hoping for the best. "All the time? Does Sasha get it right *all* the time? Does she *always* know what you would ask for? What you'd like to eat, or what you'd like to be for Halloween?"

A slow, reluctant shake of blonde curls followed.

Thank goodness for truthful little girls.

Tamara raised a brow at Sasha, speaking even softer. "You need to be more polite to your sister, and not assume as much. I know you love her, and I *know* you're just trying to help. I have zero problem with you delivering the message *if* Emma asks you to, and I don't care if she uses telepathy to ask."

Sasha's face wrinkled in confusion, but she refused to ask what that meant.

Fine—Tamara had never believed in pandering. "Starts like *telephone*, turns into the word *path* with a *y* at the end. Look it up."

She ignored them for a moment and turned to the counter, bringing forward the cookies she'd made earlier and glasses of milk. "Hungry? Want a snack before you empty your backpacks then get started on your homework?"

This was the moment where it could all go wrong. Emma reached for a cookie with one hand and a glass of milk with her other.

Sasha...

Her lower lip trembled for second before her entire face contorted. She folded her arms on the countertop, buried her face in the crook of an elbow, and began crying at the top of her lungs.

It was pretty impressive.

Only this wasn't the first temper tantrum Tamara had seen— she'd spent a lot of time on the children's ward at the hospital and had seen crying and upset tears for far better reasons than having the law laid down.

Which is why it was fairly easy to ignore the fuss and reach for a cookie. She enjoyed the sweet treat as Emma glanced back and forth between the two of them, her eyes growing wider and wider as Tamara did nothing to try to settle the shrieking Sasha.

Tamara wiped her mouth daintily before speaking to Emma. "She'll be okay. She's just feeling a little emotional. Do you want me to help you with your backpack?"

Emma took another nibble from her cookie as Sasha wailed even louder. Finally, with amazing fortitude, she patted her sister on the back then pushed her schoolwork towards Tamara, freeing both hands for her glass of milk.

So be it. They might go deaf, but Tamara figured this was an acceptable first step in the nanny process. She popped the rest of her cookie into her mouth and did the next thing.

6

$\mathcal{C}$aleb had intended to be home when the girls got off the bus, but he'd arrived a couple minutes late, which meant he walked into the house in time to hear Sasha burst into tears.

He knew his daughter well enough to recognize the sound as crocodile tears and nothing more serious, but there was still that initial sense of utter failure.

This wasn't what he wanted for them. With all the changes over the past two months—and hell, the years before—their little worlds were out of control. Having to deal with the unknown was tough at his age, let alone theirs.

He stopped in the hallway, peeking into the kitchen without showing himself. In the first two-second glimpse he caught the emotions sliding over Tamara's face. Sadness, confusion—he got that one. Sasha was not an easy person to deal with. The only thing he didn't see was frustration, so he hung back and waited another moment.

Tamara placed both hands on the island, talking a deep breath as she observed Sasha with that hint of sadness in her eyes.

Glancing at Emma, she offered a sympathetic headshake, but she didn't try to go over and hug Sasha or anything.

Then she ignored Sasha and moved to Emma's side. "One message about a field trip. I'll put it on the calendar." Tamara placed the open homework book in front of his younger daughter. "Oh lovely—spelling words."

Emma stuck out her tongue.

Tamara chuckled and patted Emma on the shoulder. "Yeah, me too, kiddo. But if you're going to write notes, you'd better be able to spell. How about you start? We'll give Sasha another minute."

Caleb leaned against the hallway wall and watched as Tamara worked on something at the stove, coming back every now and then to check on Emma. Throughout it all, Sasha continued to cry—big, dramatic gasps worthy of an Academy award. Softer, then louder again when she realized she wasn't getting any attention.

Tamara disregarded the performance other than to grab a box of tissues off the side counter and plop it next to Sasha's elbow.

By this time Emma was giving her sister the evil eye, but she also ignored the caterwauling with incredible patience.

They were more tolerant than him. Caleb's nerve endings were raw from the shrieking. He stepped forward and cleared his throat, making sure he was loud enough to give a warning before he walked into the room.

Tamara spotted him, and between her jerk of surprise and his noisemaking, it was enough Sasha glanced over her shoulder—

Miracle of miracles, the tears shut off as if she'd turned a valve. She grabbed a handful of tissues as she hurriedly reached for her backpack and began pulling things from it, all the time keeping her face turned away.

Tamara watched warily, but Emma slipped off her chair and

ran to greet him like usual, stopping inches away before wrinkling her nose then for emphasis, pinching it closed.

"Yes, button, I've been doing stinky things, and I'm not done with work for the day. I just thought I would stop in and say hello." He glanced at the island. "Are those cookies? I might have to steal a couple."

Emma kissed her fingertips then pressed them against his lips before running to the counter and climbing up to grab a glass.

She held it out to him.

"I'd love some milk. How do you eat cookies without a glass of milk?"

"Cookies without milk are illegal," Tamara agreed. "Sasha, would you please pour for your daddy?"

Sasha got off her stool quickly, grabbing the milk from the fridge and going to work to fill the glass Emma left on the counter. She paused to get rid of her tissues before turning to him, all evidence of her tears wiped clean and a beautiful smile in place. "We're having a snack before doing our homework."

Caleb nodded. "I see. Sounds like a great plan. And yum. Cookies—not something we get every day."

Emma apparently approved as she had two clutched in one fist and a pencil in the other. She'd pulled out a piece of paper and was drawing a picture.

"Are those your spelling words?" Tamara asked.

Her little shoulders rose before Emma let out an enormous sigh and slid the paper under her notebook, returning to the dreaded assignment.

It wasn't appropriate to laugh at either of his children. He exchanged a glance with Tamara, thankful he didn't have to say a word. She'd picked up on his amusement, a hint of a smile twisting the corners of her lips.

He stood and enjoyed his cookie as Sasha told him a random set of information including what she'd done in gym class, that someone in second grade had a birthday soon, and that the pillow on her bed was lumpy.

The cold milk rinsed down the sweetness of the cookie perfectly, and since world war three seemed to have been averted, he took his leave.

"Be good," Caleb warned, pressing a kiss to Sasha's head after leaving his glass in the sink.

"Always," she said without a blink.

God, he was in so much trouble down the road.

He returned to the barn, thinking hard as he went. He'd have to spend a little extra time making sure the girls were comfortable, but he wasn't about to let them chase Tamara away. He couldn't continue on his own. From what he'd seen so far, Tamara was just the type of person he'd hoped for in his daughters' lives—firm and yet with a sense of humour.

He was still somewhat distracted as he wandered through the doors and nearly walked into Ashton.

The foreman put up a hand to stop them from bumping. "Open your eyes, lad. I've no desire to be bounced to the ground."

"Sorry, Ashton," Caleb said. "You're usually a much bigger target. You don't have a horse beside you."

"Your brothers aim to put me out of a job," Ashton complained before proving his grumbling was all a show. "It's good to have Walker back. I might let him take over working with Dewdrop, if you don't mind."

Caleb shrugged. "You know the animals best, you and Luke. But I thought we'd sold her."

Ashton made a rude noise. "Luke offered to sell, but no way was I letting her go to that woman."

Caleb hid his smile. There was only one female their foreman referred to as *that woman*. Ashton and Sonora were involved in a long-standing feud.

Feud, or something else? Not that Ashton would ever admit

it, but Caleb was pretty sure the man was sweet on the woman who lived a couple of range roads over from their homestead.

"That's not very nice," he chided. "Luke said he'd sell the animal. We're going to get a bad reputation if you go back on our word."

Ashton grumbled for a moment before lifting his face sheepishly. "I gave her a different horse," he admitted. "She didn't need something young and wild. She needed something steady and reliable, so I let her have Sampson."

Caleb glanced away because there was no way he could stop from grinning this time. The man was a sentimental fool. Sampson was probably worth twice as much as the unruly young filly, at least in the short term.

Ashton seemed to sense what Caleb wasn't saying. He let out a gruff noise. "I know, but it'd be a shame to hear she'd broken her neck trying to ride a horse that was too much for her."

"I agree," Caleb said. "Who'd you fight with at Ginny's annual barbecue if Ms. Sonora was no longer around?"

Ashton gave him a dirty look. "Don't you sass me, young man, I can still turn you over my knee—" He eyed Caleb before shaking his head. "File that. I can still make your life hell, but I'm not putting my back out trying to wrestle any of you monsters to the ground."

"Good choice," Caleb said before slapping Ashton on the shoulder then heading through the barn and into the arena. The momentary distraction from worrying about his girls was welcome, and when he found his brothers working with the newest horses, he stopped and watched contentedly for a moment.

Their display of skill was undeniable. Even Dustin had the potential to grow into a great horseman.

Caleb stood with a foot up on the railing as the boys rode smoothly around the arena, taking turns watching each other and analyzing their moves. Adjusting gaits and soothing restless beasts.

Walker spotted him and waved a hand, using his knees to guide his horse to where Caleb waited. "Want to join us? We're going to work for another couple of hours then go into town to Longhorn's Steakhouse for dinner."

"I'll help, but I'll take a rain check on the steaks." Although he was sorely tempted. The opportunity to catch up with Walker was just that, a temptation. "I need to stick close to home the next few of days. Give the girls a chance to get used to having Tamara around."

Luke was there as well, sitting tall in the saddle as he listened to Caleb's final comments. "It'll be good when she's settled. I know you want to be around for your kids, but you need time to yourself as well." He grinned across at Walker, his eyes flashing with amusement. "Might have to take him out on the town and see if he still remembers what to do with a woman."

"Shut up," Caleb said dryly.

"That's right, Luke. Don't be rude." Walker waggled a finger at their brother. "You know it's not that he's forgotten, it's just it's been so long he might end up being a trifle quick on the trigger."

Luke snickered, far too amused for someone whose life expectancy was not much more than his next breath. "That's not the reputation we want bandied around about the Stone boys. Goes against our name." He gave a lewd wink.

Caleb shook his head as he wandered away, tossing over his shoulder. "You guys are a bunch of teenagers."

"That's the point. *We're* not, but right about now, you probably are," Luke teased.

"Stop slacking off," Dustin shouted from the far side of the arena.

Caleb ignored the lot of them as he grabbed a saddle and headed to work. He kept an eye on his watch, though, and made sure he was back inside the house in plenty of time to be cleaned up and ready to help before supper was on the table.

He pulled on clean jeans and a dark T-shirt, dragged a comb through his hair and called it done, hurrying in case there were any more temper-tantrum emergencies to deal with.

Instead, peaceful quiet greeted him as he left his room, the low murmur of country music growing louder as he entered the great room. The table was set and the most amazing smells floated on the air. He double-checked to be certain, but Sasha *was* in the room, playing a board game with Emma as they sat on the floor in front of the unlit fireplace. Tamara sat at the island, cookbooks and paper at hand as she wrote. A new calendar on the fridge held a bunch of bright notes written in a bold hand, and there were more cookies cooling on racks on the counter.

Caleb didn't say a word for fear there was some magic at work, and talking about the serene situation would break the spell.

Not only were the girls in their right minds, the room felt cozy. Plus, he wasn't about to regret there was food on the table he hadn't put together.

He closed his eyes and took a deep, appreciative breath. "I swear it smells better when somebody else cooks."

"Daddy!" Sasha scrambled to her feet.

Both girls came running to greet him, and he had to admit there was something soul-satisfying about the happiness on their faces and the tight squeeze of their hugs. He wasn't a perfect father, but they seemed pleased enough with him, most times.

Tamara had risen as well, and she motioned toward the table. "You ready to sit right away or you want a drink first?"

"I could eat."

He and the girls were halfway to the table when there was a brief knock at the kitchen door. An instant later it swung open, and Dustin poked his head in and smiled. His brother's face was heck of a lot cleaner than it had been a half hour ago when he could've sworn the kid had been rolling in the mud.

"Am I in the right place?" He stepped inside, basket in hand. He held it in Tamara's direction. "Fresh bread. JP sent these for you."

Tamara pulled the basket from him, motioning him toward the table. "Take off your boots then sit," she said. "You're right on time."

Caleb counted quickly and realized the table was set for five. "You didn't say you were joining us for dinner."

"Tamara invited me when I stopped by earlier." Dustin stepped out of his boots, lining them up on the mat beside the door. He stopped to wash his hands before moving toward the table, ruffling the girls' hair before dropping into the chair next to Sasha. "And we were working. I didn't want to interrupt since I figured I'd see you soon enough." He grinned at Tamara. "Man, it smells like heaven."

A tray filled with ribs settled on the table in front of Caleb, and there was no time for him to complain about not knowing what was going on in his own home.

Although he knew damn well one thing that was going on that wasn't going to continue for much longer—if Dustin thought he could flirt with Tamara, *hell no* for so many reasons.

Tamara placed the rest of the food in front of him. She'd stacked all their plates there as well, and when she sat to his right, he hesitated. Especially after she picked up the water pitcher and began pouring for everybody.

A flashback to an earlier time struck hard—Wendy in that same position. Her blonde hair pulled back, face tight. Silent as the girls babbled and Dustin, Ginny and Dare teased each other.

Tamara's expression shifted to worry. "This is right, isn't it? The table setup?"

He hurried to assure her, the tightness in his gut

uncomfortable even as she waited for his answer. "Family ritual," he explained putting a scoop of everything on the first plate. He hesitated then placed it in front of her. "I don't even remember when it started, but my dad used to serve everyone. When they passed on, I kept up the tradition."

Dustin lost his smile, thoughtfulness drifting over his expression as he met Caleb's eyes. "We needed that bit of sameness during the mess of them being gone." He glanced over to Tamara. "I was too little to remember all the details, but my guess is with seven at the table some days, and eleven when Dare's family joined us, it was the only way to make sure everybody got some food from the pot."

Caleb had kept serving while Dustin talked. Sasha glanced at him as she passed him a full plate, as if realizing something for the first time "You were as big as I am now, when grandma and grandpa died."

Dustin nodded once.

"I'm not too little to remember things. And neither is Emma. We remember *lots* of things."

Her lips twisted stubbornly, and Caleb had to laugh. "Yes, pumpkin, you remember lots of things. I think what Uncle Dustin's saying is he's gotten so old *he's* forgotten what it's like to be seven and nine like you and Emma."

Emma poked Sasha and did something under the table with her fingers, then for some strange reason, they both glanced at Tamara before Sasha gave him a pointed glare.

"Emma's seven and a *half*," Sasha reminded him sternly.

Everyone had food and drink, and conversation turned to memories and whether they were more like a TV show or a framed picture, and slowly that sense of being watched by a ghost diminished enough Caleb could take a deep breath and push past it.

The food helped. He sank his teeth into another bite of barbecued ribs and sighed happily.

Next to him, Tamara chuckled. "What would you have done if I hadn't known how to cook? You never asked."

"The fact he's on his third helping means he knows how lucky he is," Dustin teased, even as he held his plate forward. "I'm lucky too. A few more?"

"Fourth serving," Caleb pointed out, but he slid the last of the ribs to his brother's plate.

Dinner done, Dustin took over the dishes again, this time with Sasha drying and Emma putting away.

Tamara motioned to Caleb. "I figured out the washing machine, so if you've got clothes you want me to do tomorrow—"

"I'll do my own wash," Caleb interrupted.

She folded her arms. "My job, remember?" They stared at each other for a moment before she gave in. "Whatever. If it's in the laundry room, it'll get washed. Up to you. You're a big boy, and I have other battles to fight."

His gaze drifted to his daughters. "Thanks for taking on the battle. You okay with how things went today?"

Tamara nodded. "Pretty much. Can we chat after the girls are in bed?"

He agreed. Then they went different directions for a bit, the evening slipping away until the tooth brushing and other nighttime rituals began.

The quiet time while he tucked the girls in had always been when secrets and questions were shared. Sometimes because they were pushing to stay up late, sometimes he knew it was because the world was buzzing in their brains too fast to be ignored.

Tonight was bound to be a doozey.

He pulled the quilt over Sasha, then reached to turn out the light.

Sure enough, she bounced upright like a rubber ball.

"Is she really going to stay?" Sasha demanded.

Caleb took a deep breath as he settled on the edge of the bed beside her. "Was it nice to get to have supper together tonight?"

Sasha frowned. "We have supper together most nights. I don't see why she has to be here."

Speaking carefully, he worked around the problem best he could. "Sometimes Daddy hires new people to come help out when we've got a tough job to do, right? Tamara is another worker on the ranch."

She looked him over suspiciously.

"Pumpkin, I know it's not easy having your aunties gone, but because they're big enough to do the next thing in their lives, that means you have to be big enough, too."

"But I don't *like* her," Sasha complained. "We don't need a nanny at all. We can take care of things on our own. I promise, Daddy."

Caleb shook his head. "This afternoon, after enjoying a cookie fresh from the oven, I got to go back outside and help your uncles work with the new horses. If Tamara hadn't been here to get supper ready and help you with your homework, then I would have had to stay inside. That means the guys would have been doing extra work for me. I don't think that's fair."

Sasha made a face.

"Would you like it if you had to do all Emma's chores?"

She shook her head.

Caleb thought it over. "I know it's not exactly the same thing, and your uncles would never complain, but I feel responsible to do my share. And I don't want to have things not get done, whether that's with the ranch, or with you and Emma. Remember I missed signing you up for swimming lessons because I forgot?"

He was almost scared to bring that one up considering the number of tears his mistake had generated.

Sasha folded her lips into a frown "I don't need swimming lessons. And I don't need extra treats. I want you, Daddy. And Emma wants—" She snapped her lips shut, hesitating for a second before continuing, "I *think* Emma feels the same."

Caleb took another breath. "This is something you'll just have to be sad about, pumpkin, because I'm the grownup. I need help, and Tamara is who I've hired."

Sasha's lips quivered for a second, but this time it was honest emotion instead of a warmup to dramatic effect.

Then she said something so quietly he had to lean in. "Say that again?"

"What if she leaves?" she whispered.

It was like a knife stab into his gut. He wrapped his arms around her, holding her close, and he wished again he'd been smarter, somewhere along the line, even though he had no idea what that would have looked like. Wished he'd have protected his little girls from the hurt they'd experienced.

"I can't promise she'll stay forever, pumpkin. But when someone takes on a job, they make a promise to do their best and work hard at it for a period of time. Tamara said she'd stay for six months for sure. That's where we're starting."

"That's not what I mean, Daddy." Sasha was barely audible, her usually boisterous voice tight with tears. "What if... What if we don't want her to go, but she doesn't like us, so she leaves anyway?"

My god. Most of the time he managed to keep from feeling anything at all about his ex-wife, but a moment like this he lost all charity possible and wished he could rip Wendy in two.

No way in hell did he want his children thinking Tamara would only stay if they were angels. He didn't want them to think their behaviour could chase her away.

He willed himself calm before he spoke.

"We're getting a little ahead of ourselves," he said. "Let's worry about settling into a routine so we all know who's doing what. That's the first thing. Then maybe we can have a few less tears during homework time."

She looked suitably guilty before accepting his kiss and curling up under the covers. "Yes, Daddy."

Tucking in Emma was easier, only because she didn't say all the things that would break his heart, but the questions were there in her eyes.

He curled his arms around her, perched on the edge of her tiny bed.

Everyone from the teachers at school to the family psychiatrist they'd been forced to visit were worried about her speech habits, but she spoke just fine. Oh, maybe not a mess of words, but she talked. When she had something to say, she'd say it, that's what he'd found.

Caleb tucked his fingers under Emma's chin and lifted until she looked up at him. "I know you miss your aunties, but I think Tamara's a good person. Auntie Dare recommended her, and you know she wouldn't do that if she didn't think Tamara was pretty special."

Emma dipped her chin, suspicion and worry on her face, but her concerns lay in a whole different direction. "Sasha's sad," she whispered.

"Sasha likes to worry," he pointed out. "But again, do you think your Auntie Dare would send someone here who can't handle Sasha? I mean in a good way. Like who'd enjoy spending time with Sasha, and with you?"

Her head twisted from side to side.

"Did you finish the picture you were drawing earlier?" he asked.

Emma shook her head.

"Well, then, tomorrow you work on that. I'd love to see it when it's done."

"Daddy?" Sweet and soft.

"Yes, button?"

She clung to him like a limpet for a moment before putting her lips right beside his ear and barely breathing out the words. "I love you."

His chest tightened. "I love you too. Very, very much."

Emma slid under the covers, popping up once to straighten the book on her side table before lying back and closing her eyes. She looked like a porcelain doll, pristine and perfect. And as usual, he stared at her for a moment wondering why the way she slept made him feel so uncomfortable.

That uneasy sensation only continued as he wandered back to the living room to discover Dustin was still in the house, chatting with Tamara. She sat in the corner of the couch, laughing at something his brother had said. Dustin was perched on the edge of the coffee table across from her, his gaze fixed on her face, hands on his knees as he leaned in.

Screw this. Caleb walked between them en route to his chair, forcing Dustin to sit back.

His younger brother stood abruptly. "I guess I should be going. Thanks for the dinner invite. It was really good."

"You're welcome anytime," Tamara told him, smiling before shifting position. She lifted her feet to the couch and leaned back, making herself at home.

Dustin waved at Caleb then headed to the door.

"Don't be late tomorrow morning," Caleb ordered.

"I hear old people need lots of sleep," Dustin quipped back. "You'd better go to bed soon or you'll be the one who's late."

Cocky bastard slipped out the door before Caleb could find something to throw.

Tamara laughed. "Little siblings are annoying."

"Yes."

She wrapped her hands around her knees, pulling upright and changing the topic. "You caught the little cryfest of Sasha's today?"

Seemed they were going to dive right in and talk. Caleb straightened up and adjusted his mindset. "She was faking it. I figure you knew that, but just so you know, I knew it too. But she is worried."

"She's got a stranger in her house. I don't blame her." Tamara hesitated. "I told her she's not allowed to answer for Emma. That's what set her off."

Oh. Caleb let that rattle around in his brain. "I see."

"I'm not going to force Emma to talk," Tamara rushed on. "But if everyone answers for her then—"

"You don't need to explain." Another wave of frustration hit him hard. He was so *stupid*. He should have thought of that earlier. Not that he wanted to push Emma to talk more, but in a way, it was lazy of them to have let Sasha run wild.

Tamara was examining him closely. "Is that a 'you don't need to explain because you're right' look, or do you think I'm wrong? You need to give me a few more clues, because I can't read your expression."

He sighed. "You're right."

Her head tilted, concern skittering across her face. "You okay?"

Caleb shoved aside his worries and nodded, trying to look more cheerful. He was afraid it probably looked as if he was constipated, but what the hell. It was the best he could do. "How about you? Other than the crying, how was your first day? You okay so far?"

She eyed him for a moment as if she might challenge his rapid change of topic. Then a soft sigh escaped and she eased back on the couch. "Pretty good. I'll ask if I have troubles."

Tamara pulled a notebook off the table and began writing. Silence fell, and the conversation ended as abruptly as it had begun.

Caleb took a book from the basket beside his chair and tried to get into it, but having another person in the room...

Be honest. Having another person in the room who wasn't one of his brothers, or his best friend Josiah Ryder, was potent.

He was aware of every move she made.

The top of her pen worked in smooth motions, a little crease forming between her brows as she concentrated on her task. Her legs were bent halfway, tilted against the couch, her notebook balanced in her lap.

He alternated between trying to read his book and letting his gaze slide over the blurry words back to her body.

She'd taken the elastic from her hair and the heavy dark-brown mass held a hint of a curl as it lay over her shoulders. As if she'd been in the sun for a while, her cheeks had a rosy hew, lips soft and shiny. Her shirt clung to the curve of her breasts, shifting with every breath.

For some stupid reason his eyes kept being drawn to her feet. She was wrapped up from head to toe in jeans and flannel, and he couldn't take his eyes off the fuzzy socks she wore.

They were white with pink polka dots, and they matched her glasses. She rubbed her feet together, and suddenly everything inside him was tight for a whole new reason.

Damn it, he was turned on as if he'd been watching porn, and all she'd done was innocently wiggle.

When she pulled the throw off the back of the couch, he finally got it. "Cold?"

She shook herself, as if surprised to see him in the easy chair. "A little. This time of year it's tough to know from one minute to the next what the temperature's going to be."

"I can light the fire," he offered.

Why the hell did his brain have to feed him images of her naked skin highlighted by firelight glow?

Her gaze drifted to the clock on the wall. "Maybe tomorrow. I probably should head to bed. It's been a longer day than I'm used to."

She gathered her things and stood. Caleb rose as well, and suddenly they were both standing there, looking at each other. That sense of...*something* struck again.

"Well, good night," Tamara announced. Then she walked away quickly.

Walked? No, she damn near ran from the room.

Caleb sat alone in the growing silence with far too many thoughts and needs he knew had to go unanswered.

7

*T*wo days later, she and the girls were *maybe* starting to fall into what Tamara could consider a comfortable routine. They hadn't had any more huge blowups, at least. That much was good.

She put the last breakfast plate into the dishwasher then grabbed for her phone, answering her sister's familiar ring tone with a light tease.

"Tamara's Pawn shop—what you got to hawk?"

"One older sister and a slightly used dad. I already got rid of the other old biddy who was making my life miserable," Lisa said saucily.

Tamara blew a raspberry into her phone. "I love you too, little sis. What're you up to today?"

"Avoiding Dad, helping Karen move stock—the usual."

Tamara tugged on her coat then took her coffee cup with her out on the porch. It was barely warm enough, but it was sunny, and she couldn't resist the view. "Pretty typical. But I thought Dad was behaving himself better these days. What's got him riled up?"

Lisa hesitated before spilling the beans. "Karen made some suggestion about crops and animals for next year, and her lack of Y chromosome smacked him in the face a few times."

Yeah, that was business as usual. Tamara breathed out her frustration, thankful she was three hundred kilometers away. "You got any great plans for the evening?"

"Saw some of the gang last night at Traders, but stop trying to control the conversation. I called to see how it's going with you. How's the nanny business?"

Easy answer. "Better than having to deal with Dad pretending he's not throwing a hissy fit."

Lisa wouldn't let it lie. "You miss the hospital."

Tamara gave it some serious thought before answering honestly. "You know? I've been too distracted to miss the old job."

A soft chuckle echoed from the other end of the line. "He must be one fine cowboy."

Good grief. Little sisters were the worst. "Behave. That's not what I was talking about, and you know it."

"What? I was making a simple observation. I think you were brilliant to pick a boss who looks tasty in Levis and a Stetson."

The only way to deal with this was to ignore Lisa's innuendo, although...her little sister was right.

The man looked damn fine no matter what he wore, or didn't wear.

Tamara focused on the real question. "It's going okay. We've had a couple of testing moments here and there, but for the most part I think I'm surviving."

"Of course you are. I bet you're doing awesome. I actually expected to get your voice mail at this time of day. What'd you do, duct tape them to their beds?"

"Close. They're cleaning their rooms. Or more accurately, they took off the sheets in Emma's room so I could wash them, and the two of them are now working on Sasha's room. I figure they'll be done a week from Tuesday."

Lisa laughed. "So they take after you. Awesome. You should be able to offer all the tricks of the trade, like shoving the mess under the bed."

"It means I know where to find everything if they don't actually clean."

"True that. One sec." Lisa whistled sharply and called for her dog—must be walking outside and chatting on her cell. She was back a moment later. "What else you got going on?"

"We're making Halloween costumes. A rocket ship, and get this—a cat burglar."

Tamara had to smile. It had taken more than a couple of pieces of paper plus Emma bringing out a movie and shaking it at them before she and Sasha figured out Emma did not want to be a *cat*. "And now I'm going to be reading *Harriet the Spy* to them, because Emma is fascinated by the idea."

"You could have a *Spy Kids* marathon," Lisa suggested. "Only don't play the last one—and you only need the first so you can enjoy the second, so you could just watch that one."

"Yeah, one movie is really a marathon," Tamara teased.

A clatter rang in the background, and Lisa responded before coming back on the line. "I'm being summoned. Karen sends her love, and big sloppy kisses from all the puppies on the ranch, and I miss you, and call me soon, 'kay?"

"Deal. Love you too." Tamara hung up and stared happily over the view. The grazing cattle in the distance were little black specks against the faded yellow-brown of the dry grass. They needed the snow to turn everything fresh and clean again.

She took a deep breath and sucked in the cool air like a balm for the soul.

It was too nice to not share. She leapt to her feet and headed indoors to Sasha's room.

The girls had music playing in the background, and the entire contents of Sasha's closet were piled in one enormous heap on her bed.

Tamara raised a brow. "Interesting cleaning method."

They glanced at her guiltily from the floor where they were both ignoring the mess and had their noses tucked into books.

"We were just—" Sasha started before Tamara interrupted.

"No excuses. You need a break from cleaning, but not more indoor time. Grab your coats and pull on your boots. We're going out for some fresh air."

The girls scrambled to their feet, and they were all outside in under two minutes.

Sasha headed toward the cottage her aunt had lived in, but Tamara called her back. "Let's go to the barns."

A quick twist and Sasha was racing in a new direction, Emma hard on her heels. Tamara followed more slowly, the trail in the grass well worn by previous trips. She smiled, wiggling her shoulders under her fall coat. She'd need to break out something more substantial soon.

They passed an old chicken coop, the fencing broken in a few places. Tamara paused to examine it, but the girls were far enough ahead she only took a moment. It hadn't been used for a few years.

She caught up with them, but instead of heading into the barn they were climbing on a tire swing hanging outside the arena.

Tamara stopped to let them play for a bit, and that's when she realized that there was no door into the barn anywhere close to them.

"Hey, Sasha. How do we get into the barn?"

The dark-haired girl stared at her in surprise. "Daddy takes us."

What? "You mean you never go into the barn unless Caleb is with you?"

Emma answered this time, shaking her head slowly, her eyes wide.

She was missing something. "Then how do you do your chores?"

"We don't have chores in the barn. We have chores in the house," Sasha explained, a tiny bit of smugness coming into her voice that she knew something Tamara didn't.

"You don't take care of any of the animals?" Oh. Maybe there was a reason for that. "You don't *want* to take care of any of the animals, is that it?"

Once again, the girls exchanged a glance and this time Emma snuck close to her sister, motivated enough to make her point clear. She put her hand around Sasha's ear and whispered.

Sasha turned back with a shrug. "Emma and I like the cats, and I like horses, but Daddy says they're too big, and we're too little. He takes us riding, though. Him and Uncle Luke, and sometimes Uncle Dusty."

"So you don't go in the barn, and you don't have chickens— did you used to have chickens?"

Sasha's face closed up like a thunderstorm had hit. "Not for a long time."

Then she caught Emma by the hand and the two of them headed back toward the house as if they were on a mission. Emma glanced over her shoulders a few times, her sad little eyes burning into Tamara's soul.

Okay, something was wrong. The girls obviously took that path often enough that it was still easy to see, but they weren't mucking about in the barn? They weren't climbing up into the hayloft to chase down kittens?

Simmering began in her belly, but Tamara didn't say

anything as she followed the girls to the house. She made them a snack before getting them back on task in Sasha's room.

Only by lunchtime, the simmering had turned into a small pocket of very hot coals, and if she didn't do something about it she was going to explode.

Maybe it was the phone call from Lisa that morning—a reminder that her father was still making her sisters' lives miserable. But she hadn't thought Caleb to have been of the same old-school bigotry that controlled George Coleman hard enough to have sent Tamara off the ranch.

She got the girls settled with sandwiches and veggie sticks in front of a movie then headed out to the barns to track down Caleb.

She ran into Kelli around the first corner.

The young woman stopped and gave her a smile. "Hey, girlfriend. Heading for a ride?"

"Need to talk to Caleb."

The words came out a little clipped, and one of Kelli's brows rose. "Oh?"

"Know where he is?"

Kelli extended an arm deeper into the barn, pointing the way. "Give a shout if you want backup."

Tamara did her best to keep from stomping. "I'll be sure to tell him that."

A soft snicker reached her ears, but it wasn't enough to make a dent in her level of frustration. And when she poked her head into the room at the end of the hallway and discovered Caleb working on saddles, she marched right up and got in his face.

"I think I missed a few things. I need you to clarify for me."

He blinked in surprise. "Tamara. Everything okay?"

"I don't know." Her voice was laced with sarcasm, so she pulled back enough to not dig herself too huge of a hole in case she was wrong. "I asked the girls when we were going to do their chores, and they informed me they only go into the barn when you're with them. Which makes me think they probably don't have chores."

"They have chores," Caleb said, looking confused. "We talked about this. You said that they were already doing them."

"Dishes and cleaning inside the house. What about outside chores?"

"They help weed the garden in the summertime. I guess they could probably shovel snow, but there's been no use for that because Dusty uses the tractor."

He was not listening, and her temper kept rising. "There's always a lot of chores taking care of animals. What're they responsible for in the barns?"

Understanding came into his eyes. "Oh. Yeah, they don't have barn chores."

Caleb turned his back, lifting the saddle into place on the wall as if the conversation was done.

Hell no was this conversation done. Tamara tugged on his arm, attempting to get him to face her. She'd have more luck rotating a tree, but she was angry enough to try.

"You live on a goddamn ranch. What if they want to take care of it with you? And if you say they can't because they're girls, I will find where you keep the castration tools and prove that a girl can learn to do any task she sets her mind on—"

"We have horses, and hands, and I don't want little people wandering where they can get hurt."

She planted her hands on her hips. "There's this awesome concept called supervision, darling."

Caleb stared at her from his full height, locking his dark brown eyes on hers. But instead of the fight she thought she'd get, he spoke softly.

"Right, *darlin'*. Now that you're here, you can give them the supervision I couldn't before. You want to add outdoor chores, go ahead."

And that was it.

Huh.

It was bit of a hollow victory considering he didn't even raise his voice.

He was turning away when Tamara spoke again. "What animals can they help with?"

His shoulders drooped for a moment before he straightened and moved closer. "You ever listen?"

"When there's something worth hearing."

His eyes flashed before he was back to hooded lids and an unreadable expression. "We've got too many horses around here that are untrained. I don't want them—"

"I said I'd supervise."

For a second his hands moved toward her, urgent and wild. Not in a way that scared her, but in a way that made a pulse go off, deep in her core.

Then it was gone again, that fire in his eyes, and he was back to calm. Reasonable. He dipped his chin once. "Fine. No horses, but you're in charge of whatever else you want them to do."

She was in his body space. He put his hands on her upper arms and held on tight, and another explosion went off in her core, heat blossoming outward in anticipation.

When he basically picked her up six inches then rotated on the spot, Tamara was shocked into stillness.

He lowered her to the ground then turned his back and walked out of the room.

No word spoken in anger on his part, no real emotion other than those brief glimpses, while she stood there damn near shaking with adrenaline. Half from anger and half from being far too turned on when all he'd done was touch her arms.

She rushed from the barn, thankful for the cool air brushing against her heated cheeks as she marched back to the house. He was the most infuriating, sexy, annoying, *desirable* ass she'd ever had the misfortune of meeting.

But he had given her permission, and he hadn't defined what that meant, so she was going to use this opportunity to make sure the girls got what they needed.

She wasn't thinking at all about how much this might piss off a certain cowboy who had a stick up his ass. Nope, not thinking that at all.

She pulled out her phone and tapped in a familiar number.

"Hey, you. What's going on?" Her older sister Karen asked with a touch of concern. "Everything okay?"

"Everything's peachy," Tamara informed her. "Today I'm a paying customer. I need a favour."

As she shared her idea for outdoor chores with her sister, Tamara felt a sense of satisfaction. A certain grumpy cowboy wasn't going to like this one bit, and she didn't care.

She entered the house with a lighter step than she'd left with, anticipation turning her grin into something slightly evil.

He wasn't going to know what hit him.

8

*P*eacefulness soaked into Caleb's bones. Early-morning chores had gone well, and none of the animals had tried to kill him, which was always a bonus.

He strolled back to the house to find the coffee was on but Tamara nowhere to be seen, although the scent of bacon was building in the kitchen.

He grabbed a cup then headed to the front porch, pulling to a stop when he discovered Tamara curled up in one of the Adirondack chairs tucked out of the wind. "Mind some company?"

She shook her head, gesturing to the second chair that already had a cushion on it. "It's your view. I can't get enough of it."

Caleb settled into place. He'd worried for a moment she would break his lovely mellow mood by starting in again on the chore issue, but like the night before at dinner, she didn't say a word.

Only, it wasn't as if she was refusing to speak about it. More as if she wasn't stewing over the topic. Definitely not pouting.

He had to admit he wasn't quite sure how to deal with the woman.

She let out a happy sigh. "I could come here every day for an entire year and not get bored of that view. I've never lived this close to a lake before. I mean, we have water on the Whiskey Creek property, but it's constantly moving." She turned her face toward the lake, smile widening. "You have to go find a quiet fishing hole to get that kind of sparkle on the water."

"You fish?"

Tamara snorted, taking a sip of her coffee before she lifted her head to answer him. "You don't have to sound so surprised."

"It's just... My sisters don't like fishing. Ginny and Dare enjoy plenty of other outdoor activities, but they weren't partial to putting bait on a hook. And since that's one of the requirements, they tended to not join us when we went."

"Everybody pretty much likes what they like, and sometimes it doesn't make any sense. Do your girls fish? Because there must be killer fishing around here." She pointed at the lake "That stocked?"

He didn't know which question to answer first. "There's rainbow in the lake and trout in the river." It was horrible to have to confess it, but he was honest. "They've been a few times, but I don't know if the girls *like* to fish."

He knew they liked to play dress-up, and they were both moderately terrible at helping in the kitchen. He knew Emma hated storms, and that Sasha would rather be skinned alive than admit she was afraid of anything.

"Seems whenever it's just me-and-the-girls time, outside of the usual, you know, special-like, I try to do things I know they'll enjoy."

Tamara spoke softly. "But sometimes you can't tell what you like until you've tried."

He nodded, even as temptation said she was partially wrong.

There were plenty of things that he'd never tried he was positive he would absolutely love. She'd turned her face back to admire the lake again, so it was easy to pretend to be gazing toward the barn and instead study her out of the corner of his eye.

She'd pulled her hair back into a ponytail, and her lips were curled in a gentle smile. He was pretty sure he would enjoy pressing his mouth to hers. He was fairly certain that if he got a chance he would thoroughly enjoy tasting every inch of her body. And although he shouldn't let his mind even begin to head in this direction, he was damn positive if he ever got her naked under him, he'd like that a whole hell of a lot too.

He eased his legs forward, gaining extra room as he turned his thoughts to other matters in the hopes time would allow his body to settle.

What he should be doing instead of sitting here with her was making headway on the mess in his office, but part of him couldn't bear to leave. "What have you got planned for the day? I'll be around if you need me. I try to take a couple days off each week, or at least the morning or afternoon. Me and the boys rotate. I've got Sunday and Wednesday when it works—the girls have early dismissal most Wednesdays."

"I need the girls this morning, if you don't mind. If you'd take care of them this afternoon, I'd appreciate it. My sisters are coming to visit, so that means we could go to town. But don't worry. I'll still have dinner on the table for six."

He was going to get to see more of the Coleman clan? "They're welcome to stay and eat with us," he offered before snorting. "Which is kind of ironic because you're the one who's going to cook it."

Tamara grinned then eyed her watch. "I'll extend the invite. I'd better run. I've got a few things to do before breakfast."

She rose to her feet and vanished.

Caleb sat back down, successfully ignoring the office chores as he spent another half hour thinking about how nice it was to have a reasonable conversation with a woman.

The final days of his marriage with Wendy had been all about drama. It was strange, though. Tamara had shouted at him louder yesterday than Wendy ever had. His ex-wife's complaints had been delivered in quiet, well-modulated tones alternated with soundless judgement.

In spite of Tamara's temper, she didn't seem to carry a grudge.

Later that morning he was checking supplies when Kelli marched past at high speed. "Visitors, boss."

Caleb put aside his clipboard and stepped after her, watching with curiosity as a truck hauling a small trailer pulled in next to the barn. The trailer slipped close to one of the arenas, and Caleb watched in admiration as the driver tucked it in sweet as possible before stopping perfectly next to the fence.

The doors opened and two people got out, and he moved forward to greet them, recognizing them from the family resemblance. Dark hair, dark eyes, similar images to Tamara, who was marching across the yard at high speed with Sasha and Emma following a little slower.

The next moment Tamara was wrapped in a three-way hug. The Whiskey Creek girls liked each other.

Caleb moved within hearing distance as Tamara stepped back to introduce the girls. "Meet Sasha and Emma. Girls, this is my big sister Karen and my little sister Lisa. Although I think we're pretty much all the same size these days."

Karen waved at the girls.

Lisa pulled off her hat then squatted to eye Sasha and Emma more closely. "Nope," she said. "You two can't be Sasha and Emma because you're way bigger than I thought you'd be. I'm sure Tamara isn't allowed to be a nanny for any one old enough to drive a car."

Emma snickered.

Sasha raised a brow, and Caleb jerked to a halt, recognizing his own expression on his daughter's face.

Tamara noticed him then, gesturing her sisters toward him. "Guys, this is my boss, Caleb Stone."

Karen shook his hand. Lisa rose to her feet with a grin, brushing her hands against her thighs before coming forward to offer another firm handshake. "Nice place you got here," she said.

"Thanks."

Karen assessed the ranch with a judgmental eye. "You keep separate barns for the horses and the other animals?"

Caleb glanced at Tamara to discover she was rolling her eyes. He was tempted to wink at her for some strange outlandish reason. "We do now. Don't have a lot of animals other than horses at the moment. Cattle are on the range with their own shelters where needed."

Karen nodded before glancing back at Tamara. "I hope you know what you're doing."

"Hush. I know plenty." She turned to Sasha and Emma. "Remember those extra chores I was telling you about?"

Sasha's stoic expression faded into suspicion. "More chores?" She glanced over at Caleb. "Daddy?"

Oops. "I said it was okay."

Dustin strolled up right around then, smiling appreciatively at the three women. Caleb considered leaning over and smacking him one across the back of his head.

"Ladies." Dustin tipped his hat before twisting to Tamara. "Ashton says he's prepared the side shed for you. Next to the old chicken coop."

"Point me in the right direction, and I'll bring the trailer. Probably the safest way to get them into the yard," Karen said.

Tamara waved at the girls. "Lead on."

They all had to wait because Emma had grabbed her sister's sleeve and was tugging on it hard, shaking her head.

Sasha turned back hurriedly. "Emma doesn't like chickens."

That was news to Caleb. Damn—he'd gotten rid of the chickens because of his ex's complaints, but she'd never said a word about Emma's fears. He hesitated. Maybe he should override this idea of Tamara's before it was too late.

But Tamara took the news in stride. "No worries. We're not getting chickens."

The slow smile that curled over Emma's face was reassuring, yet not. She gave her head a happy toss then caught Sasha by the hand and led her back at high speed across the yard and toward the chicken coop.

Meanwhile, Caleb eyed Tamara and wondered how she'd managed so much mischief in just twenty-four hours, including corrupting his foreman and, it appeared, his brother.

The rest of the group followed except for Karen who returned to her truck to back in the trailer.

Ahead of them, the small shed still needed some work, but the fence was once again vertical, and there was an additional lean-to roof over one side. He could've sworn it hadn't been there the day before.

Caleb and Dustin took up the rear. Lisa and Tamara were chatting away happily, talking over each other in that way that women did without being annoyed. They both wore form-fitting jeans, and he wasn't about to admit that his gaze lingered far too long on Tamara's hips as they swayed from side to side front of him.

Then he glanced at Dustin, elbowing him hard in the ribs when he noticed that his kid brother was also eyeing the women's butts.

"Stop that," he ordered.

"Huh?" Dustin said in a shock before grinning. "Oh, come on. You were doing it, too."

Caleb wasn't about to admit any such thing.

They all gathered at the gate outside the pen, waiting as Karen backed the trailer into position.

Tamara turned to him. "Ashton said you used to raise fryers. Maybe when spring comes around, if you want to start that up again, we can decide if this is still the best place for Eeny, Meany and Miney."

Caleb was curious as all get out by now. "What? No Moe?" he asked.

"She's pregnant, so I left her back at our ranch. Figured you didn't need that kind of trouble right off the bat," Karen told him, joining them at the doors to the trailer.

Dustin pushed ahead of Caleb, as eager as the little girls to see what would happen next. "What did you bring?"

He leaned around Tamara just as Karen opened the doors and they were all greeted with a chorus of *mahhh*s.

Goats.

Three of them, judging by the names, and they must've been tired of sitting in the trailer because they rushed forward at high speed, barreling into Dustin and knocking him to the ground.

The following aftermath was hard to describe. The entire area was full of little girls screaming, young ladies shouting, and his brother starting a half-dozen times to swear then remembering his nieces were present.

The goats ran in circles, jumping over each other and anything in their way. If they'd run away in a straight line, it would've been a lot less chaotic, but for some reason the creatures remained close to the familiarity of their trailer. Although they didn't want back in it, and they didn't want into the yard that was now open to them after Caleb had fought his way through the squirming horde and pulled the gate aside.

Considering it was chaos, Caleb couldn't help but be pleased because while Sasha was making most of the noise, screaming at the top of her lungs with a wide grin on her face, she wasn't the only one.

Emma wasn't screaming, but she let out the occasional sharp bray as one of the goats brushed by her hard, sending her off balance. She toppled over into Dustin who had just about made it up to his feet.

Lisa went one way and Karen went the other, and finally the three grey and white creatures were somewhat contained in a square between the trailer, the girls, and the yard.

Over the screaming and bleating rang the soft sound of laughter, and he glanced to his right to discover Tamara clutching her stomach, her entire body shaking. Her gaze was pinned on Dustin as he rolled to his feet, arms flung wide as he stampeded after the smallest and darkest of the animals.

"Dusty, for God's sake, stop chasing them," Caleb ordered.

His youngest brother straightened up so hard and fast that he tripped again, and just when it seemed he would regain his balance, the biggest of the goats lowered his head and took aim at his butt. It was a firm enough tap to send Dustin sprawling to his face on the ground.

Tamara covered her mouth with her hand, but it was too late. She couldn't stop, and now he was chuckling along with her.

It was almost anticlimactic when Tamara grabbed a bucket from beside the fence and gave it a shake.

The sound of grain against metal was all it took for the three goats to turn in her direction. She made a few clicking sounds with her tongue, and the goats stepped forward as if she were serving gourmet food.

She backed up, clicking again before glancing at Caleb with a soft-spoken message. "For the love of God, don't do anything like flap your arms. I thought Dustin was trying to fly there for a minute."

Caleb didn't move except to offer a wink.

Her eyes widened for a second before she focused back on the goats, backing up steadily as they followed her into the pen.

The instant they could, Karen and Lisa closed the gates, trapping them all in as Tamara emptied the pail into the feed trough then stepped aside to let the goats enjoy their first dinner in their new home.

She glanced at Sasha and Emma. "As long as you don't ask Uncle Dustin to help, you won't have nearly that much excitement when you're taking care of them."

Dustin was back up like a yo-yo, brushing himself off and smiling good-naturedly at his own downfall. "If I'd known what you were doing, I wouldn't have gone off half-cocked."

Lisa looked him over before pinning her lips together, as if refusing to grin at his expense.

It appeared all the Coleman girls were a bit of trouble. Caleb glanced at Karen. "I'm surprised you didn't pull out a harmonica and Pied Piper them into the pen."

Karen brushed her gloves against her thigh. "I'm the horse whisperer, not the goat whisperer," she teased back.

The next half hour was spent teaching Sasha and Emma what they had to do to take care of their goats.

Caleb backed off and left Tamara and her sisters to the task. He ended up on the far side of the fence with Dustin. Ashton joined them as well, checking the proceedings with great curiosity.

"Like my fencing repairs?" Ashton said with a bit of a gloat.

"You might've warned me we were getting goats," he chided Ashton.

The silver-haired foreman shrugged lazily. "Tamara said you

told her she had total responsibility if the girls wanted animal chores. I figured you put this one on yourself."

Huh. Caleb had to agree. "You're right, I did."

Dustin rested his arms on the railing as he watched the girls and the goats with fascination. "How come I never got to have goats?" he asked.

"Because you had everything else, I guess."

Oh hell. Tamara was right.

At Sasha's age and earlier, Dustin had already been in the barns with their father. Maybe the situation had been a bit different because there'd been a lot more adults around, but still.

Caleb glanced at the girls working excitedly with the animals, and when Emma put her hands to her cheeks and laughed out loud, he felt that same sense of hopeless wonder strike all over.

There was no way he could do this without screwing up, but at least now he had someone helping him see the forest through the trees.

TAMARA SLIPPED into the bench seat at the coffee shop, putting down the tray and dividing the food among them.

"I still can't believe you asked me for goats," Karen said. "Those things are going to make your life miserable."

Tamara shrugged. "I want the girls to have chores. Caleb doesn't want them in the main barn, and you said goats would be better than pigs."

"I said the girls would probably *like* goats better than pigs, but raising pigs would've been easier," Karen corrected her.

"Cute kids," Lisa slipped in. "I know you tried to get away without spilling details on the phone, but now you have no choice but to answer, or I'll hold your coffee hostage." She held it out of range while Tamara waited patiently. "Go on. How are you enjoying being a nanny slash housekeeper slash cook?"

Tamara glanced at her sisters. They were both waiting, true interest on their faces. She was lucky to have them in her life. "It's not much different than being a nurse. I mean, at the hospital I didn't have to cook, but there was always cleaning involved. I don't mind the cooking, and the girls are...we're getting along."

"Is it weird living in someone else's house?" Karen asked.

"Yeah, it is, but did you see that *lake*? I can't get enough of the view."

Lisa had been admiring the coffee shop, and now motioned toward the opening between the area where small tables and comfy chairs were arranged and the space next door filled with knick-knacks, candles and glorious flower blooms. "Well, I think it's neat you've got new places to check out. Buns and Roses—cute name for a shop."

Karen made an appreciative noise as she took a bite from the enormous cinnamon roll in front of her. "And tasty. Yeah, I can see you're enjoying spreading your wings a little."

"Things are going well," Tamara assured them. "Still got to figure out a few things with the girls. Caleb's a bit of a stick in the mud at times, but I knew that when I signed on for the job. He's fine to work for. I'm glad I'm here." She took a deep breath and asked the burning question. "Is it bad back home? I mean, the rumours about me?"

Karen and Lisa exchanged glances before Karen spoke. "It's not *terrible*, but it's a good thing you're not there."

Lisa nodded her agreement. "I think it'll die down sooner with you not around, but speculation is running wild. Everything from you seduced a patient, to you absconded with the hospital fundraiser money."

Tamara leaned her head against the wall beside her. In a way, she was surprised her secret had remained buried for as long as it had, but she'd known when she did it she was risking her career.

Years ago she'd discovered a good friend's mother was dying of cancer. That had been tough, but when Allison's mom failed to tell her children the news, that had been the straw that pushed Tamara over the line.

Allison had already lost her dad to the disease, and the pain of not being there for her mom would have been heartbreaking.

So Tamara had ignored her nursing vows, and instead of keeping a patient's information confidential, she'd let it slip to Allison who had been able to return to Rocky in time.

Tamara's actions were wrong, and she'd been fired when the news finally came out. Didn't matter that it was years earlier—she'd screwed up.

And with one fell swoop, years of training and her career were history.

She sighed. "You know if I told the truth, that wouldn't make it any better, because somehow, someway, people would still get it twisted."

"Worse, it would hurt Allison and her family. We know." Karen laid a hand over hers. "Hon, we don't think you did anything wrong. Allison got to be home with her mom during her last months. I'd have been tempted to do the same thing."

Lisa nodded. "We won't tell anybody what you shared, but I am glad you told us. Makes it easier to put up with the bullshit." Her sisters and Caleb's sister, Dare, were the only ones Tamara had told the truth.

"Well, I know you guys can keep your mouths shut."

The three of them looked at each other. They'd never complained in public about how annoying their particular...*situation* was.

"I just think it's better nobody knows."

"We agree."

But they were still thinking about it. "Dad's having a hard time, isn't he?"

Lisa nodded reluctantly. "The guys at the coffee shop keep poking him for details, so whatever you do, keep your mouth shut with him. Sharing what happened is not an option because that would end in a big old mess."

"You seem extra distracted." Tamara poked her older sister. "Dad troubles?"

Karen shook herself. "What? No. He's been grumpy lately, wondering what the truth is about you leaving, but he hasn't been any worse than usual when it comes to the ranch. Working with the cousins has made life a lot better, and the rest of the ranches are more than happy to take my advice. With Jesse back, I think we're going to do some good things with the stock. In fact, I was thinking about combining bloodlines more—"

Lisa shoved the plate of goodies toward her and spoke loudly to cover her words. "Eat. No breeding talk at the table."

Coughs of surprise rose from the two men at the table next to them. The one with dark hair smiled before looking away, but the blond made eye contact, a wide smile on his handsome face. Lisa flushed, then wiggled her fingers in greeting.

Tamara smacked at her sister's hands. "Stop that. I live around these people now."

Lisa leaned around her to check out the guys again. "Which is why I'm perusing the menu."

Good grief. "Karen was about to tell us why she's moping," Tamara reminded Lisa.

Lisa waved a hand, easing her chair back so she had a better view of the neighbouring table. "Oh, *that*. She's pouting because old Freddie Wilson crawled out of that ancient RV he's been entombed in for half of forever and asked her to a Halloween party."

"Lisa," Karen snapped.

"Frankly, I think she should go because while she's there, she can ditch him and find somebody younger."

"I'll ditch you somewhere on the drive home," Karen threatened.

Without moving her gaze off the hotties at the next table she was batting her lashes at, Lisa reached into her pocket. She swung a keychain around her finger. "Going to be hard to kick me out when I'll be driving."

Karen slapped her pocket before eyeing Lisa evilly. "Thief."

"We all need hobbies."

Tamara sat back, positive her smile went from ear to ear. "I love you two," she said impulsively. "I'm glad you're my sisters."

The two of them responded instantly, hands sliding forward to meet in the middle of the table. Fingers grasped, surrounded by empty plates and latte cups. "We're the three Whiskeyteers forever," Lisa proclaimed.

"That nickname makes me think you're calling us mice," Tamara confessed.

Karen snorted. "I always figured we were opening a barbershop."

A hoot escaped Lisa. "God, you guys. It's our family cheer. Get over yourselves."

Tamara squeezed her fingers. "To the three Whiskeytee— Nope, can't say it with a straight face."

Lisa rolled her eyes, and Karen snickered, and they were all laughing too hard to say much after that.

Tamara finally got it together enough to speak. She lifted the last bit of her coffee in the air in a cheer. "To family."

"To family."

They sent Lisa to the counter to get more goodies in an attempt to keep her out of trouble. Karen shooed her off. "We need dessert."

Lisa raised a brow. "Pie after our cinnamons rolls?"

"You arguing with that idea?"

"Hell, no. Just wanted to make it crystal clear I won't be held responsible for my actions after the sugar rush hits." Lisa turned her full smile on the blond at the next table as she rose to her feet. She looked him up and down then made her way to the counter, hips swaying in an exaggerated matter.

Karen and Tamara glanced at each other, then at the poor man seated next to them. He'd just taken a deep breath and stretched out his legs, eyes pinned to Lisa's ass.

It was impossible to stop from laughing all over again. Warm happiness, familiar and perfect, filled Tamara to the brim. Even though they were many miles from what had been her home, this was right.

They were together as a family. That made it home.

9

aleb wasn't sure how they'd gotten along before Tamara arrived.

Her presence was everywhere. Tasty food hit the table three times a day, the house sparkled—well, maybe not that, but it was a lot cleaner than it had been.

The girls were tolerating her okay. Emma had taken to following Tamara around like a hesitant puppy dog. His little girl would settle in and play somewhere near enough to keep an eye on what Tamara was doing. Sasha stuck close as well, but she didn't seem as charmed, as if waiting to defend her sister in case Tamara's true colours appeared.

So far he'd managed to stop from following in their footsteps. His issue was he couldn't get near the woman without wanting to tug her against him and bury himself in her softness. She looked good, she smelled even better, but he refused to give in to the caveman-like urges that woke him in the middle of the night.

Woke him in the morning with a hard-on that would not quit.

Distraction. Now.

Instead of joining Tamara on the porch he forced himself into the office, the mess taunting him. He could deal with just about everything else on the ranch in an orderly fashion, but this was the one area he'd never been able to tackle to the ground.

It was the section of the ranch where his mom had reigned, and for a moment he got lost in the past. Images returning to mind of walking into the office and finding his mom and dad sharing a kiss. His dad thanking her for the work she'd done, and her winking back.

They'd been connected—so united in everything.

The knot of ancient pain Caleb kept under tight wraps in his core got in a sudden jab before he ruthlessly shoved it away. What his parents had must've been one in a million, because it certainly hadn't been the situation with his wife. That oneness, or complete connection.

Oh, he'd had all kinds of hopes when he'd asked Wendy to marry him. Even though she'd been accidentally pregnant when he asked, he'd honestly felt they had a chance at love. Whatever the hell that meant, because it'd become clear pretty quickly her idea of being a rancher's wife and reality were very different things.

He stared at the paper in front of him to discover he'd been doodling hay bales or some such nonsense. He ripped the page off and tossed it behind him.

It was better if he didn't think about the woman. It was better if he didn't think about his parents, or anything else he couldn't have.

Instead he'd focus on what he did have. Wendy had given him the two most important things in his entire world. He wasn't sure he always told them that, but he was trying. Sasha and Emma were the reason he got up every morning and headed out to get things done. They were the reason, even though he hated the task with a fiery passion, he reached for the bills and the chequebook, and forced himself to put numbers on the page so that he could accomplish *something* before they got up.

Shockingly, he got distracted enough that the next thing he knew someone was tugging on his sleeve.

He rolled the office chair back and brought Emma into his arms. "Hey, button. Did you have a good sleep, or do I need to go dig some nasty peas out from under your mattress?"

A giggle escaped as she buried her face against him and cuddled closer. "No peas."

"But it's morning? Wow. The sun keeps getting up earlier and earlier."

Emma laid her head on his chest and held on tight, and Caleb felt his frustrations and sorrows slip away. There was nothing better for a man's soul than the innocent love of his child.

He ignored his work and happily cradled her until the clock on the wall warned time was ticking.

Caleb gave her a squeeze. "Okay, we'd better move. You have a full day ahead of you. We should go see if Tamara slept in."

Emma snorted and shook her head.

"Oh, you're right. I think she's up. Do you smell muffins?"

Emma's nose rose in the air like a little bloodhound.

He laughed, setting her on her feet before joining her, enough paperwork dealt with he could ignore the mess for another day. "Let's check the kitchen and see if Sasha left us anything for breakfast."

Sasha sat at the kitchen island looking as if butter wouldn't melt in her mouth as she scolded Tamara. "We don't eat muffins for breakfast," Sasha said haughtily.

"There's those ham-and-egg-type muffins as well, but if you don't like either of those option, I guess you're cooking for yourself this morning," Tamara responded in a light tone. "Because that's what I made. You want something else, feel free."

Emma scrabbled up on the chair next to her sister and reached eagerly for the fresh baking.

Sasha glanced guiltily at Caleb before smiling primly and pretending she hadn't just been a stinker to Tamara. "Good morning, Daddy."

Heaven save him. She was going to be a handful once she reached her teens. He spoke softly, but sternly. "Apologize to Tamara. You may state your opinions as bold as you'd like, but you'll do it politely. Yes?"

Her fake bravado bled away and she was back to being his sweet, protective, worried little girl. "Yes, Daddy." Sasha lifted her gaze to peek at Tamara's face. "Sorry I was rude."

"Apology accepted." Tamara lifted the coffee pot. "Caleb?"

He nodded at Tamara as he stepped close enough to give Sasha's shoulders a squeeze. "Yes, please. Hey, Emma. You plan to leave any of those muffins for me? They look amazing."

Tamara made a noise, but when they looked her direction, she was wiping innocently at her mouth. "Sorry. Swallowed wrong."

"You're taking us Halloweening, right, Daddy?" Like a resilient perennial, Sasha had returned to her favourite topic.

"We had this conversation last night."

"But you're still taking us."

He tweaked her nose. "Nothing changed in the past eight hours."

She nodded firmly then glanced over to see if Tamara was looking. When the coast was clear, she snagged a muffin and gobbled it down.

It was his turn to fight to keep from snorting in amusement.

Caleb was well into his afternoon work when he ran into Josiah Ryder, co-owner of the local veterinary clinic. The man had moved into the community right around the time Caleb and Wendy's marriage had fallen apart, and once the dust settled,

Josiah had become Caleb's closest friend. It was the best thing to have come out of that time.

Josiah had been off on holidays for the past couple of weeks, just returned on Sunday, meaning Caleb hadn't caught him up on the most recent developments. Specifically, the full-time nanny situation. Josiah knew Tamara was there, but they hadn't talked about how it was working out.

Caleb shook his head—had it been only two weeks since he'd agreed to have Tamara join them? Everything had changed in the blink of an eye.

For some reason Josiah was lying flat on his back in one of the horse pens. An empty one, thank God.

Caleb raised a brow. "Good thing you're not any uglier, or I might have wondered why there was a pile of shit in the middle of an otherwise clean pen."

Josiah laughed as he rolled to his feet. "Jackass. One of your dogs has lead poisoning. Ashton mentioned a few of the pens got redone recently, so I was checking them out."

"That's not the source of the problem." Caleb frowned. "I had extra time so I did them myself—all new wood, no old paint or toxins."

Josiah whistled. "Extra time? You invent a thirty-six-hour day since I've been gone? Because I've never noticed you slacking off with the twenty-four the rest of us mortals get, and you've never had extra time before."

"It's the new nanny," he admitted grudgingly. "It's amazing how much more I can get done when I don't have to keep breaking off in the middle of a project."

"I'm glad." Josiah clapped him on the shoulder. "You deserve a break for a change, so I'm happy to know it's working out. Maybe I'll be able to convince you to come spread your wings and start to enjoy life a little more."

"I enjoy life plenty," Caleb insisted.

"Let me rephrase that. I wouldn't mind seeing you outside of a work setting, or have you forgotten how to have a good time?"

Caleb wasn't sure if he'd forgotten, or if it had been beat out of him. "Always ready for a game of cards. Luke would join us, and Walker, since he's home."

"That's all good and well, and I like your brothers, but I like doing stuff with you even if it's just us, remember?"

Amusement struck, and Caleb pursed his lips to make a crude smooching noise. "Yes, darlin'. I love you too."

Josiah retched exaggeratedly. They grinned at each other then put aside the teasing and ran their way through the animals Caleb wanted checked. Easy talk flowed, except when it didn't, but the entire time they worked.

The two of them were good enough friends that the silent moments were as comfortable as conversation. Men of the land, working with their hands, helping without a comment when needed. Caleb could fall into that same rhythm with Luke or Walker. Even with Ashton, but it seemed extra special having a friend he hadn't grown up around who inspired that same feeling of comfort.

They'd nearly finished for the day when Josiah brought up the topic again.

"I have to admit it. Every time you say the word nanny, it throws me. I keep picturing someone slightly crazy. You know, like Mary Poppins, with strange outfits—"

"—magical bag of tricks?"

A voice that was already familiar rang in the air as Tamara stepped into view.

She waggled her fingers at Josiah before holding out a hand. "Sorry, but this is one nanny who has not yet figured out locomotion by umbrella."

Something in Josiah's eyes lit up as he took Tamara's hand willingly. A grin crossed his face, and for one fevered moment

Caleb imagined what it would be like to gut his best friend from nose to knees.

Because Caleb could see it coming. The damn bastard planned on flirting. The way he flirted with everyone of the female persuasion whether they were two years old or two hundred, so the idea shouldn't burn as hard as it did.

But that was a logical thought, and logic could get the fuck out.

Sure enough, Josiah lingered over the handshake. "I recognize you from the coffee shop the other day. You do not look like Mary Poppins, but I bet you could make the medicine go down just right."

Caleb rolled his eyes.

A smile slid over her face. "I know a thing or two about making people's days brighter. So does my sister."

Sister?

Josiah looked positively gleeful. "Yes, about your sister. She moving to Heart Falls as well? Because I know someone who'd be mighty interested—"

Caleb coughed abruptly. "You need to take a look at this, Josiah."

His friend had forgotten about the animal in the pen behind him, so Caleb pushed the vet into the pen and closed the gate after him as if worried about keeping the colt in.

Then he turned so he stood between Tamara and Josiah. "Need something?"

Tamara shook her head. "Not really, although I wanted to check if it works with your schedule for me to go out tomorrow night. Kelli suggested it. I think things are going well with the girls, but it would probably be good to have a little space for a night. I didn't want to confirm plans until I talked to you."

Caleb was nodding when Josiah, the right bastard that he was, popped up again, resting his arms on the top of the gate and whipping out his lady-killer smile. "Sounds like a great plan. Caleb was saying that the girls were settling in well to having you around, but I bet they would appreciate some quality family time." He aimed the full potency of his flirting at Tamara. "As it happens, I'm free tomorrow. I'd love to escort you and Kelli to Rough Cut."

Tamara looked confused for a moment. "Is that somewhere we want to go?"

"Local bar. Because of the coal in the area, and the nearby town of Black Diamond, but yeah, it's a great place to hang out for a while. Drinks and dancing. I do it all."

He was getting a boot up his ass if he kept this up much longer, Caleb thought darkly.

He'd had enough. "No objections, but if you're planning on going out with Kelli, maybe make it a girls' night out. Luke's fiancée is around." He ignored the sudden coughing from the pen where Josiah stood. "Or I bet Kelli could introduce you to some of her other friends. Be good for you to get to know more women in the community. You'll mostly spend time around guys here at Silver Stone."

Tamara leaned a hand on the nearest post, looking Josiah up and down for one long, deliberate moment as if to poke Caleb in the ass before she smiled at them both. "That sounds like exactly the thing I need. The girls' night out, and all. Josiah, I'll take a raincheck on the dancing, if you don't mind."

"No problem. I'll give you my number. I should give it to you anyway in case you ever need to reach me. I hear you've got goats on the property."

"I'll call if it's necessary," Caleb offered.

"I am the vet," Josiah pointed out, completely deadpan. "And I have a phone, *and* I happen to especially like goats."

Caleb was going to kill his friend later. "Oh look, there's Penny."

He put as much enthusiasm into his voice as he could muster, but it took a lot of energy, and he didn't think he did a very good job because both Tamara and Josiah stared at him as if he were possessed.

Yeah, his tone had been forced for more than one reason. Penny was a nice enough girl, he supposed, but he wasn't quite sure what Luke saw in her. And the fact they planned on getting married somewhere down the road but never seemed to make any further commitment than that made Caleb uneasy.

Luke insisted it was because he was still working on their house, which was true. The place was not much more than skeleton framing with a roof, but there'd been so many changes to the plans...

Enough. Penny hadn't done anything *specific* Caleb could point a finger at, but she always seemed to rub him the wrong way.

Course it wasn't that difficult to rub him wrong when it came to marriage.

She wore an outfit that was perfectly suitable for the barns, yet still somehow smelled of money. Her boots were that bit shinier, the cut of her blouse something *more* than off the shelf at Walmart.

Caleb checked himself—he didn't want to dislike her on principle, because it wasn't wrong to like to wear nice things, and her family had the money.

It was just something about how she came across. Even now as they stepped forward, she and Luke weren't holding hands like a couple in love. She'd rested her hand on his arm as if he were escorting her down a grand staircase.

Luke seemed oblivious, chatting happily. His eyes lit up as he spotted Caleb and Tamara.

"Hey, Caleb. We were looking for you." He turned his attention on Tamara. "And you being here is a bonus. I'd like you to meet my fiancée, Penny Talisman. Penny, this is Tamara Coleman. She's Caleb's new nanny."

"Sasha and Emma's new nanny," Josiah corrected. "Although if she's available for grownups, I'd like to put in a request."

Tamara's cheeks flushed at Josiah's comment, but she extended a hand to Penny. "Nice to meet you."

"You too." Penny slipped her other hand farther around Luke's arm, as if she were staking a claim. "Is that something you can take actual training for? Nanny school?"

"Maybe. I'm not sure. I'm a registered nur—" Tamara broke off abruptly before smoothing her hands over her hips as if straightening her clothes. She started again with a bold smile. "Well, I have nurses' training, and that works well for some parts of being a nanny. But probably more importantly, I grew up on a ranch. Lots of training opportunities there that apply to working with the girls."

"Which ranch?" Penny asked with a little more interest.

"Whiskey Creek, near Rocky Mountain House."

Penny frowned. "I don't recognize that name. What do you breed?"

Tamara laughed. "A bit of everything. We're connected with the larger Coleman spread, but all the family holdings are generalized. Although my sister Karen is great with horses. She does a lot of work with rescue animals, and she's looking into starting an equine therapy stable on the side."

"She could make more money working with purebreds or show horses," Penny pointed out. "If she's that talented."

"Oh, she's that talented, but she likes helping people. But philanthropy isn't for everyone," Tamara said dryly.

The other woman blinked for a second before responding sweetly. "I suppose not. Good for her. She sounds...lovely."

Light conversation continued as Luke and Penny discussed something with Josiah. Tamara adjusted her position casually until she was leaning against Caleb's side. He willed his body to not react, especially when she pressed even closer and twisted her head so her lips brushed his ear. "If you mention girls' night out to that woman, I will discover your least favourite meal and serve it for a week straight."

Caleb coughed to cover up a snort.

Penny squeezed Luke's arm. "I probably should be going. Walk me to my car?"

"You're heading home?" Luke laughed. "Okay, then I guess we don't need to talk to Caleb."

"It's been nice meeting you," Penny tossed over her shoulder, already walking away.

"It was peachy," Tamara purred.

Josiah blinked in surprise then snorted, returning to work.

Caleb refused to laugh, but he wanted to. "So. Girls' Night Out will be Penny-less?"

Tamara grinned. "Appropriate, since we no longer accept pennies as currency in Canada."

Damn if she wasn't right. Amusement rose again, and a touch of admiration for her quick wit and snark, because she was so alive and—

Caleb jerked his body to the side, hurriedly busying himself with a task. Maybe if he put some distance between them, he could stop the unasked-for rush of emotion flooding his system. It was bad enough he wanted her physically, he didn't need to complicate things even further.

"Take a key. I won't be up late," he ordered gruffly.

When he chanced a glance over his shoulder a few moments later, she was gone.

10

They paused in the truck outside Rough Cut, and Tamara tilted the rearview mirror so she could put a final layer of war paint on her lips.

Kelli eyed her with interest. "It never fails to surprise me how makeup changes a person. I mean, you looked good before, but somehow you're even shinier now."

Tamara glanced at the other woman. Kelli's baby face shone with enthusiasm and youthful beauty. "Makeup on you would be a waste. You're pretty enough without it."

Kelli shrugged. "All I know is when I do put it on, it doesn't sit right. I'm more comfortable without it. I've got no issue enjoying how it makes other people feel about themselves. I just end up more like the Joker than a beauty commercial." She shoved her door open then twisted to jump from the high cab, turning in a circle as she wiggled her hands over her torso. "Like you said, what I've got ain't too shabby, so I'm not worried."

Tamara joined her on the other side of the truck. "No false modesty here," she teased.

The other woman pursed her lips before offering a cocky

smile. "Before we go in and get deafened, let me know when we need to head home. I can go all night, but if I show up for work looking like I had too good of a time, the boys will give me all the shit jobs just to make me bleed."

Tamara understood that as well. She'd deliberately driven her own vehicle so she could leave when she was done, but she didn't think timing was going to be a problem. "I'm not looking to stay out all night. Cinderella limit?"

Kelli grinned. "I like you."

The bar was an old-fashioned place on the edge of town, with a false front and an authentic wooden boardwalk. An old chair sat to one side, weathered and worn from use and the sun.

But as they pushed through the heavy slab door, they stepped into an entirely different setting. Still a Western, but everything shone. Dark gleaming wood and black wrought-iron fixtures.

Wall sconces burned as if they were chandeliers with real candles, and Tamara was dragged forward into the heat and light, mesmerized at how charming the result. The main areas were well lit, although below full brightness. The dance floor that took up half of the space was darker and crowded with couples dancing vigorously.

Kelli nudged her on the shoulder and shouted above the music. "This way."

Tamara followed her to the side of the floor where long wooden boards created tables to put drinks on. There were hooks attached to the support posts, but she patted the wallet in her back pocket, content to keep her things close where she wouldn't forget them.

Two women at a tall table waved, and Kelli led her there, tugging Tamara by the sleeve when she got distracted by the new sights and sounds.

It took effort, but she finally focused on the people they were headed toward. She'd have plenty of time to come back and examine Rough Cut more closely.

The two women waiting for them were mixed opposites. Short and tall, blond and dark, fair skinned and sun-kissed brown. They greeted Kelli with wide smiles before their gazes shifted to Tamara and a great deal of curiosity drifted in.

"Girls, this is Tamara. Tamara, this is part of my crew. Tansy and Rose are sisters, and they make the best damn cup of coffee in town."

"Notice she didn't mention the flower shop," the blonde teased her sister before offering a hand. "I'm Tansy Fields, that's Rose."

Tamara did a second take. "I know who you are. You were at the coffee shop."

"I was behind the counter," Tansy agreed. She jabbed her thumb at her sister. "Rose was trying to convince Josiah and the boys that she's legal for trade."

Rose had her beer stein halfway to her mouth. She didn't even blink as she smacked the back of her hand against her sister's arm.

"Ouch."

Rose blinked brightly, smiling at Tamara. "Then this is your official welcome to town. And thank you for your patronage."

Tamara laughed. "Buns and Roses is the best name ever for a coffee shop and flower store. Not sure how you came up with that combo, but it's brilliant."

"Leftover coffee grounds make great fertilizer," Rose informed her.

"And Rose is too lazy to come over to my place to pick them up, so she tore down the wall between the two shops. Also, she couldn't stand to be apart from me."

Kelli shoved her way between the sisters, rolling her eyes at Tamara. "They're inseparable. Twins, even."

Tamara eyed the women closer. Nope. Not believing that one. "Sorry, you'll have to explain how that works."

They smiled. "We're both adopted, but we have the same birthday. Sisters who were born on the same day? We have to be twins."

"Got it." Tamara liked how they handled that. She liked that they were tight—not everyone got along with their sisters as well as she did with Karen and Lisa. Tamara turned to check out the room. "Nice place."

"Busy all the time," Rose said. "A lot of ranches in the area where the guys work shifts, so there's no Friday or Saturday night parties around here. It's pretty much every night is a good night if you need a distraction."

"Strange." Tansy examined her sister closer. "I would've said every night is a good night to come out dancing. Whatever do you need to be distracted from, sister dear?"

The back of Rose's hand slapped into her upper arm again, and Tamara said *ouch* at the same time as Tansy, the two of them exchanging a grin.

"My sister is forlorn and sad about being alone," Tansy informed her. "And by alone, I mean male-less."

"So you're teasing her about it?" Tamara pretended to think about it for second. "Yup, definitely sisters."

Kelli eyed the crowd, her feet moving and shoulders wiggling. "Okay, I've introduced you, and y'all are getting along great. I don't need to stick around to make sure you behave? Of course not. Good. Because I'm going dancing."

She swallowed the last of her beer and set the empty glass down on the table before wiping the back of her hand across her mouth. She headed across the dance floor like she was on a mission.

"You need to see this." Tansy tugged Tamara next to her and

they all pivoted to watch Kelli in action. "It is a thing of beauty when she gets her eye on something she wants."

What Kelli wanted involved a table of young men, all them broad shouldered and wild. Pitchers of beer covered their table and laughter rang loud and clear over the music.

Kelli sauntered up and draped an arm around one of the guys, casually sitting on the edge of his chair.

A second later he was out of his seat, taking her by the hand, and as the table hooted, he pulled her on the dance floor. A rapid two-step followed, bodies dipping and whirling with incredible skill.

Rose leaned in closer to be heard. "What you've got to realize is that somehow in the past five minutes, Kelli figured out exactly which guy had enough moves to be worthwhile hauling out to dance."

"I have no idea how she does it, but Rose is right. She should have a fifty-fifty chance of ending up with someone with octopus hands or three left feet, but no. Every single time, Kelli picks the twinkle-toes from the crowd." Tansy leaned forward to smile up at Tamara. "Which *we* like because we dance with her leftovers all evening, and it saves our ankles and shins a world of hurt."

Tamara grinned. Too funny Kelli could do that. "But what if I like getting stepped on a little?" Rose's eyes widened. Tansy covered her mouth and laughed.

Then they both waved, and Tamara turned to discover a tall brunette making her way toward them. Tansy introduced her. "Brooke. Local mechanic, and all around good gal. Tamara is the Stones' new nanny, or I should say the Stones' first nanny, because they haven't had one before you."

Brooke said hello then helped herself to a glass of beer from the pitcher. "I see Kelli is in full swing already. Which of you girls claimed him second?"

The twins pointed at themselves before pointing at Tamara.

"I have no objections. I like dancing,"

"Perfect. Let's do it." Brooke took her by the hand and whirled her to the floor. Behind them, Tansy's and Rose's laughter rang out, probably at what must've been a very shocked expression on Tamara's face.

She got herself together and caught hold of Brooke, and allowed the woman to lead her around the floor, quick-paced twirls and all.

Actually, dancing with Brooke wasn't that bad.

"This is fun, but I don't swing your way," Tamara said, still smiling because it was the truth. Both parts.

"I'm not swinging any particular way. I get tired of waiting for the guys to stir up enough courage to come ask me to dance. Plus, I figured it was the easiest way to get a chance to talk to you. You enjoying Heart Falls?"

Tamara ignored the questioning glances they were getting. "So far, so good. You like being a mechanic?"

"Love it. Someday I plan to take over the shop for my daddy."

"Wow. Good for you." Tamara wasn't sure if she was more impressed or jealous. Obviously Brooke's daddy had no issue with a female in a nontraditional role. "That sit okay with the locals?"

The woman grinned. "Sometimes not, but there's more than enough work for us with the guys who prefer to have the job done properly the first time. And the slow-to-learn, well, I enjoy making them see the light when they have to drag in someone else's mistake for me to fix."

"I hope you charge double for that."

"Yup."

They both laughed.

Then someone tall, broad shouldered and most definitely male tapped Brooke on the shoulder. He had a buddy at his side, and the next thing Tamara knew, she was twirling around the room in the arms of handsome stranger.

It was fun and lighthearted, and even when he stepped on her toes for the second time, she somehow kept from laughing.

The next couple hours flew by between dancing and chatting, and when midnight rolled around, Tamara was ready to call it a night. Kelli came willingly enough, pressing up on her tiptoes to plant a kiss to her favourite dance partner's cheek before cleverly evading his grasp.

They slipped outside and said their farewells to Tansy and Rose.

"Stop by the shop anytime," Rose ordered.

"And I'll bring out that thingy I promised later this week," Tansy reminded her. They took off, striding back to their shared apartment over the stores.

Brooke walked with her and Kelli to where they were parked close to each other.

Kelli rolled down the window. "Come out the ranch tomorrow," she said. "I can show you—"

They all cringed as Tamara turned over the engine and a horrible grinding sound rang out.

Brooke's brows rose. "Lovely."

Tamara swore. "I wasn't expecting that."

"Pop the hood," Brooke ordered. Before long she was clicking her tongue in that annoying way mechanics always did when the trouble was something more complicated than adjusting a few screws. She shut the hood and walked forward, brushing her hands together. "Come on. Lock it up and I'll drive you guys home tonight. I'll check it out tomorrow."

Tamara and Kelli climbed into Brooke's vehicle. "Do you need me to get the guys to tow it over for you?"

Brooke shook her head. "I'll get it to the shop easily enough in the morning. I'll call to let you know what's wrong and the cost before I do any work."

The trip home went quickly, with more conversation and laughter, and when Brooke dropped them off, it was easy to agree to get together again soon.

Tamara accepted a hug from Kelli, the young woman squeezing her before stepping back with a grin. "You were good company."

"Thanks, Kelli. I had a great time. You have awesome friends."

"They're your friends now too," Kelli pointed out. She waved goodbye then sauntered toward the bunkhouse.

Tamara snuck into the house, hoping she wasn't going to disturb anyone. She glanced into the living room, but there was no sign of Caleb, so she headed down the hallway, pausing to peek in the girls' rooms.

Emma lay flat on her back, an old, worn-out stuffed monkey sharing her pillow. Her lashes rested easily against her cheeks, but the sheets were tangled, so Tamara covered her up again carefully.

She smiled as she closed the door and slipped down the hall. One quick peek into the next room and she discovered Sasha sitting upright on her bed, flashlight in her hand as she stared across the room at the closet.

Tamara didn't want to scare her, so she made a little extra commotion before twisting the door farther open.

"You okay?"

Sasha glanced up, chin rising. "I heard a noise," she complained.

"I hate when that happens," Tamara said. "Did it wake you?"

Sasha nodded again.

Tamara opened the door a little wider. "Can I come in?

Sasha's gaze darted toward the closet.

Tamara took that as a yes. "I can take a peek."

When Sasha agreed, Tamara stepped around the room, double-checking to make sure every bit of the room was clear before coming back to Sasha's side. "I think we're good. Maybe something fell over outside. Do you want me to leave a light on?"

Sasha shook her head.

It was like pulling the last bit of toothpaste from the tube. "Do you want me to sit with you for a while?" Tamara asked, wondering if that was pushing it.

Only to her surprise, the response was a definite yes, so she moved to the side of the room and settled in the chair near the head of the bed. "Did you have a fun evening with your daddy and Emma?"

Sasha nodded but didn't answer. It was strange to have her silent the way Emma usually was.

"I met some nice people tonight," Tamara told her, working the distraction angle. "You probably know them. Tansy and Rose Fields, and Brooke the mechanic."

"I like Tansy." Finally, a solid, Sasha-like statement. "We did a field trip to Buns and Roses once, and she taught us how to make cinnamon buns."

"Well, you're going to have to help me with that recipe because I like cinnamon buns."

"Daddy loves cinnamon buns, but we never got to have them because *she* said they had too many empty calories."

Tamara hesitated. She had a pretty good idea who Sasha was talking about, but she didn't want to jump to any conclusions.

"Then I'll ask and we'll make sure we have the right recipe. I know Tansy would give it to us."

Sasha was eyeing her with great intensity.

"What?"

"When are you going to leave?"

The question didn't sound nearly as belligerent as it had a

week ago. Less of an order, and more...concerned. "Don't have plans to leave anytime soon," Tamara said. "I don't know that I can promise that I'll always work here, but I like Heart Falls, and I like taking care of you guys."

"*She* left," Sasha pointed out.

This time Tamara didn't have to ask who the nefarious *she* was. "I'm sorry."

That was about all she could say.

For a little girl, Sasha was capable of the most adult-like expressions. "She wasn't very nice," she declared. "And she didn't like us."

God, Tamara thought, horrified any child would talk about their mother in that way, even though she knew there were times it was justified.

"I'm sorry," she repeated, not wanting to get into a discussion about the absent Wendy.

"I'm *glad* she's gone. She was mean to Emma. Emma's glad she's gone too, and I'm not just saying that. I *know* because Emma told me."

Tamara couldn't take anymore. "Sasha, I'm very sorry that your mom wasn't nice, but I don't want to talk about her with you."

"Because you think I'm too little."

A rush of anger struck so hard Tamara nearly shook, and her fury probably snuck out in her voice. "Yes. Because grownups aren't supposed to use bad words when little people are around, and the idea someone was mean to you and Emma makes me want to track *her* down and nail her to the floor until she learns to be nicer. I don't like very much of what I've heard about your mom, but it's not my place to say bad things, especially to you."

Sasha blinked.

Tamara held her tongue. Too bad she hadn't managed it thirty seconds earlier.

They sat in silence for a bit then Sasha settled back on her pillow. Eyelids slowly closing before they popped open, forced there by one determined little girl. "Emma won't go in your room because it was *hers*."

"Well, it's mine now. You're welcome to visit me, although I'd appreciate if you knock first. Maybe if you visit, Emma will as well."

A decidedly un-childish snort escaped. "Doubt it."

She sounded so much like Caleb, Tamara blinked.

Silence fell. Sasha's eyes stayed closed for longer and longer each time until Tamara thought it was safe. She went to stand—

"Don't go," A childish, soft request. More longing in the tone than demand.

Tamara smiled as she gave in. "I'll stay, but I'm tired. I'm going to lie down next to you. Are you okay with that?"

Sasha nodded, wiggling to make room.

Tamara took a moment to remove her slippers before settling in position. She wondered if she dared rub Sasha's back, then chose instead to slow her own breathing and close her eyes most of the way.

One exhausted little girl was asleep in under thirty seconds. Tamara remained next to her, though, fully dressed on top of the sheets. Her brain whirling until sleep came to claim her.

11

$\mathcal{C}$aleb stumbled up the steps in the evening darkness, cursing solidly as his thigh met the edge of the railing with a bruising smack.

He was cold, he was tired, and every inch of his clothing was soaking wet. As a final *fuck you very much*, he was still annoyed as hell...for what had turned out to be no reason at all.

Yup, he would admit it. Right now he was one cranky bastard.

After a day from hell it made sense he wouldn't be a happy camper, but he'd started off in the foulest of moods, and things had only gone downhill from there.

Last night waiting up for Tamara to return from her girls' night out while pretending he *wasn't* waiting up had been sheer torture. He'd finally kicked his own ass and took himself off to bed.

She was a grownup. She was old enough to know what she wanted and who she wanted to be with...

...and all the platitudes in the world didn't help settle the fury in his gut when he walked outside at four a.m. and didn't see her truck in the yard.

Soft curses turned the air around him blue, and the ranch dogs had stepped gingerly out of his way. He'd decided to find her and rain down fire and brimstone as hot and wild as any revival-tent preacher when he stomped back to the house two hours later and found—

The scent of coffee and baking filling the kitchen, like usual.

Tamara curled up in one of the outside chairs, like usual, gazing contentedly over the lake. She'd greeted him happily then explained about her broken truck.

He clearly had no reason to be upset, but it wasn't easy to turn off the pain that had begun to fester inside.

Followed by said day from hell, which had started moments after finishing his coffee before he'd even gotten to say good morning to the girls. Rushing out the door to an emergency call from one of the crew who'd been in an accident not far from home.

So now at whatever ungodly hour it was, Caleb stripped down not even two paces into the kitchen. He threw his filthy clothing on the floor in the laundry area before grabbing a towel off the rack and wrapping it around his hips. A quick glance at the wall clock said it was two a.m., and he strode toward his bathroom, planning to crank the heat as high as possible to chase away the chill in his bones and maybe boil off some of his festering temper at the same time.

He rounded the corner, and caught a glimpse of movement in the shadows right before a solid body made impact with his. Adrenaline rushed his system as he caught hold to stop from falling over, jerking them against him, one arm locked high, the other low.

"Oh my God, Caleb, stop. It's *me*. Tamara."

Shit.

"Sorry."

He went to let her go, then froze. The towel he'd hitched around his hips hadn't been fastened very well, and with his quick actions, he must've loosened the knot.

The fabric drifted downward over his thighs to land silently on the floor, leaving him naked.

Tamara grasped his forearm with her wrists and shook it. "Caleb. Let go."

It was sweet heaven and hell, her soft body held in front of him, the clean fresh scent of her in his nostrils an aphrodisiac. Not that he needed anything to get his motor going. Knowing she was in the house was enough to make him go off, even after his shitty day.

"Don't move," he ordered.

"You're scaring me. Where the hell have you been? And why are you creeping in at this time—?"

Dammit all. He lifted one hand to cover her mouth, the other still locked around her torso. "Shush. Don't wake the girls."

She stiffened, but her lips closed under his fingers, so he loosened his grip.

She spoke more quietly, but the anger in her tone was ozone sharp, the scent of lightning on the air. "You're right. I wouldn't want to wake them, especially since they spent the last hour before going to bed crying."

Caleb just about jerked her around to face him before remembering he was naked. "What the hell are you talking about? What's wrong? Are they hurt?"

Tamara let out a dramatic sigh. "No, physically, they're fine, but are we really going to have this discussion with you holding me like you're practicing to become a ninja warrior? What is *wrong* with you? Let me go."

He might have loosened the grip on her mouth, and she'd spoke in a near whisper, but the whole time she'd continued to wiggle, which was exactly what he didn't need. His body reacted to the warmth and softness of her rubbing against his body. Frustrated with himself, still pissed at her, his response was sharper than it should have been.

"I've been chasing runaways for the past twelve hours, and everything I own is wet or muddy, including me, but if you'd like to continue this conversation, by all means. I'm naked, so you go ahead and strip down as well, and we can get in the shower together."

Dead silence.

Ha. So that's what it took to make her go tongue-tied.

Tamara straightened her spine. "Oh."

He still wanted answers. "Go put on the kettle," he ordered. "I need a shower before we can talk."

Caleb released her then turned and headed silently for the bathroom. Wondering if she would stand there motionless until she heard the door safely close.

Only this was *Tamara*. A quick glance over his shoulder proved she'd turned as well, and even in the shadowy darkness of the hallway, he could tell her eyes were taking him in from top to bottom. Some devilry tempted him to pause and let her gawk. See if she could maintain a straight face, or if she'd be blushing before they were done.

Because as cold as he was, it was amazing how quickly his body had hardened. There was no mistaking his response.

A soft noise escaped her before she scurried from sight into the living room.

He kept the shower short, and a few minutes later met Tamara in the kitchen. Steaming hot chocolate waited for him, and he took it gratefully, drinking deeply before putting the cup back on the table.

She wouldn't meet his eyes, and a small note of satisfaction rose in his belly. Maybe the unflappable Ms. Coleman wasn't so unflappable after all.

"Did you find the horses?" she asked quietly.

"Not all of them. Couple of trees came down and took out a section of fencing. We didn't find out until it was too late. I think the horses headed to the neighbours' land." He glanced at her. "I was damn grateful to know you'd be here for the girls. I'm sorry I didn't call—we kept going in and out of reception areas—but I did think about that."

Tamara nodded but didn't speak.

For once it was him who fought to fill the quietness. He couldn't seem to stop, even getting hazy with exhaustion. Truthfully, something inside him wanted her to know he hadn't just been out for all hours without a good reason.

"Hopefully we can find them over the next few days because the weather is supposed to turn for the worse, and a couple of them have foals." He took a long drink before continuing. "Of course, *that* happened after the morning call out to deal with a transport trailer that went off the road not even fifteen minutes after leaving the ranch."

"Kelli said the driver was okay, but she didn't know much more than that," Tamara told him.

"Thankfully, he was just shook up. It was a steep section of road, and could have been worse." Caleb paused. "I had to put one of the horses down."

His attempt to keep his regret from showing was a failure because she wore an all-too-knowing look. "I'm sorry."

He shrugged. "Part of the job. Now, what happened with the girls?"

Tamara tilted her head. "You lost track of what day it is?"

Between his frustrations last night and the whole shitstorm of today, Caleb was half-asleep on his feet. "I'm too tired to play games. Just tell me."

"October thirty-first." She glanced at the clock on the wall. "Oh, excuse me. We're after midnight, so it's now officially into November, but we *weren't* a few hours ago."

A sick sensation stole through his exhaustion. Halloween. The girls. "Ah, *fuck.*"

"They still got to go trick-or-treating but it wasn't quite the same as going with you. They were excited enough to be out they didn't realize how disappointed they were until bedtime. Thus, the tears."

Nothing he could do to change the past. "I'll apologize in the morning."

Tamara shook her head. "Good start, not enough."

If he hadn't been so bone-weary, he would've reached across the table and shaken her. "Remember that part about I'm *too tired for games?*"

"They were really upset—"

"Yeah, I got that. Thanks for making it abundantly clear that I'm a shitty dad. Enough with the guilt. I'm going to bed."

Tamara was out of her chair, slapping her hand down on his shoulder before he could rise to his feet. "For a man who asked me to help, you're damn quick to get snarky. I'm *not* trying to make you feel guilty. I'm trying to tell you to plan for more than just an apology."

He grabbed her by the wrist, words coming out quietly. Softer, but the intensity went up. "Are you getting some kind of sick entertainment from dragging this out? Because I swear I will pull you across my knees and spank your ass. Get *on* with it."

Sudden silence filled the room. A hot beat lingered in the air, full of sexual tension. Her pulse raced under his fingertips and his mouth went utterly dry.

Forbidden images. Deliciously dirty thoughts.

Thank God Tamara ignored his comment, and instead of giving him a piece of her mind, she shared in detail what she thought he needed to do to apologize. Even on the verge of passing out from exhaustion, the wisdom in her plan was clear.

He still had a grip on her wrist, so he gave it a grateful squeeze. "I'll help put out the—"

"No way. You're exhausted," Tamara chided him. "Go to bed. I'll take care of things in the morning. I already have everything ready."

Of course she did. Extra guilt would have snuck in if he'd had any energy left to protest. "Thank you," he offered sincerely, more grateful than he could say. Smoothing over his stupid mistake with the girls was so important.

Tamara patted his hand then wiggled free, making some excuse about heading to bed, although she hardly needed one considering the time.

She vanished down the hallway as if she were being chased, and even brain numb as he was, Caleb wondered what he could do to make Tamara forget his inappropriate comments.

But more importantly, how could *he* forget the gleam of heat that had risen in her eyes at his words. How could he not think about it the entire time he was trying to convince his body that enough was enough. It was time to sleep.

He woke late, joining the girls for breakfast. He gave them extra kisses before apologizing for missing the night before.

"It's okay." Sasha glanced at her sister before answering. "We're glad you found the horses, Daddy."

"Did you have a good time trick-or-treating?" he asked. "Did you get lots of your favourite candies?"

Tamara lowered her coffee cup. "They haven't gone through their bags yet. I suggested they wait to do that with you today."

Caleb gasped. "What? You mean you still have full bags of goodies, and you haven't even looked to see what you got?" Sasha and Emma both eyed him curiously as he pretended to have a great idea. "That means Halloween isn't over yet."

His oldest daughter spoke up. "Daddy. Halloween was *last* night."

Caleb shook his head. "Nope. If you didn't go through your bag, Halloween's not officially over, which means we should go and see if we can get more loot."

He winked, glancing over their shoulders to see Tamara give him a nod.

Emma tugged him down to whisper in his ear. "Where?"

He turned to Tamara. "Emma would like to know *where* it would be possible to find Halloween still taking place. I think they don't believe me."

Tamara managed to look dramatically shocked. "What? They've never heard that rule before? As to where to go, well, it has to be somewhere they haven't been yet. I know they've been to town, because I took them. And they went to the bunkhouse."

"Because Uncle Dusty and Uncle Luke took us there. Daddy, Kelli gave me two full-size chocolate bars. And Kelli says everybody who gives out little chocolate bars are just chintzy." She informed Emma, "That means cheap. I looked it up."

Caleb didn't ask Tamara why she was snickering. "I agree," he told his daughter. "But if you went to town, and you already went to the bunkhouse, what's left?"

Tamara tapped her lips and pretended to think. "I *suppose* you could check with the goats."

Emma snorted. A clear, sharp, little-girl sound that drew all their attention. She covered her mouth, her eyes going wide.

Tamara pointed at her, smiling widely. "Ha. I see you don't think goats like Halloween, but I am pretty sure they do. Almost as much as horses."

Sasha's eyes were the size of plates now. "Really? We've never gotten treats from the horses before. We never *had* goats, so I guess it makes sense we never got treats from them, but I'd think that the horses would probably—"

Her words cut off as her little sister jammed a hand over her mouth before dragging her toward where their bags were stashed on top of the dining room table.

"Hey, you're forgetting something," Tamara interrupted.

They froze.

Tamara looked them up and down. "You think anyone's going to give you Halloween candy when you're not wearing a costume?"

Bags abandoned to the floor, the girls raced back to their rooms.

Caleb couldn't stop a grin from stretching his lips. "The horses and goats are in full cooperation, are they?"

Tamara nodded. "Except the goats were little *too* interested in participating, and Meany lived up to his name. He'd already found one of the bags I stashed this morning, so I moved new ones to where not even he could reach it. Unless the three of them work together, and stand on each other's shoulders."

"Don't go giving them ideas," Caleb returned. "Those goats are far too smart."

Tamara muttered under her breath. "Far smarter than me at five in the morning."

He glanced at Tamara. "Where's your costume?"

She laughed, grabbing her hat from the laundry room and plopping down on her head. "There. I'm going as a cowgirl."

It felt good to grin. "Look at that, I barely recognize you."

She snickered. "Oh, wait. I should go as a *cowboy*."

She adjusted her stance, placing her legs wider on the ground. Then she contorted her face into a strange scowl.

He looked her over quickly, trying not to dwell too long on the curves under her well-cut jeans or the soft flannel shirt flaring over her breasts.

"What's that all about?" He flicked a finger at her expression.

"Cowboys don't go around making faces. That one would scare the horses."

She straightened with a laugh. "I was going for an *I'm serious, don't mess with me* macho cowboy look."

He shook his head. "Stick with the sweet cowgirl."

One brow arched skyward. "Now about *your* costume." She turned to the kitchen and pulled open a drawer. "I happen to have just the thing right here."

She came forward with a pile of bright red fabric.

Caleb backed up until he remembered strong, manly cowboys didn't back down from anything. "I don't know that I'm cut out to be Little Red Riding Hood."

She gave material a sudden snap, straightening the fabric as she moved in closer.

"We'll switch jobs for the morning." She tipped off his hat, looping a strand of the fabric over his head. She stepped behind him as he glanced down with a grimace.

"I need to record this somewhere so when the girls are teenagers I can prove how much pain and suffering I was willing to go through for them."

Tamara stood behind him, tucked in close against his back as she did the ties snugly around his waist. "Hey, it's just a costume, I don't actually expect you to cook."

"I can cook," he protested.

"And I can cowboy."

She gave him a swift pat on the butt, and he just about cleared the floor in surprise. He pivoted on the spot to discover her face had gone red.

"Oops?" She stepped back rapidly. "Sorry. Too used to joshing around with my cousins."

He nearly reached for her to drag her into his arms. What happened after that, he wasn't sure. Oh, he knew what he'd like to do, but the exact order wasn't down pat yet.

Something of his thoughts must've shown on his face, because her breathing gave a little hiccup, then she inhaled unsteadily. Her throat moved, and she blinked hard, and if the girls hadn't chosen that moment to ram straight through the four inches of space separating them, Caleb was damn sure he would've done something regrettable.

The girls grabbed their bags off the table and rushed out the door.

The entire time they were marching to the barns, Caleb scolded himself thoroughly.

She was his employee, for God's sake. Even if they *wanted* to get involved, they couldn't, because no way in hell was he doing more to put his girls' hearts in jeopardy.

Didn't mean he could stop his eyes from being drawn back to Tamara again and again.

They swung past the goat pen and rescued two bags that were tied over ten feet off the ground to a yard-light post.

"How on earth?" Caleb muttered at Tamara as his girls shoved the find into their bags then took off again at a run.

"You don't want to know."

He laughed softly.

Emma literally bounced when she found the first bag of candy in the barn, hanging on the outside of Moonlight's stall. She turned, shaking a Ziploc baggie that held a full-sized candy bar along with other treats.

"Daddy, look," she called out loud, delight in her eyes.

Tamara didn't make a fuss over Emma's talking, just stepped forward with a smile and pointed the girls in two different directions. Chaos ensued for another five minutes until all the bags were found and his children were grinning from ear to ear.

And the morning wasn't over. Tamara called the girls to her side, holding a bag with cut pieces of apple in it. "I'm pretty sure the horses don't want any tricks, but you could give them all a treat."

The girls came rushing back, their goodie-filled pillows tossed on a nearby shelf as they went down the line and, with his and Tamara's help, offered up apple slices on their stretched-out palms.

Tamara patted the neck of her horse as Emma reached up her offering. "Stormy says *thank you.*"

Emma held her hand with the apple rock-steady until the treat had been daintily nibbled away, then she happily patted Stormy's nose.

"You want to pet him some more?" Tamara asked. When Emma nodded her agreement, she brought them around to the side so Emma could stroke her hand along the horse's strong neck.

Stormy turned his head to bump Tamara, and Emma giggled, sliding her fingers into Tamara's.

Caleb wasn't quite sure what to do with the sensation churning in his gut. It was fine to want the woman. Any man would want someone as beautiful and direct as Tamara. But this felt like more than sexual desire, watching her with his children.

A pulse of something definitely *not* desire struck, icy cold along his spine.

He cleared his throat, shoving away the emotions. "Time to get back to the house and let Tamara get on with her day. Halloween's got to come to an end sometime."

Two little girls made disgruntled sounds, but Tamara gestured them forward. "Go on. You have to sort your candy, and you can't keep your daddy from his day forever."

Walking back from the barns was a lot less pleasurable than the excited trip there. Uncomfortable, uneasy, at least on Caleb's part. The girls and Tamara seemed oblivious, strolling at a comfortable pace as Sasha dramatically recited everything they'd just done, in spite of Tamara having been there.

Emma no longer held Tamara's hand, but she was walking close enough to bump into her every other step.

When they got in the house he was far more brisk with Tamara than necessary, all things considered. "Why don't you go take a break for a while? You've been up since early. I'll sort the candy with the girls then get them started on their chores."

He turned his back, dismissing her.

Sasha and Emma were busy upending their pillowcases on the table and making sounds of delight at their treasure trove. He watched for a moment before glancing over his shoulder to see Tamara had vanished.

But that strange uncomfortable sensation in his gut refused to leave.

12

A week into November the snow lay like a beautiful fresh page over the land, and while it might be out of the norm, Tamara bundled herself up and took her coffee to the porch every morning.

They'd settled into a routine. Every day was a little different, and Tamara found she enjoyed the ebb and flow of daily life at Silver Stone. She rose, got her chores going, dealt with any number of things throughout the day. Spent time with the girls, then every evening she relaxed in the living room with a fire burning in the hearth.

Caleb was there most nights. Dustin dropped in on a far more regular basis than she expected from a youth in the final year of his teens. Luke and Walker as well more often than not stopped for in a few moments, as if touching base with their older brother was an important part of finishing their day. Luke would laugh and joke with her. Walker—he tended to eye her as if she were a fish that had been left in the sun a little too long.

She'd thought she'd worked hard at the hospital, but the hours at the ranch seemed to last forever. She wasn't the only one putting in long hours, though. Caleb was out of the house by four a.m. most days.

She wasn't even sure why she knew that until she realized after leaving the house through the kitchen door, he'd walk the perimeter of the house on the covered porch. As if checking his territory before heading to the barns.

The solid impact of his boot heels on the wooden platform echoed in a steady rhythm until the moment he'd take the stairs, *click, click, click,* then nothing.

The first day she'd woke it probably had been the silence that stole her attention. She'd been trained to stay alert for nighttime sounds, and she'd already learned that in nannying, the quiet moments were more dangerous than the noisy ones.

When it sounded as if World War III was taking place in Sasha's bedroom, Tamara could continue with her tasks. When the house went deadly silent, that's when she had to worry.

She smiled as she sipped her coffee, bundled up with a throw blanket over her legs as she stared at the water. Thin traces of ice had formed at the edges of the lake, but the river flowing from the far end kept most of the surface from freezing.

It was late enough in the year that, at this time of the morning, a hint of sunlight was barely visible at the edge of the eastern horizon. Crisp, cold. Breathtakingly beautiful.

Staring over the lake had become a vital morning ritual.

Other changes continued, but her connections to family back in Rocky stayed strong. Lisa called on a regular basis, and Karen as well, checking to see how she was. She loved that they were interested, and that they cared.

She wondered at times if she was imagining the touch of jealousy in Lisa's voice as her sister asked about all the new places and people she was meeting.

"You're welcome to come visit anytime," Tamara assured her.

"I know. I don't want to encroach on your new adventure."

A snort escaped her. "Please. It's just a job."

Her little sister said nothing, but a round of coughs resonated from the phone, sounding an awful lot like the word *bullshit* over and over.

Tamara laughed at the memory.

A creaking noise echoed in the quiet stillness, followed by another sharp snap, this one directly overhead.

Strange. There shouldn't be enough snow yet to affect the gables.

She put down her coffee cup and stepped to the edge of the porch, leaning against the railing to peer toward the sky—

"Oh my *God.*"

The words burst out of her as a pair of boots swung off the roof and past her. Walker Coleman did a crazy acrobatic move, letting go of the eaves trough and twisting in mid-air to land with both feet on the porch.

He pulled himself to vertical and offered a calm, expressionless look, as if jumping off roofs at five-fifteen in the morning was perfectly normal behaviour. "Morning."

She went for nonchalant as well. "Morning. Like a coffee?"

"Love one. Don't get up, though, I can grab it. Want yours topped up?"

"Sure."

He was back a moment later, steam curling skyward from the cup he handed back to her before settling in the second chair.

They stared over the land in shared silence for a bit. Peace returning.

Only Tamara couldn't resist. "Your brothers said you were on the circuit. Do they know you're actually a rodeo clown?"

A sharp snort of amusement rang out. "I don't have the guts to be a clown. They're the ones racing toward the bull when everyone else is running like hell the opposite direction."

"They are incredible, aren't they?" Tamara agreed.

"Dangerous line of work, but I've seen the results. They save lives."

"They do."

Tamara looked at Walker closer, not even pretending she wasn't examining him. And when he turned his face toward her, as if assessing her right back, she ignored him and went on with her consideration.

She had spent a lot of time over the years getting into strange circumstances. She'd volunteered her nursing skills to people who'd been beaten up, broken down or otherwise abused. And, at times, she'd worked with the people who *liked* to get beat up and put themselves in dangerous situations.

Some people craved that kind of adrenaline rush—a lot of the guys on the circuit thrived on it.

Walker didn't play out right in her mind. Something was off.

"Do I have mud on my face?" he asked, dark brown eyes meeting her eyes boldly. A challenge.

"Nope. You look like a Stone, though."

His lips twitched. "That didn't sound like a compliment."

"You ever hear what happened the first time I met your brother?" Tamara asked.

Now she had his attention. "When was that? I'd assume this past summer."

"He showed up to check on your foster sister. She was in the hospital, and I was her attending nurse."

"An angel of mercy. I can see it now," he said dryly.

"An *avenging* angel—Caleb overreacted and made a feint at my cousin. I got in the way and flipped him. He hit the floor hard. Knocked the wind from his sails long enough for his brain to come back online."

Walker snickered. "I assume you know I will use this information to tease the hell out of him. You flipped him? That had to hurt his ego."

"Tease if you want, but I told you that so you'd know—I can take care of myself. And I'll take care of your nieces. I'm not here to mess around with anyone."

He raised a brow. "Did I say you were?"

"Not in so many words, but yes."

They sat in silence again, Tamara refusing to be the first to look away.

He finally turned his head and took a deep drink, humming appreciatively. "That's good coffee."

Which Tamara figured meant, *they* were good. "And I didn't even poison it."

Walker paused in the middle of a sip, pulling the cup back to flash her his first real smile. "This time."

She laughed. "If I ever decide to poison you, I'll warn you, how 'bout? Give you a fighting chance."

"Deal. Better odds than riding a bull."

A car pulled into the yard, and Tamara rose to her feet. "And that would be Tansy."

Walker had stood as well, cup in his hands. "Tansy Fields?"

"Yeah. She said this was the best time to stop in. She has to be back at the store at six a.m. to open the doors." She wondered at the expression on his face. "Are you feeling okay?"

He shook his head as if trying to clear cobwebs before offering her a slow smile, far politer than he'd been up to this point. "Of course. Let me get the door for you."

Which put them both at the kitchen door right as Tansy walked up. Walker held the door for her as she stepped past, a huge towel-covered metal bowl in her arms.

"Walker. I didn't know you were in town."

"Off and on, like usual. How's the family?"

Tansy's expression went unreadable. "Oh, they're all great."

"That's good. Real good."

He stood there in the doorway, fidgeting with the cup in his fingers until he realized Tamara was watching him. He put it down on the counter then stepped back, reaching behind him for the door.

Suspicion snuck in. He was acting an awful lot like a nervous suitor. Did Walker have a thing for Tansy?

"You're welcome if you want to stay," Tamara said. "We're making cinnamon rolls. You could have another cup of coffee—"

"No, that's fine. I should be going. Thanks for the coffee. Bye, Tansy."

And with that, he was gone, the kitchen door swinging closed after him with a snap. Tamara moved forward to watch out the window, amused that the man was all but running. He was past the road before slowing to a cowboy stroll.

"Well, that was entertaining."

Tamara turned to discover Tansy wore a pleased smirk. "There's got to be some history I don't know about happening. Are you and Walker—?"

Tansy's eyes widened and her jaw dropped open. "Oh no. Not me, my big sister. Ivy and Walker had a thing back in high school before she went away to university."

Ha ha. The plot thickened. "So *how's the family* was code for *how's Ivy doing but I don't really want to ask?*"

"Yup." Tansy pointed toward the side counter. "Come on. We'll get started on the next step while we talk. I can only stay for half an hour."

Half an hour was long enough to get the cinnamon buns in the oven and share some quick talk time, which turned out to be not about Walker and his past love life. Instead they shared a little about their training—Tamara's time as a nurse and Tansy's baking adventures.

It was far too short, but when Tansy waved goodbye, the scent of sweet cinnamon and fresh bread was rising on the air, and Tamara felt as if she'd come that much closer to putting down roots.

A SOLID KNOCK on the wooden panel to his right brought his attention up from where he was cleaning stalls. Tamara stood patiently until he met her gaze.

"Everything okay?" he asked.

"Yes, just wanted to make sure it was okay if I pick the girls up from school. We need to go shopping, so I may as well save them the bus trip home."

And with that one comment, he felt a little out of touch. "They need new clothes? I thought—"

"No. They're good. But they have a birthday party, and we're down to the wire. I have no idea what eight-year-olds want."

"According to Sasha, most of the store."

Tamara smiled, and something inside him twisted. She'd let her hair down since he'd seen her that morning, and the ends curled around her face like a picture frame. She had a hint of something shiny on her lips, and he had to look away before it became too clear he was considering how much trouble it would cause if he were to press his lips to hers, just to see if there was a flavour to go with the shine.

Hell, the thought of kissing her had a certain portion of his anatomy reacting, and he stepped awkwardly back into the stall to grab his rake in self-defense.

"We'll be back before four," Tamara finished, speaking to his back as if he weren't being rude.

Only he couldn't turn around because if she happened to look down, she was going to wonder what it was about horse stalls that gave him indecent hard-ons.

Then he remembered. "Wait."

Hell. On. Earth. He reached into his back pocket and hauled out his wallet, gritting his teeth as the movement pressed his jeans tighter over his erection.

Caleb held the wallet high as he opened it and pulled out some cash. "Here. I know we got you set up with household money, but this kind of stuff is extra."

"If you're handing out change..." Luke slipped into the space next to Tamara. "My hand is always willing and ready."

"That might not be something you want to advertise too loudly," Kelli teased, jumping out of reach as Luke took a mock swing her direction. "You sound as if you're..."

"And hello to you two," Tamara interrupted, lifting the cash in the air and nodding at Caleb. "Thanks. I'll add it to the record in the kitchen, but I figured twenty-bucks-as-a-gift limit?"

He paused. "Each, or together?"

"Together."

Kelli raised a brow. "Wow, you two are just as tight with the coin as each other. I like that."

"Until you ask for a raise, at least," Luke returned.

"They'll take my raise out of your earnings. Since I'm the one who did your work today."

Caleb glanced between the two of them. "Luke?"

His brother sighed as if he'd been hard done by. "She out-roped me."

"Tell him how many times," Kelli said perkily. She was gloating. *Definitely* gloating.

Luke ignored the question, turning his back on Kelli, probably so he didn't have to see her grin. "I vote we find out what Tamara's got happening. What's on your agenda for tomorrow?" Luke asked.

Caleb considered returning to his raking, but this was too interesting.

"Birthday party with the girls for someone in Sasha's grade

two class. Of course, that means twenty-four girls and a dozen chaperones, so I get to meet all the young mothers in town."

"Should be fun." Luke nodded approvingly.

Kelli laughed. "Watch yourself. That group is only fifty percent sweet, homegrown sunshine."

"What's the other half?"

"Homegrown noxious weeds. No way to get rid of them but to burn them to the ground."

"Kelli," Luke chastised. "You don't even know who's going to be there."

"I know their type," she insisted. "Dangerous, all while looking like peaches and cream."

"Don't judge so fast. Maybe Tamara will make some good connections in the group. Be nice for her to have friends nearby instead of being stuck out here on the ranch without any women to chat with."

Tamara opened her mouth to protest, but Kelli's spine had gone rampant straight, cheeks flushed as she glared at the man who seemed oblivious to his impending doom.

"Yeah, right. Because I'm chopped liver." She gave Tamara a quick farewell wave. "Have fun, stay safe. Talk to you soon."

She marched past Luke, stomping extra hard at the opportune moment.

"*Owww.* What the hell?" Luke lifted his foot and shook it as he glared after her. "What is wrong with you? Watch where you're going next time."

"Oh, I think she hit where she was aiming," Tamara said coldly, raising a brow.

"She's a cranky creature these days."

Caleb stepped out quickly. His brother was one step away from being skinned and stuffed. "Luke, go grab Ashton for me."

Luke blinked at the rapid change of topic. "Why don't you—?"

"*Go,*" Caleb snapped.

Warning bells must have finally filtered through his thick skull because for once his brother headed out without making a smartass closing remark.

Caleb and Tamara were left alone in the relative quiet of the barn. He glanced at her.

Her lips twitched.

"I didn't want you to kill him," Caleb explained.

"Good timing on the interruption, then, because I had a feeling he was about to make some crack about Kelli having PMS."

He bit down his amusement. "You know how to operate a backhoe, don't you?"

Laughter burst free. "Are you offering me forty acres of unmarked land to bury the body?"

"Possibly."

She slapped a hand on his shoulder good-naturedly. "Fine. You've saved him for another day. I don't get how your brother can be so smart ninety-nine percent of the time then completely stupid."

"Prolonged puberty." He winked and watched as surprise rippled over her face.

And that bubble of something *other* rose in his gut again, and he didn't know what to do with it.

So he turned his back and grabbed the rake, working far more vigorously than necessary.

By the time the dust settled and he glanced from the pen, he was alone.

13

$\mathcal{T}$amara pulled her borrowed truck into the parking spot outside the community center, taking a deep breath before offering the girls a smile. "Okay. Who's ready for a birthday party?"

"Us, us, us," Sasha declared loudly enough for a dozen little girls as they escaped the cab, tumbling out like clowns from a stunt car at the circus.

Brightly wrapped packages in hand, they led the way with so much enthusiasm Tamara caught herself grinning. Oh, for youthful resilience. Any tears from earlier disappointments were gone, and their anxiety and distrust was easing day by day.

Or at least moment by moment. Sasha hadn't completely let down her guard, but she was too excited to stay on point one hundred percent of the time. Emma was...Emma. Quietly watching and assessing, and so far, she seemed to be weighing in favour of Tamara.

Tamara, on the other hand, was nearly as confused and conflicted as she'd been the first week, and no simple solution would make her particular issues go away.

Caleb Stone was driving her mad.

He also made her mad, for far different reasons. He was a faulty furnace. Damn intriguing—steaming, blisteringly attractive, and she'd sternly warned herself that whatever animal magnetism she imagined between them was all in her mind because if it were real, the house might spontaneously go up in flames.

Yet for every time she thought she caught him undressing her with his gaze, he'd just as often turned as chilly as a January cold snap.

It was like living with the physical embodiment of the Chinook wind. Unseasonably hot followed by icy blasts.

But the worst thing about him? He was a truly shitty fighter. Seriously—she loved a good debate, and wrestling down details to figure out what was important was part of the fun in her books. Didn't matter if it was something big, like the chores, or something small like favourite meals, she wanted to discuss it.

Anytime they came head to head on an issue, though, Caleb had the same response. He'd walk away, leaving her talking to an empty room.

"Damn annoying," she muttered.

He'd probably figured out how much she hated it and was now doing it on purpose. A fight she won because the other person refused to...well, *fight*...was a hollow victory.

Enough dillydallying. Today was not about the maddening man, although she had to admit he'd arranged a very nice temporary vehicle for her to drive while Brooke worked on her truck. The repair parts had taken longer than expected to arrive—typical small town trouble—and Tamara would have hated to be stuck without a vehicle the entire time.

Tamara caught up with the girls in time to guide them toward the table where other gifts had been placed. Children were running wild around and over the play equipment scattered in the open space of the gym.

This kind of birthday party she could approve of. Nothing over the top—no rented bouncy house or one-upmanship. She walked forward with a slightly more optimistic spirit, even though Kelli's warning lingered.

Some of the moms gathered near the snack table extended smiles, one face more familiar than the rest. The day she'd gone into Emma's class to help, Hanna had been there as well. Tamara had enjoyed working alongside the quiet woman.

Hanna waved happily. "Good to see you again."

Tamara returned her greeting with an enthusiastic smile, slipping into the empty chair beside her. A quick round of hellos and introductions followed before the conversations reverted to child wrangling and coordinating the partygoers for small bursts of games.

Over the next hour Tamara kept a close eye on Sasha and Emma, making sure they minded their manners but had a good time. Sasha stayed near her sister, which didn't surprise Tamara much.

Once the birthday cake and presents had been dispensed with, the kids were back to unorganized fun until the party time was over. Tamara caught Sasha all but mesmerized by one of the games the bigger girls had started on their own. She snuck over, catching hold of Sasha's shoulder for a moment as she knelt to speak privately to them.

"I thought I'd take Emma to the colouring table. If you're okay on your own for a bit."

Sasha glanced at her sister before shaking her head. "I don't mind staying with Emma."

This time it was Emma who made it clear she had other ideas. She leaned in and whispered something to Sasha.

Sasha frowned. "You sure?"

The little girl nodded then slipped her fingers into Tamara's.

Still Sasha hesitated, glancing at Tamara with a warning expression. She waited as if ready to return to her position as guard dog the next moment.

Emma rolled her eyes and propped her free hand on her hip.

It was the final nudge Sasha needed. She nodded, joining the crowd of jumping and bumping older girls.

Tamara gave Emma's fingers a squeeze. "There's a big girl. Your sister will be back in a bit. She'll be happy, and so will we. I peeked through the colouring books earlier, and saw a book with a picture of a goat, if you can believe that. Want to track it down?"

Emma's smile widened.

As an added bonus, Hanna was at the small table with her daughter, and the two girls sat next to each other like little puppies, content to use the coloured pencils and work side by side in silence.

"Crissy talks about Emma all the time," Hanna admitted quietly. "I think some of the noisier girls in their class scare her, so she and Emma buddy up a lot."

"They look as if they get along well," Tamara agreed. "You guys want to come out to the ranch sometime for a playdate?"

"Crissy would love that." Hanna smiled sweetly. "Honestly, so would I. It's been a long time since I got to wander a ranch."

After double-checking to be sure Hanna would keep an eye on both girls, Tamara snuck away to the washroom.

She paused as she exited the room to take a slow look over the gathering. Voices sounded in her ear, loud enough to make her jump, and she spun, turning back in surprise when no one stood anywhere nearby.

It took a moment before she realized where she stood formed a perfect sound tunnel. With the gymnastics equipment stored along the side wall, the very intense discussion being held half a gym away was being magically carried all the way to Tamara's ears as if she were sitting in their midst.

The longer she listened, the tighter the knot in her belly became. Because three of the moms Tamara had just briefly met were talking about Caleb.

Caleb, and the girls.

Her feet were frozen to the ground as she stood and listened.

"Maybe now that fine man will get out more," offered Carrie, mother of the birthday girl.

"He gets out plenty. He needs to spend more time *in*." Natalie winked lewdly.

The third woman, Joleen, leaned over and slapped her on the leg. "You are so bad."

"But I bet *he's* good, if you know what I mean. Knows what he likes—that's sexy in a man." The three women exchanged glances. "Wendy always was a complainer. I don't think anything she bitched about was real."

"Especially considering the way she took off. *I'd* have no trouble with that man being demanding in bed."

"You wish your husband would do something other than missionary," the friend teased.

"I'm not complaining about my situation. I'm thinking of that underappreciated hunk of manhood. Now that he's got the nanny, maybe he'll come back on the market. Lord knows my sister could use a strong, sexy rancher."

"If the nanny is good enough to stick around. Poor things, especially that littlest one."

"She's not quite right in the head, is she?"

Tamara's spine straightened with a violent snap. What the hell? There was nothing wrong with Emma.

"They need someone who's going to take care of them."

"My sister loves kids."

The other two women laughed at the same time. "Your sister

likes money, *and* sexy men," Joleen pointed out. "Your sister would keep the nanny if she could, and focus on spending time with a certain sexy rancher."

"Wouldn't we all?"

"Wouldn't you do just about anything to put a smile on that man's face? I imagine once he makes a move, you'd spend the rest of the night with every muscle in your body screaming for more."

"Tell your sister to drop by Silver Stone one evening. I bet Caleb would be happy to see a friendly female face," Joleen insisted. "It's been a long time since he had a good time with a woman."

"Unless he's getting some when he's gone on business," Natalie said.

Carrie shook her head. "I doubt that. Besides, he's rarely the one who leaves the ranch. You know, he's kind of like your prize stud bull. Give him a comfortable, well-fenced area. Feed him and keep him happy so he'll be at his peak performance anytime he's needed."

"Amen. That's definitely what my sister needs—"

There was more, because the women were still laughing, but Tamara couldn't hear them because she was marching across the floor, feet propelled by anger.

Oh, she had her issues with the man, but to hell with other people talking about him as if he was a stud for hire. And Emma—

Tamara took a deep breath and slowed her step, casually making her way to where the ladies were chatting madly. She pretended her goal was the lemonade, smiling as sweetly as she could at the group.

The laughter hushed as she approached, all three offering exaggeratedly friendly faces.

"Are you enjoying yourself at Silver Stone?" Joleen asked.

It was tempting to respond with something snappy and rude,

but Tamara held herself in check. She did have to live in this town, and in spite of these being some of the *noxious weeds* she had to deal with, there was no use in burning everything the first time they faced off. "It's beautiful."

"It's a big place to have to take care of." Carrie leaned forward, resting her elbows on her knees. "You must be exhausted."

Okay, she hadn't expected that. "Why?"

The woman blinked. "It's a lot of work to take on two little girls when you haven't done that before. And the house, and taking care of Caleb."

Tamara laughed. "Oh well, there's one of your mistakes. Caleb doesn't need to be taken care of."

"But it must be tough dealing with Emma."

Her banked fury escaped a little around the edges, but she pulled it back to a reasonable volume and attitude. "Emma? That sweet little thing? Well, in a way you're right, because between her and her sister I have to stay on my toes. They're so smart I'm working overtime to make sure their environment is challenging. No use letting all that potential go to waste."

The women's mouths opened and shut in a lovely fish imitation, as if she'd caught *them* off guard.

Tamara pressed her advantage. "And in terms of Caleb, I suggest you not worry about him. The man is more than capable of looking after himself and his...*needs*. I doubt there's a woman alive who could resist him."

She finished pouring another couple glasses of lemonade, balancing all four precariously as she returned to the colouring table.

Hanna eyed her as she accepted two of the glasses. "What was that all about?" she asked in a soft tone.

"Just people being catty."

Her new friend's lips twitched. "That's why they look as if you squirted them with a water bottle."

Tamara snickered, turning toward Emma who had laid a hand on her shoulder even as Crissy crawled into her mom's lap.

"Yes, sweetie?"

Emma held up her finished work proudly. The goat was accurately depicted in his debonair grey and white, with a bright red bow newly drawn on the page—the same one Emma had attached around the little creature's neck the day before.

"Beautiful. That looks like Eeny."

The little girl's enthusiastic nod was a reward all in itself.

A moment later, Tamara found herself smiling even harder. Emma glanced at her friend in her mom's lap then peeked over her shoulder to check where Sasha was. Discovering her sister was still hard at play with the older girls, Emma tugged Tamara's arm out of the way and proceeded to crawl into her lap.

Emma picked up her glass of lemonade and drank it as if her seating arrangement was the most natural thing in the world.

Something not right with the child? Baloney. Emma was smart, just like Tamara had claimed. Whatever reason she had for not speaking it was a deliberate choice not a mental issue.

It was too easy to put an arm around her and cuddle her close, the sweet scent of little girl making Tamara feel all sorts of emotions she hadn't expected.

She cared about the girls, no question about that. But something seemed—

Different.

The party was over, and the day came to a conclusion. Happily, two tired little girls headed to bed without any trouble, but Tamara was far too wound up to sleep. Caleb had gone back out to the barns immediately after dinner, leaving Tamara restless with nothing to distract her.

She wandered the house for a while before giving up. She might as well make some long-term plans.

She slipped into Caleb's office to grab some paper—

One of the precarious stacks fell over.

"Dammit."

Tamara bent to scoop them up, moving too quickly, and her butt nudged over another pile. Now she had twice the paper on the floor, and twice the frustration.

No getting around it now. She had to clean up the mess.

Tamara ended up on the floor, gathering the papers around her into piles. She avoided the details, peeking quickly to discover whether it was a bill or an invoice as she slowly created new stacks.

There was a kind of peacefulness in the task, though. In fact, when she had one corner of the room straightened, it was tempting to continue, but she decided a little trouble was all she was willing to borrow this time around.

If she had a chance, though, and Caleb approved, she'd be back. Finishing the task would be Zen-making to her brain.

For now, she lay the completed filing neatly on the top of the credenza she'd dusted while it had been empty.

She took one of the newly discovered sticky notes and left him a message.

Caleb.

I knocked over some of your paperwork, so I had to straighten up a bit. Sorry if I overstepped my boundaries.

T.

It wasn't a great excuse, but maybe he wouldn't mind.

Maybe he would…

Another rush of frustration hit. She was accomplishing good things in this nanny job, but it—it wasn't enough, and at the same time it was far, far too much.

Not the work, but all the other sensations that struck out of the blue. The sweet moments when Sasha forgot to be aggressive. The heart-rending touch every time Emma treated her as if she belonged.

The confusing-in-every-way-possible moments with Caleb. Sensual tension and laughter and body-aching need and mind-tangling frustration.

Too many longings tugged Tamara in new directions, and she wasn't ready to look them square in the eye, and that alone was the most frightening fact she'd faced.

More than losing her job. More than leaving what had been her home for nearly thirty years.

She didn't want to admit, even to herself, what she had begun to long for...

Tamara ran from her own thoughts, escaping into the kitchen to mindlessly scrub the already clean countertop until it was late enough she too could take herself off and fall into a restless sleep.

CALEB STRUGGLED with the bolt he was trying to remove, swearing as the wrench slipped from his fingers for the twentieth time. Dustin was helping brace the gate, and the wrench bounced off his arm and slammed back into Caleb's knuckles as it fell.

A rush of pain chastened him for being distracted. Maybe it was punishment for avoiding his office for a week, choosing instead to torment himself by sitting on the veranda each morning with Tamara in the quiet time before she'd rise to finish getting breakfast ready.

It was peaceful and relaxing, but tempting, which set him

into feeling guilty and now, distracted. But he couldn't seem to stop himself from making the same stupid mistake. He was stuck on repeat.

When something hit him in the side of the head not even two seconds later, Caleb was sure the world was trying to make a point. What exactly, he wasn't sure.

"Now I understand why you were all growly." Josiah marched up and slapped Caleb on the back. "Why you didn't you just say something?"

Caleb stared at him in confusion. "What the hell are you going on about?"

Josiah snickered. "Don't think you can keep things secret in a small town like this. I'm surprised it stayed *undercover* this long, and yes, that was a dig."

Dustin glanced between Josiah and Caleb. "What's he talking about?"

"No idea."

"Oh, come on now. Don't play the innocent. I know about you and Tamara."

His youngest brother looked shocked. "Are you and Tamara...?"

"No."

"Yes."

Caleb and Josiah spoke at the same time,

Caleb glared at his friend, narrowing his eyes. "Who the hell is telling you bullshit stories? There's nothing between me and Tamara."

At least a whole hell of a lot less than he wished was going on.

Josiah leaned back and folded in his arms over his chest. "That's not what I heard. I was at the Sinclairs', and word is you're taken. So's she, and considering how growly you've been the last while, it all kind of made sense."

"I don't think you and Tamara should be fooling around," Dustin piped up.

"We're not fooling around," Caleb snapped. "It's just damn small-town rumour. I'm surprised, Josiah. You know better than to listen to gossip and take it as gospel truth."

"Hey, let's just say I was hopeful." His grin widened. "But if it's gossip, then she's not taken, which means I can ask her out, right?"

Caleb wasn't about to rip his best friend apart, but the urge was there.

The urge was damn strong.

Instead he shrugged. "Don't know that she's got a lot of time to be off gallivanting at the moment, so maybe you should put that on hold for a while."

Josiah's knowing look was enough to send Caleb scrambling to find something for them to do that would be enough of a distraction.

They got into a task, and between the happily finicky labour and Ashton joining them, there was plenty enough work to change the topic to safer ventures, but word of the gossip nagged him.

Small-town rumour *was* a thing, but even that usually had some kind of a starting point. He was still stewing over it when Josiah was getting ready to leave.

Caleb jogged up and knocked on his truck door.

The window rolled down and Josiah rested his elbow on the sill. "I'll send out one of the staff to finish the vaccinations, if that's okay with you. I've got a couple of things I need to complete before the office closes."

Caleb waved it off. "Not a problem." He eyed his friend. "You mind telling me exactly who said what about me and Tamara? It's the kind of thing I don't want getting back to the girls without having an idea of what to tell them."

Josiah's lips twitched but he kept his expression under control. "A few days back Tamara was at some event with the girls and claimed you were well *satisfied*, if you know what I mean. And no, I'm not talking about her abilities as a nanny. People figure your bed is plenty warm these nights."

A swear escaped.

That was the last thing he needed—actual encouragement straight from the horse's mouth. And it was encouragement, of the roughest kind.

The images crowding his brain were as dirty as all get out. Tamara warming his bed? Exactly the dreams waking him in the middle of the night. The ones where he'd find himself with the sheets kicked off, body covered in sweat. Fingers wrapped around himself before he realized what he was doing.

He dipped his head. "Appreciate it."

Josiah paused. "I was teasing you earlier, but you know, maybe the two of you getting involved wouldn't be a bad thing."

Caleb couldn't believe his ears. "She works for me. What part of that is a good idea?"

His friend wavered but still forged ahead. "Right, that does make things difficult, and yet it's not the working-for-you bit I was thinking about. You've been alone for a while."

"There's a reason for that."

"Not all women are like Wendy."

"Thank God, or the human race would have died out years ago."

A snort escaped Josiah. "Okay, looking at this from a different angle. You realize Tamara grew up on a ranch? She knows how much work it is, and hey, look. She hasn't run screaming yet."

"She's here to take care of the girls."

His friend nodded. "And from everything you've told me, she's doing a great job at that." Josiah looked him over. "So why is it not a good thing for you to act on how hot she makes you?"

"She doesn't..." Caleb couldn't bring himself to lie. Not to his best friend.

"Thank you for not continuing that bullshit. But seriously, I know it's not the easiest of situations, but you've got an opportunity here—"

"Thanks for coming out this morning. Talk to you later."

He turned and walked away.

That Josiah recognized his attraction to Tamara wasn't a good thing. Especially in light of the fact that the rumour mill would now be going wild.

My God, what if the girls heard? What if they thought their world was about to be flipped upside down all over again? Their memories of Wendy were bitter and hurtful.

This was his own damn fault for not being stronger. It should have been crystal clear from the first moment he wasn't interested in Tamara except on a business level.

But it was *Tamara's* fault too, for speaking out of turn, and right then he was angry enough to march into the kitchen and shout at her. Of course, that would cause all sorts of other problems.

No, this had to be dealt with in a big enough way to make an impression on the hardheaded woman. Something private enough he could get through to her *exactly* what she'd done.

It was strange. All the times he and Wendy had fought left him aching and angry, but never hot like this. Those fights had been icy-cold, polite and sterile.

What burned in his belly now was red-hot, laced with sexual tension.

It might not be right, but for once in his life he didn't care if he was doing the *right* thing. The way to prove his point without a shadow of a doubt was simple, and perfect. Terrible and yet wonderfully justified.

He couldn't wait. She wasn't going to know what hit her.

14

$\mathcal{T}$amara pulled back the quilt and crawled on her oversized bed, leaning against an enormous stack of pillows and settling into her book. She'd barely finished the first chapter when the floorboards outside her room made a distinctive creaking sound.

She glanced up to see the doorknob turn, and wondered which one of the girls needed her. She wasn't shocked when the door opened—

Not until Caleb marched in.

Marched in, turning to close the door behind himself.

Tamara stared, positive her jaw was hanging low. "Need something?"

"No." He strode to the side of the bed, gaze fixed on the wall behind her.

Tamara shoved away the impulse to grab a pillow to cover herself. "What... What are you doing?"

"Getting ready for bed."

The impossibility of that statement combined with the dirty daydreams she'd been having about her boss mixed into one enormous cauldron, and Tamara found herself, for the first time in a long time, speechless.

Her silence was based on utter confusion, not helped at all by the fact he was deadly quiet as he reached to undo the buttons of his shirt.

Somehow she forced herself to form words. "Caleb, this isn't funny. You shouldn't be here."

He shrugged the flannel off leaving a plain white muscle shirt behind, the broad muscles of his shoulders and massive biceps far too close. "I don't know what you're talking about, darlin'. Where else should I be when it's time to get ready for bed?"

"Your own room. *Caleb*—"

Tamara's mouth went dry as the final layer covering his torso lifted away. Far, *far* too much naked, gorgeous skin was right there beside her. A light dusting of hair covered his chest, another darkening and narrowing as it headed lower and disappeared under his beltline and—

Oh my word, he was putting his hands on his belt and loosening the buckle, and...this was not happening.

Tamara abandoned her book and slipped out of bed. She had some idea of hiding in the bathroom until he came to his senses, but he stepped in front of her, blocking her path.

Maybe she should have been afraid. Maybe she should have screamed, but he wasn't *scaring* her, scaring her. Just making every nerve in her body tingle and sending her pulse into orbit.

His gaze slid down, then up, until he was once again staring into her eyes. When he spoke, his voice had gone low. "I think that's my favourite nightie. Although I don't know why you bother to wear it since I won't let you keep it on for very long."

Maybe she'd fallen asleep and was having a deliciously dirty dream. Tamara reached up and pinched the skin of her forearm. "Ouch."

Awake. Definitely awake.

"What the hell have you been doing?" Suspicion rushed in. "Have you been drinking, Caleb Stone?"

He stepped closer, his gaze dropping from her eyes to linger on her breasts. The traitorous things reacted, nipples jerking upright to press against the cool material of her nightgown.

"Nope. Not a drop. Only, you see, I hear you and I are an item. I hear you're warming my bed at night, and I'd hate to think of you as a liar. So we should make it clear where we stand. Or should I say, where we lie?"

Tamara stuttered for a moment. "S-s-someone said we're sleeping together? Oh my God, who? Wait, *what?*"

His answer was wordless. His hand no longer hovered between them. Instead he touched her, tracing the thin strap of her nightgown down her shoulder, continuing to the swell of her breast. His fingertip slid over the hard peak of her nipple, and a shiver rippled over her entire body.

Her brain was not working, that much was obvious. She forced herself to speak. "I have no idea what you're talking about."

"Seems someone at that birthday party you went to got the idea that I'm sleeping with my nanny. I figured since you were the one who started the rumour, you wouldn't mind if—"

The birthday party? "I hate small towns."

Tamara jerked back two steps, instant fury heating her blood. Now she knew what he was talking about, the memory clear and sharp.

She was mad at herself for having spoken out of turn, but she was even madder at Caleb for what he was doing. "Look, there were a bunch of catty creatures there that day who were not being very nice, making remarks they shouldn't about all sorts of things. So, yeah, I got a little snarky with them, but I did *not* say we were sleeping together. I said you had no reason for them to farm out your services like a stud bull for hire."

"Well, *baby*, your smart comments caused trouble."

Really? He was going to come in here and go asshole on her? She might find it difficult to think straight with him shirtless and all, but this was not happening.

He was right...but he was totally wrong.

Fine if he wanted to punish her for screwing up. But not like *this*. This was so far over the line the other direction she was actually shocked he'd gone through with it. If she hadn't been as annoyed as a cat stuck in a rainstorm she might have been impressed at the level of his game. Then she realized...

Caleb's expression might be unreadable, but his eyes—

He couldn't hide the fire burning in his gut. Lust, not anger.

It appeared his little lesson had backfired.

Inspiration hit—a bad, wicked idea that was so wrong. So *very* wrong, but now that it was fully formed, stopping was damn near impossible.

She needed to turn away.

Need to grab on and take a bite.

God, she needed a bite of Caleb Stone.

Do it. Take a bite.

Fine, it was a bad idea, but she'd blame the stupidity on the heat in her veins, bubbling now with sexual frustration as well as anger.

She lifted her chin and looked him in the eye as she adjusted position. Closer. Closer, until she could skim her fingertips over his impossibly hard chest. Circling and teasing the light dusting of curls and the tight surface of his nipples.

"I'm sorry, *baby*. You're right. I misspoke. You *are* just fine without a woman. Your bed isn't cold and lonely." As she spoke she slid her hand down. Slowly, lower, until her thumb stroked the thick ridge she found waiting, pressed to the front of his jeans. "You don't spend the night with your fist wrapped around your cock."

Caleb swallowed hard. His pulse raced at the base of his throat.

"*Tamara—*" The word was a harsh growl.

But he didn't move away.

"Or maybe you do. Taking care of yourself—I'm sure you *take care of yourself* no problem." Tamara unsnapped the button on his jeans. He grabbed her wrist. "Not that I blame you. I do the same thing."

The sound of his zipper being lowered meshed with a dangerous rumble deep in his chest. He let go of her hands, and then, oh my God, he was touching her. Skimming his palms up her waist, slowing as he passed her breasts.

She ached. She waited, no longer angry, but on fire with desire.

Caleb sucked for air, chest heaving as he fought—for control? For strength? He slid his fingers into her hair and tightened, lifting her face.

Then his lips crashed down and he was kissing her senseless. His rock-firm body met hers as his other hand jammed against her lower back, locking them together. It was incredible, like cool wine on a hot day, all delicious sweetness and tingling pleasure.

Tamara tangled her hands in his hair as he took the kiss deeper. Tongues fighting, bodies wrapping tighter.

She was nothing but aching need on the inside. An empty aching need waiting to be filled. Tamara was tempted to climb him like a tree, clinging tight until they were both satisfied. A shiver raced up her spine as he lifted her skyward, and she wrapped her legs around him, wishing the layers between them were gone.

His kiss was fierce and possessive, one hand cupping her breast, and she wasn't sure how it happened but she was on the bed, hot male draped over her like a sexy, *sexy* blanket.

He caught the hem of her nightie, scrunching the fabric

upward as if ready to strip it from her. She could go along with that. She could shove his jeans down and roll them until—

Caleb jerked back, just enough to separate them. Chests brushing as they fought for air.

Her entire body tingled as he rolled off. He kept moving until he was on his feet, standing beside the bed.

He shoved a hand through his hair, the strands sticking up wildly.

"I'm sorry." The words fell like an avalanche. Crashing, unexpected.

She grabbed a pillow, clutching it in front of her like a shield. Her brain wasn't quite working, bewilderment and sexual frustration swirling.

He was apologizing? God, she didn't know if that made her more angry or frustrated.

It certainly made her confused.

He stared down for one more moment, his body tight with need, his erection clearly visible. Frustration and desire dogged her, and she opened her mouth to say something, but he snatched his shirt from the ground and fled.

Tamara sat there, stunned, her heart pounding in the silence that followed the click of the door.

She hadn't expected any of that, and she collapsed to her pillows and let out a long sigh of frustration.

Frustrated, confused and at a total loss.

How on earth could she face him tomorrow?

CALEB CRASHED INTO THE HALLWAY, somehow closing Tamara's door and taking a dozen steps before his shaking legs forced him to put his shoulders to the wall. Deep breaths shook him as he fought his desires.

Three more seconds and he would've been beyond the point of no return. As a man who prided himself on his control, at that moment there was nothing he wanted more than to go back, jerk open the door and pick up where he'd left off—

The fire burning in her eyes had said she wouldn't stop him. The way she'd gripped his shoulders in passion as they'd kissed...

He dragged a hand over his skin, feeling the welts she'd left with her nails.

Caleb's head thumped the wall again before he pushed to vertical, shuffling down the hallway. He needed to do something. He needed to do *anything* that would take him away from temptation, because it was clear the two of them had an awful lot of kindling piled up, and it wasn't safe for them to be in a room alone. Not unless he was going to blow this entire relationship to hell by stripping her and driving into her like a man possessed.

God, what he wouldn't do to be able to take her.

He stepped five paces farther down the hallway then three paces back, trying to decide where to go. He wasn't about to drop into his own bed, or hit the shower—in both those circumstances, he'd be taking his unruly hard-on to completion in the saddest and sorriest of ways considering there was a hot-blooded woman down the hall willing and interested. No way would he stroke off while thinking about her.

So he took the only guaranteed boner-killer and shoved open the door to his office. He flicked on the light, prepared to let the chaos in the untended room cool his fires as he pondered once again what a pathetic excuse for—

It was clean.

Shock nearly as strong as the passion he'd just experienced struck, and he crept forward, wondering if he'd stepped through a time machine.

The last time he'd seen the office this tidy, his parents had still been alive.

Bitter grief swamped him, and he clutched the back of the chair to keep from wavering. He was overwrought, emotion churning through him with his brain not fully engaged.

The woman he wanted more than his next breath was interested and yet utterly unavailable.

He closed his eyes, focusing on the mental images of his children. Their sweet smiles the center of his universe. A balancing place.

It took a moment, but when he glanced around again nothing had changed—the room was still strangely neat, and he moved forward with caution.

The side credenza held papers, stacked and in order. A quick glance through showed they were not only separated into bills and statements, they'd been sorted by month, and any he'd scrawled his name on in an attempt to have a way to remember which were paid had a red line under the total.

Around the edge of the room were more piles, neatly placed in folders, and on the desktop itself, his ledgers were out. The ones he still filled in by hand because that was how his mother had done it, and learning how to transfer it all over to a computer had seemed more work than it was worth with the limited the time he had.

A trembling moment of displeasure struck. One of his brothers could have snuck into the room and straightened things, but he doubted it. No reason for them to do that now when they hadn't done it anytime during the previous ten years.

It had to be Tamara's work.

He wasn't sure what to think about her looking through the family finances. Having her know what their financial bottom line was made him uncomfortable in ways he couldn't quite articulate.

He should be mad. It was an invasion of privacy. It wasn't her place to come in and do such a thing, especially not without asking permission.

But as he flipped open the journal he discovered there were no additional entries in the book. The last thing in there was in his somewhat legible handwriting.

Tucked between the pages, though, was a printout with the numbers from the statements on the side credenza. A running assessment, with no totals but a place to check off if the balances had been entered. She'd left that part blank, meaning her organization had gone only so far.

Still a stretch, but not as invasive as it could've been.

Caleb sat in the chair and considered hard. A riot of emotion rolled through him. The fierce passion he'd felt was still there, but it was muted with something else.

Looking around the room he realized she'd given him a gift he hadn't expected.

Hell if he was smart enough to know what to do with it.

15

*I*t had taken a long time to fall asleep. Long enough that when Caleb's footsteps woke her, she should've been able to simply roll over and go back to sleep.

As if.

Hearing him disappear from the house just brought back all the feelings that had swept in when he'd disappeared the night before.

She wasn't sure how she was going to get through the day. Heck, how she was going to meet his eyes for the first time.

She'd wanted him as much as he wanted her. She couldn't even blame him for the stupid situation they'd ended up in because it had been her foolish attitude that had started the trouble in the first place.

Maybe he shouldn't have assumed, but she was just as good at jumping to conclusions—as usual.

No surprises there.

Tamara stared at the ceiling, trying to plot ways this could possibly not end up a shitstorm, but all she saw in her mind were two little girls being disappointed yet another adult was abandoning them.

She and Caleb had to get over their impossible attraction and do what was right for the girls.

That was the solution. She'd make it clear she accepted her responsibility in last night's debacle, but going forward they'd have to work extra hard. They'd make a commitment to talk things out and not let local gossip cause problems. That's the last thing the girls needed, and she of all people knew better.

Tamara was still scolding herself when Caleb failed to march into the kitchen at six a.m., and she wondered if he was going to hide out and avoid her all day. In some ways that would be fine, but she couldn't stop from peering out the window as she continued working, prepping meals and making plans for the girls.

She topped up her coffee and headed toward the door. She might as well get in a little sit time out on the porch. In case it was one of her last opportunities—

Oh my God. It was entirely possible Caleb could fire her.

Shock and reality smacked together, painful and horrifying. If it happened, she wouldn't complain. Being fired from her last job had been an indignity because she'd meant well, but her mouthing off at the birthday party had been nothing but personal exasperation and not really helpful.

She pushed open the door and muffled a shriek. Eeny and Miney were standing shoulder to shoulder, noses tucked forward as if they planned on joining the family for breakfast.

"Go on, go on, backup," she ordered, shoving against them and pushing them outside as she closed the door, coffee cup abandoned on the counter.

She caught the goats by their collars, glancing down at the slippers on her feet with regret. It was better than being barefoot.

Tamara shuffled off the deck and into the snow, tugging and pulling to get them headed in the right direction.

Only to become stuck when she hit the pen. How was she supposed to open the gate without letting Meany out?

"You're not a goat, you're a turkey," she told the old-timer through the fence. "You taught these two how to be escape artists, then you convince them to go AWOL while you stay back and act all innocent. I know your type."

"Need a hand?"

Tamara whipped her head around to see Caleb striding closer. "I need four hands, so yes, please."

Between the two of them they got the animals behind the fence. Caleb watched closely as the goats bounced happily around the pen. "I'll get Ashton to take another look to see how they're getting out."

"Meany hasn't escaped lately, so maybe it's something small enough for these two and not for him."

She stopped. They glanced at each other, the easy moment vanishing as her cheeks heated. "I'm sorry—"

"Last night—"

Tamara figured he'd stop talking, so she kept on rolling. "—I was totally out of line. It was my fault for misspeaking at the birthday party, as well, and I promise I won't let it happen again. And I'll make sure any rumours die in the bud."

He stared at her feet as she spoke.

Icy-cold radiated through her soaking-wet soles, but while she was on a roll she wasn't going to stop. "I hope you'll forgive me. I would hate to leave and the girls have to get used to another nanny, and I really love—"

He held up a hand, and this time she choked to a stop.

"I'm not having this conversation with you while you're standing without shoes in a snow bank."

Oh God, she was totally fired.

"Caleb." Sheer misery in her voice. "Please let me stay."

"You're not fired. Get in the house," he ordered gruffly. "*Now.*"

It wasn't right that when her job was on the line, him being all bossy made her tingle.

She abandoned her slippers before stepping on the porch. Her socks were soaked through as well, so she stripped them off, and followed him obediently into the house.

He motioned toward the fireplace, tossing a blanket her way. "Wrap yourself up."

He didn't say anything else, just settled into the chair opposite her. She sat, draping herself in the throw that had landed beside her, hands in her lap as she waited for the verdict.

Caleb took a deep breath. "I have one question. No, two."

"Anything."

"I wondered if you'd consider—" His gaze met hers firmly. "You got any experience with bookkeeping?"

Not the direction she expected this conversation to go. It was enough of a surprise that Tamara simply answered the question. "Not much more than accounting in high school, and a couple of business-management classes in university. Administrative math. I've helped Karen look over things on the ranch, but Lisa's the Whiskey Creek girl with the numbers brain."

A soft sound escaped him, not his usual sexy grumble, but more of a frustrated sigh. "I didn't do well with math back in school, and accounting still doesn't make me very happy."

"Why don't you hire a business manager?"

His lips twitched. "Probably hire them to get things straightened out only to have them tell me I need to fire them because I can't afford to pay their salary."

A flutter of concern struck. "Are things that bad? I mean, I know I did a running tally, and I'm sorry for invading your privacy, although I didn't look at the numbers *that* close, just put them down for you." She was rambling and knew it. She caught herself. "My dad does the same thing. In fact, I think every single business owner who gets into it because they love the other parts of the job has an office like yours. My cousin's quilt shop was a mess."

"Would you take over?" The words burst from him as if a plug had been pulled from a well, gushing over her, earnest and sincere. "I need someone to help, and if you're interested in getting things straightened out, it would sure be appreciated. I'll hire somebody to come in and clean if that would give you more time. Same as before—the girls are your first responsibility, but if you put this second on your list... Well maybe third, because I like having food on the table."

Not what she'd expected at all. She figured she'd be getting the boot this morning, and here she was being given more responsibilities?

"I don't mind," she told him honestly. "As long as you understand I'm not an accountant."

He visibly relaxed, settling back in his chair as if he could breathe again.

Only, they weren't done. Not really. They still needed to address the elephant in the room.

How should she start?

Then wonder of wonders, he did.

He lifted his eyes to hers and spoke as politely as if he were facing a very demanding review board. "I was wrong last night. You're a woman in my home who deserves to be protected and treated with courtesy. What I did was beyond disrespectful. You shouldn't feel you need to defend yourself from me, verbally or physically"—he held up a hand to ward off her protest—"which is all you did when you turned the tables. I'm sorry."

Well then. Tamara had to think that over for a moment. It was odd to have him basically apologize for a kiss that had turned her world on end, but...nice he had taken responsibility for his actions.

But this wasn't all on him.

When she was around? It was never all someone else's fault.

"I was wrong as well." She took a deep breath. "You're a good-looking man, and there's an attraction between us. But—"

"It won't happen again." He rose to his feet. "If you want to work on the office stuff, just let me know what you need. I'll call the bank later this morning and make sure you're cleared to make inquiries."

"But—"

"I'll be out until dinner."

He was gone.

From what seemed to be a deep connection to not even sharing the same air space in under fifteen seconds. Tamara sat back and felt the room reel.

He really was the most annoying man, but she had to admit she admired him for sticking to the priorities. Plus, any morning that started with expectations of being fired that didn't finish that way was okay in her book.

An easy truce returned. That edge of sexual awareness between them lingered, but they both did their best to keep it locked down tight. Their evenings by the fire after the girls went to bed became a time of deep peacefulness. Sometimes chatting, sometimes just sitting.

Caleb didn't talk much, but they didn't have to fill the room with conversation to have it feel comfortable.

For once in her life Tamara was learning that silence had a

rhythm and flavour. It was cozy, and sweet, and instead of ending each day like a running fool, she crawled into bed satisfied and content with her work.

Satisfied, except for that *will not be spoken of or thought too hard about* craving she felt for the big, gruff rancher.

And her days...

Full of activity, and energy, and two little girls she enjoyed more and more as time passed.

Tamara rounded the corner, pulling to a stop inches before she slammed into Caleb.

A rapid stop that turned into a disaster as Sasha and Emma slammed into her from behind, shoving her the last couple of inches forward so she connected top to bottom with Caleb.

He'd been in the process of taking a step backward, and the combined momentum of three bodies hitting him out of the blue meant his legs folded, and he tipped toward the floor while Tamara desperately tried to brace herself.

They landed in a pile. A solid grunt escaped Caleb as Tamara ended up the filling in an Oreo cookie, Sasha laughing heartily, and Emma offering a snicker.

Under her was one hundred percent hard male body.

Tamara forced a lighthearted smile to her lips she attempted to roll away. "Oops. Sorry."

"We caught you," Sasha gloated, twisting herself free and pulling Emma to her feet.

Caleb placed a firm grip on Tamara's hips and lifted her.

Was it only her imagination, or was there a caress in his touch before they both made it to their feet?

"Running in the house?" he grumbled.

Tamara raised a brow. "High-velocity acceleration for short periods of time. We didn't expect to see you home so soon."

"Obviously."

Well, now. Somebody was extra grumpy this afternoon. "Go on, girls. Grab the carrots and raisins."

They scurried past, digging into the pantry and fridge as Tamara bestowed her best nanny look upon Caleb. "What can I help you with?"

He turned sideways to speak privately. "I won't be here for dinner and might not get back until late. Put the girls to bed for me tonight?"

Tamara hesitated.

Caleb sighed. "I know it's your night off, but Penny just called, and her family's got some animals they're considering selling. Talisman will give us first dibs, but they're shipping tomorrow, so we have to drive to Calgary to check them out."

Luke's woman was not growing on her, except maybe like a fungus. Sheer frustration on Caleb's behalf struck. "Nice of them to give you so much lead time."

Amusement rolled before he tapped it down. "Yeah. I guess Penny forgot."

She didn't have the strength to hide her growl of annoyance. "Twit."

Caleb glanced over her shoulder to where the girls were consulting the recipe she'd pinned to the fridge, slipping into the pantry to gather supplies without help. "I'm surprised you picked *that* word."

"You already know what I think of the woman. She must be freaky in bed. Either that or she's keeping Luke drugged."

"Tamara," he scolded, but his lips twitched.

"What? My money's on the drugs. She looks as if ice cream wouldn't melt in her mouth." She raised her hands and backed up a step. "But the family raises some fine horses. Don't worry about it. I'll take care of the girls."

"You can rearrange your days off—"

"Enough. It's okay. Just...she doesn't have an older sister, does she?"

Caleb looked confused.

Tamara forced a smile, fake all the way. "I don't think you should eat or drink anything when you're around their place. Who knows what they might slip into your food."

She turned and left him to rejoin the girls, guiding them through making a healthy salad before pulling out the miniature marshmallows and fixings for ambrosia.

It was a quiet supper with just the three of them, at least until Dustin dropped in, and then it was chaos until bedtime.

The girls were off brushing their teeth when Dustin cleared his throat. "Can I ask you something?"

Tamara stacked the games they'd been playing in a pile and stood to put them away. "What's up?"

"There's someone I like, but I don't know if they like me, and it's hard to figure it out because there's not a lot of events I go to that she's at."

Dating advice with a nineteen-year-old guy. This could be all sorts of trouble. "Go on."

Dustin scuffed his feet on the floor. "Well, Caleb's tightening the purse strings, so I'm not about to ask for extra money. I'm trying to save everything I can, but that means I don't have the coin to be able to go asking people out for fancy dates all the time."

Warning bells were going off like crazy in Tamara's brain.

When he continued with "she's not part of the crowd I used to hang with in high school. She's a lot more"—hesitation—"mature than that," Tamara's heart fell all the way to her toes.

"Dustin. I—"

This was so many kinds of awkward she didn't know where to start. She refused to lie. She couldn't straight-up say she wasn't interested in dating, because the honest-to-God truth was if

Caleb asked her, she'd be opening the door in spite of how bad an idea it was.

She wasn't looking to date *Dustin*.

Something of her misery must've shown on her face because his eyes widened and he raised both hands in protest.

"Oh hell, no. I learned my lesson about that one. You are a mighty fine woman, but you are out of my league. And besides, I have no desire to have my skin stripped off me and woven into leather straps."

She was saved but still confused as ever. "What are you talking about?"

Dustin cleared his throat as the girls came rushing back into the room, and the conversation was over, at least for that moment.

He scooped up the girls in his arms and gave them both a big hug. "Since your daddy's not around, want me to tuck you in tonight?"

Sasha and Emma agreed excitedly.

"Crawl in. I'll be there in a minute."

They raced off, waving to Tamara.

"That's sweet of you," Tamara said.

Dustin smiled sheepishly "I don't mind. They're more little sisters to me than nieces, in a way, since Caleb brought us all up." He looked her over, a curious expression on his face. "You like him, don't you?"

Tamara blinked in surprise. "Who?"

"My brother."

Oh boy. Nope—not discussing this. "Of course. Caleb's a fine man and a good father."

Dustin tilted his head and gave her a dirty look. "That's not what I meant, and you know it."

She couldn't help it. She snickered before raising a brow and giving him a pointed look. "Don't you have some little girls waiting to be tucked in by the Dust-man?"

He paused, his expression far more like Caleb's than usual, before giving up and turning toward the hallway.

A second before he stepped from the room, though, and his parting shot sent her teetering once again. "I wouldn't mind if you liked him."

16

Silence filled the corners of the room like a windless snowfall. With both girls asleep and Caleb not back yet, Tamara sat all cozy in the living room, intending to fall into her book for a relaxing evening.

Not an empty silence, though. It was the sounds of peace and home. The fire crackled. A furnace fan kicked on somewhere in the background, adding a low thrumming noise to the room. The scent of chocolate from the girls' last cup of cocoa lingered on the air along with wood smoke.

It should've been perfect, but it wasn't.

She glanced at Caleb's empty chair far too often, the seeds of discontent growing. It felt strange to be in the room without him, and knowing he was off dealing with the Talisman family didn't make it any better.

She prided herself on being a fair judge of character, but she still couldn't see why Luke was with that woman. He was sharp-witted and entertaining, and headed straight for disaster.

It was time to tell herself to stop being meddlesome. Luke

was a grown-ass man. He could make his own mistakes. Just like she could make hers.

Although she was trying hard to avoid the biggest mistake ever—

A shiver ran up her spine as a terrible cry rose from down the hallway, and she was out of her chair and rushing to Emma's room. There'd been fear and terror in the sound, and she wasn't sure what she'd find when she entered the room.

What she got was an armful of little girl as Emma launched herself like a projectile missile, tangling herself around Tamara's neck.

Tamara sat on the bed and patted her back, soothing best she could. Emma clung like a burr, weeping as if her heart was breaking.

Tamara wasn't sure what to do. She checked for a fever, but other than being hot from crying, the little girl was fine.

But the tears—

Sasha's fake crying had been easy to ignore because it'd been dramatic and attention seeking. This was as if Emma couldn't stop herself, but there was nothing she wanted more than to hide away.

"Sweetie. It's okay. I've got you, and you can cry all you want."

That turned the faucet on higher than a moment before. Quiet, violent tears rocked Emma's body.

"Oh baby, I don't know what's wrong, but I'm here. I'm here." She caught Emma tighter, one hand cupped around the back of Emma's head to tuck her little face against Tamara's neck.

It took a long time before the crying faded to slow, gasping breaths.

They were tangled close, yet Tamara barely heard Emma's whisper. "Bad dream."

Such a sweet voice to be so filled with misery.

"It's over," Tamara assured her. "Bad dreams can't hurt you."

"Hurts inside," Emma insisted.

Well, there was that. "You're right. Sometimes bad dreams make us think of things that hurt us, or remind us of sad things." Tamara pressed her lips to Emma's cheek and adjusted her to sit more comfortably. "You want to talk about it?"

It was a long shot. The fact Emma had said as much she had was a miracle.

Sure enough, Emma shook her head, but her lips quivered and her face scrunched up again.

What was the etiquette for dealing with bad dreams? All Tamara had to go on was how she would've dealt with it at the hospital. Working in the children's ward had always been equal parts heartbreak and reward. Their fears were often caused by not knowing what was about to happen. Or from the pain of treatment—real and vivid horrors no child should ever have to face. Soothing and comforting them, even for a little while, had been worth every minute of Tamara's effort.

Tamara tucked her fingers under Emma's chin and lifted until their eyes met. "Was it a scary dream or a bad memory?"

"She's not my mommy anymore," Emma gasped before the tears began all over.

Oh my God. Tamara held on tight, rocking gently until the little girl calmed down enough to suck in another rattling gasp. "It's okay," Tamara repeated over and over, even though it really wasn't.

Whatever reasons Wendy had for leaving, Tamara didn't like her. Not one bit.

It seemed to take forever because the whispered words came between heavy bouts of crying, but in the end Tamara learned at some point Emma had been shouted at by the woman. Told that *she* didn't want to be a mommy, and to stop calling her that, and that Emma needed to *shut up.*

The fact this verbal assault had taken place in the chicken coop explained another mystery, but the final result remained that Emma firmly believed Wendy went away because of her.

"She told me to stop." Emma refused to lift her eyes to Tamara's. "I was noisy, and she went away."

A strange sense of utter control caught Tamara, even as icy hot flames roiled in her gut. There was no way to do this without being blunt, but she was going to make sure Emma understood the truth.

Tamara spoke gently. "Mommies don't leave when their babies are noisy. Do you remember hearing how noisy Auntie Dare's baby was when you visited them? Do you think Auntie Dare or Uncle Jesse would ever leave Joey?"

"*She* left."

"Not because of you. Relationships fall apart for many reasons. One reason is when a person is sick and not thinking right. They leave because they're broken inside. And you didn't break anyone."

Emma had her fingers tangled in Tamara's shirt, her face streaked with tears. Exhaustion was finally taking its toll as she laid her head on Tamara's chest.

"I mean it, Emma. Wendy was broken, and that wasn't your fault, or Sasha's, or Daddy's. I'm sorry you have that sad part in your life, but it's not because of anything you did."

Emma let go with one hand and stroked Tamara's shirt smooth, as if it were of vital importance to get all the wrinkles out.

She caught the little girl's fingers in hers and lifted her hand, kissing Emma's knuckles gently. "You can let that bad dream go. It's not real. What's real is you have a daddy who loves you very much, and the best sister in the world, and uncles and aunties and Kelli and Ashton and *me* who all love spending time with you. And as far as we're all concerned, you can be as noisy as you'd like, although I doubt you can be as noisy as Eeny and Meany when they get to complaining about their dinner being late."

The smallest of snorts escaped Emma, but nothing else until her eyelids fluttered and a yawn broke free.

"You ready to go back to bed?" Tamara leaned back as if to lay her on the mattress. Emma caught hold of her again with an ironclad grip.

Or, maybe not.

The only solution of course was to take Emma to bed with her. But which bed? Emma's was far too small, and this probably wasn't a good night to attempt to bring her into Wendy's old room.

Tamara headed to the couch to curl up there when Emma tugged on her shirt. "Daddy's."

So that was where they went.

It was strangely intimate to carry Emma down the hallway and into Caleb's bedroom. The place was still neat as a pin, but Tamara didn't spend any time looking around. Just pulled back the covers and lowered Emma to the pillow.

The little girl must've used up all her words because she didn't say anything, just clung to Tamara's shirt.

"I'll stay with you," Tamara promised. "Let me take off my jeans."

She crawled into bed, and Emma curled up against her like a kitten in a nest. Her breathing slowed, the occasional lingering hiccup shaking her body as she burrowed in tight.

Tamara's earlier restlessness had been burned away by sadness and anger and now. With the precious child in her arms, she ignored all the thoughts trying to overwhelm her. She focused instead on that pulse of warmth beating in her heart, steadily growing.

CALEB PUT his truck into park then glanced over at his brother who had been strangely quiet the entire drive home. Add that to Caleb's usual lack of conversation, and it had made for a very long silent trip.

Did he say something?

Ahh, to hell with it. "You know what you're doing with this woman?"

Luke glanced up, blinking out of his stupor. "I'm sorry Penny made a mistake and the sales had already gone through."

"She made more than one mistake, but I'm not talking about tonight and our wild goose chase. I'm talking about you being engaged to her. Why are you with her? You're not in love."

Luke looked away from him, staring out the front window over the lake.

"I think you have some hard realities to consider." Caleb spoke carefully. "She doesn't seem to be in love with you, either. You get along, and maybe you're friends, but it doesn't seem as if you can't bear to be apart from each other. That you can't wait to be together at the end of the day."

"And that's what it looks like when you're in love?" Luke demanded. "Because if that's the case, what are you planning to do about Tamara?"

What the hell?

Luke let out a rude snort. "Yeah, don't give me that innocent look. You spent all evening looking at your watch as if you couldn't wait to be back here. You've become a complete homebody, and you should see your face any time you're around her."

"I appreciate what she does. It's been a relief having her—"

"I would've accused you of wanting to get into her pants, but it's more than that. And I'm not saying this is a bad thing, but you know, before you start messing around with my life you should fix your own first. Because maybe *you* have some hard decisions to make."

The urge to tell his brother to shut up and mind his own business probably wouldn't go over well considering Caleb had just been a nosy body himself.

The two of them got out of the truck, doors slamming with well-timed synchronization.

He glanced over at the same moment Luke looked up, both of them scowling, both of them stomping their feet.

Both of them suddenly grinning because it was too funny not to notice.

"Ass," Luke said nonchalantly.

"Goat." It was the most offensive insult Caleb could think of.

His brother's lips twitched before he broke into laughter. "We're both not thinking very straight these days."

"Maybe that's something we need to change," Caleb suggested.

"Maybe." Luke stepped in closer and laid a hand on Caleb's shoulder. "We didn't want any of those horses anyway. We should lay low on the spending until the finances settle in the spring. In a way, Penny mixing up the sale dates worked to our advantage."

"That silver lining is going to come out your ass if you keep pushing so hard," Caleb warned.

"And I will think about it. My relationship with Penny, although I don't think it's as bad as you suggest. We've both been a little distracted, is all."

Luke waited as if it was Caleb's turn to make some grand confession.

Hell, no. Not happening. Instead, Caleb punched Luke on the shoulder. "Good."

He turned and walked back to the house, Luke's laughter drifting after him.

It was far too late to expect Tamara to still be up, but he was surprised to find she hadn't tidied the kitchen like usual, her cup and her e-reader abandoned in the living room. The fireplace was still glowing with coals, the damper left open.

He moved quietly down the hallway, peeking in on Sasha. When he opened the door and found Emma's bed empty, he stood there for a moment, shocked. She'd gone to sleep in it and left the sheets tangled and messy, but she wasn't there now.

And when he carefully cracked open the door to Tamara's room and found it empty as well, he was even more surprised. The first flicker of fear slipped in.

He shot to the window to double-check, but Tamara's truck was in the parking space, and he didn't think she'd have left Sasha unsupervised if they needed to rush away.

Discovering his missing persons in his room sent that tension in his heart a foot lower, pulsing in his gut as if something were wrestling there as he stared at two sleeping faces.

Tamara's hair lay across his pillow, and Emma's blonde curls peeked from under the covers where she was curled under Tamara's chin.

It was wrong, perhaps, to have such a visceral reaction when he didn't know what had brought them there in the first place. He didn't think Tamara would simply pop into his bed without a good reason.

His bed. God, Tamara was in his bed. What he wouldn't give to have her there for real. He wanted what was best for his girls, and he knew they had to wait, but...

He just *wanted.*

He stepped in closer, intending to silently grab a change of clothing and escape, but Tamara woke, big brown eyes shining as the light from the hall fell across her face. She met his gaze, and his heart leapt into his throat because he was pretty sure what he saw there was *want* as well.

Caleb stepped close enough he could brush his knuckles over her cheek, tenderly. Slowly.

Forbidden, and yet he couldn't have stopped himself if he tried.

Tamara struggled to move upright, Emma a lead weight pinning her down. He sat on the edge of the bed and curled an arm around her shoulders and helped her to sit.

"Let me take her," he offered softly.

She turned, and Caleb reached for Emma, his hands brushing Tamara's body. A small noise escaped her lips, and his system went tight as if he'd been poked with a cattle prod.

Somehow he managed to get to his feet. He stood there for a moment, arms full of his little girl as he stared at the woman in his bed. The sheets covered her, but every curve was there if he wanted to look. Soft shoulders, her hair tumbled down. Warm from sleep, vulnerable—

Sexy enough to make a saint want to dally for a spell.

Their eyes met again, and he wasn't imagining the heat in them. The need—the same urgent desire roiling in his gut.

She licked her lips, and they parted, as if she were going to say something, when Emma wiggled.

"Daddy?"

All attention went to his little girl. "Right here, button. I got you."

"I was scared and sad."

"You're safe now."

"Tamara cuddled me."

"I saw that. You want to stay in my room with me?"

She shook her head. "Professor G needs me."

Ahh. The stuffed monkey. "He's in your room. You want to go cuddle with him?"

A sleepy nod.

She was nine-tenths of the way asleep again when he laid her on her bed. As soon as he tucked the stuffed animal under her arm, she breathed out long and hard and her eyes remained closed.

He sat with her for a minute, listening to her settle. Thinking about the small moments of conversation she'd slipped in.

The fact she'd accepted Tamara's comfort blew his mind.

When he rose from the bed and stepped down the hall, he wasn't sure what he'd find, but he knew what he was hoping for.

Alas, it seemed angels only appeared in his bed once a night. The sheets were tugged back into place, and Tamara was gone.

He was ready to go after her—took two steps toward her room in fact before he realized he couldn't. This didn't change anything.

But he wanted to. He wanted to go join her so badly his entire body ached with it.

And when he crawled under the sheets and found they were still warm, the scent of her lingering, it pushed the madness over the line.

There was no ignoring the truth anymore. He wanted Tamara. She was a good woman, and a smart one. Strong and sexy and stubborn, and everything about her drew him in like a moth to a flame—

He would be man enough to admit it, at least to himself. He was scared shitless he was about to be burned all over.

Luke was right. This was something more than sexual craving. It was closer to what he'd felt at the beginning with Wendy, that hopeful tangle with longing for a great future.

But when did the potential for *more* become a dream? Relationships were a complete potshot in terms of lasting, and he didn't know if he was strong enough to fail again.

He couldn't ignore this situation, though, Caleb realized. At some point in the coming days he and Tamara needed to redefine their relationship. He'd have to be brave enough to decide which fork in the road to take.

But not tonight. Not this minute. Maybe not until the holidays were over...

As if setting a date released the pressure, he could suddenly breathe again. It was right to wait—there was too much going on, and changing anything before the holidays was out of the question.

But now that he was forced to look at the situation with his eyes wide open, Caleb acknowledged this could be a huge turning point.

He wanted Tamara. He trusted her with his children.

Why was it so hard to trust her with his heart?

17

"They're finally asleep." Tamara spoke softly as she slipped into the living room, pausing at Caleb's expression. He was staring at the tree, a dozen decorations laid on the table beside him.

Sheer misery took Tamara's heart out of her body, tied it in a knot then put it back in place far more worn. She backed up slowly and made extra noise as if she were just coming around the corner.

"I'm ready to be Santa's elf," she quipped cheerfully, giving him time to pull himself together.

It had been the strangest couple of weeks. Ever since Emma's nightmare, it felt as if the house had been slowly filling with pressure. She'd shared with Caleb what Emma had told her, and he'd been suitably upset then achingly tender with his little girl.

Emma had bounced back far faster than the rest of them. Part of that had been the distractions of the season. With Christmas programs and holiday gift-making, there was always something going on that took her and the girls out of the house.

They hadn't decorated, though, which was odd to Tamara.

But the Stone tradition was for the tree to magically appear on Christmas morning, and while not having any decorations up was different, she understood where Caleb was coming from. Waiting until Christmas Eve to deal with the tree had meant there was a single deadline to meet. Some of those early years, it had probably had come down to that final, last-minute rush.

The girls had been amazingly patient. More patient than Tamara as they eagerly worked on secret gifts for everyone in the family.

Now here they were, Christmas Eve, when the magic needed to happen.

Caleb met her eyes, and in that instant, instead of returning to being reserved and shut off, he allowed his sadness to show. Then he nodded briskly and dropped more decorations on the table. "If you want to put the kettle on, I'd love a drink."

Gruff, gruff, stubborn man. Whatever had hurt him, he was going to move ahead as usual and ignore it.

Fine. She would do all she could to help. "Is that a Christmas tradition? Hot chocolate while you set up the tree?"

He paused before the smallest of smiles snuck out. "Truth be told, you're the one who's got me drinking hot things in the evening. I'd have been more likely to grab a beer."

"Well then, I guess this is us putting some new traditions in your life." She moved toward the kitchen to put on the kettle as requested. "That hot drink is going to have a kick," she warned.

She glanced at him and was rewarded as, for a split second, a full-out grin broke over his face. Tamara treasured it as if she'd been given an enormous bouquet of flowers.

She liked making him smile—

A wave of clarity hit, and she nearly fell back against the counter, awareness digging in deep. She didn't just want this man. Although she did—utterly and completely.

She *liked* him. She thought his sacrificial ass needed a firm talking to most of the time, and yet she couldn't fault him for the things that he cared about and put his energy toward.

Selfless, caring, *stubborn* man.

She fussed as she went to make the drinks to cover up the emotions bubbling inside her, bringing everything to the coffee table as he finished wrapping the final strand of lights around the enormous tree.

Tamara nodded in approval. "Is the tree from your property?"

"Josiah's spread. He's building a trail through a batch of royal spruce, but he's in no rush. Every year we take down a couple of trees to make it a little longer. In the meantime, we get to enjoy the benefits."

She eyed the pile of decorations. More than half of them were handmade. "I see the girls have been busy."

"Don't try to pretend you haven't been encouraging them. Dare and Ginny used to spend most of December making ornaments with them as well." Caleb gave her a dry grin. "And my girls aren't so good at secret keeping as all that."

"You're right. There'll be new ones under the tree in the morning. Any particular order these are supposed to go?" She gestured toward the collection.

He shook his head. "Anywhere is fine."

Things were going well until she picked up a matching set of small silver ovals. In them a young woman held a newborn baby in her arms. The woman wasn't exactly smiling, although she was very pretty, and it was clear that in one ornament the baby was Emma and the other, Sasha.

Tamara held them, staring at what were the first pictures she'd seen of Wendy. Blonde curly hair, cupid's-bow mouth. Her first thought had been *beautiful*, but there was something in the woman's eyes that didn't look remotely like what Tamara would've expected in a new mom.

Wendy looked...lost, as if she were pretending.

Tamara slipped back in time to when she'd seen that expression on a woman's face before. She opened her mouth to ask if Wendy had suffered from postpartum depression, but decided it was far too personal to blurt out, even for her.

"I've never known what to do about those damn ornaments." The words escaped Caleb like a confession, soft and low. "They're the first pictures we have of the girls, and Dustin saved up his money to give them as a gift. Dare thought I should keep them because of that, but it's never sat right with me. I always hide them in the box so the girls don't see them every year and be reminded all over."

Caleb stared at the ornaments in the palm of her hand. Tamara swallowed hard, throat tightening. The girls might not see them, but keeping them meant *he* did.

He kept staring down, away from her gaze. "She left us."

She knew that from the night with Emma, but he seemed to be talking about something more. Tamara sat motionless on the couch beside where he knelt on the floor.

"Emma was right. Wendy just up and left. I knew she wasn't happy. Hell, she hadn't been happy except for brief moments since we finished saying *I do*, and instead of going away for a big honeymoon, we came back here."

"Caleb."

He shook his head. "No, you gotta hear this, because if things get bad tomorrow, you need to know."

Panic shot through Tamara. "Wendy's not coming here, is she?"

His eyes widened. "Hell, no." Absolutely firm. "She has no rights to the girls. Gave them up completely, but sometimes she gets it into her head to call on Christmas, or their birthdays." He gestured at the ornaments in her palm. "Like a reminder in a box that everything fell apart. I've never let her talk to them. She doesn't deserve to be a part of their lives."

Tamara took a deep breath, curling her fingers around what was pain in trinket form. She laid her other hand on his shoulder. "You want to tell me about it?"

She expected to get a gruff denial, maybe even have him walk from the room.

Shockingly, he nodded. "She wanted me to sell. I think she had a whole different idea of what it meant to be a rancher's wife than the reality. Or at least *our* reality. I couldn't buy her every frilly thing she wanted. I couldn't afford to make the house fancier. My sisters tried to help, but they were finishing high school, and Dusty was still a teenager, and I was having to be a father to them as well, and..." He dipped his head. "I swear I tried, I really did—"

God. He felt as guilty about this as Emma had, for as little reason. "Of course you did. Damn, Caleb that's the last thing you have to convince me of. I've seen you with your family. You work yourself into the ground to try and make them happy. You've done so much."

"Wasn't enough," he muttered.

The unspoken *I wasn't enough* hung on the air.

With an explosion of energy, Caleb shot to his feet. He took the ornaments from her hand and marched to the kitchen, and she watched as he silently opened the trashcan and threw the mementos away, shoulders rigid, body tense.

Tamara waited until he returned, settling on the couch beside her and staring into the fire.

She ached to find a way to comfort him, but it didn't seem her time to talk.

He was the one to keep sharing. "Last time we had contact she was based in Edmonton with her new husband. A sixty-year-old with a well-established bank account."

Tamara didn't like to think poorly of a person without ever having met them, but actions spoke damn loud. Between the bullshit Wendy had pulled on Emma and leaving Caleb to find a sugar daddy, it was pretty clear this wasn't a simple relationship misunderstanding.

Sometimes people were horrid. This was one of those times.

"As long she's fully and legally out of the girls' lives, and yours, I think it's perfectly fine to move forward."

"I should've told you all this months ago," he grumbled. "Don't know if I was acting the fool, or trying to not overload you, or trying to protect my ego."

Confusion rushed in. "Why would I think less of you because your wife decided she didn't want to be married? Do you really think I care much for the opinion of a woman who would leave her daughters?"

"I wasn't enough to make her stay, not even the girls were. She didn't want to be a mom; she didn't want to be my wife." He stared at the tree sightlessly. "Hell, she didn't *want* me, period."

He turned to face her, as if shocked at all the words that had escaped him. She stroked a hand over his stubble-rough cheek as she examined him closely. A small furrow had formed between his brows, the muscles under her palm twitching lightly as he stared back.

"Trust me, Caleb, any woman who doesn't *want* you— It's not you who's got issues. It's them. It's one hundred percent them."

She stroked her thumb over his lower lip, trembling as he snuck his tongue out to lick across the pad.

Silence surrounded them but for the music drifting from the speakers and the crackle of the fire.

He wasn't going to say anything, and she'd pretty much said anything that needed saying, so she leaned forward and let their lips connect.

A sweet, gentle caress, a kind of amen and hallelujah all in one. Enough that the flutter in her heart kicked up a notch as she pressed forward the slightest bit. She wasn't going to push, but as the taste of him slipped through her system, she wasn't ready to stop.

His fingers drove around the back of her neck and into her hair, tightening as he took the kiss deeper. Harder. Using his lips and tongue to seduce her senses, and that fluttering heart rate—a flutter no more. It raced like a driving piston on an old-fashioned steam train, blood pounding through her system with the only connection between them two hands, and two lips.

Caleb closed his fingers, tugging her hair as he pivoted to his knees and between her legs. Pushing her body to vertical so their chests connected, her breasts brushing the rock-hard plane of his body.

She'd dreamed about repeating this moment, this kiss—but she'd been wrong. Completely wrong, because it wasn't enough to make everything in her turn on, she was in overdrive. Aching and needy, her skin craving his touch.

He kept kissing her, and a low moan of pleasure escaped as a second hand slid around her torso and under her shirt. His big palm pressed her bare back and urged her body tighter against his.

She was on the very edge of the couch cushion, knees spread wide. His body rested between her thighs, and the thick line of his cock made contact with her aching core.

Her very sedate and proper pyjamas were cute and festive, with little green and red bows, but they were thin, and ridge of his jeans pushed against her hard enough she was tempted to rub. Oh God, she wanted to rub.

She still had one hand on his face, and she let the second rise so she could slide her hands over his shoulders, tracing the firm muscles there. Smoothing her hands back and forth as she rocked.

Or attempted to rock. He didn't let her move. He kept them zipped up tight together, which was good, but not good enough. She wanted to pick this up a few rooms away.

In his bed, *her* bed—she didn't care which, but when his fingers tightened that last bit and tugged their lips free from each other, they were breathing as if they'd finished a marathon. Foreheads touching as he stared at her face.

"Point proven," he said softly.

Her head was spinning hard enough she wasn't sure what he was talking about? "Caleb?"

"I know you want me. I want you too." He stole his hand out from under her shirt, and she damn near whimpered in disappointment.

He made a soft shushing noise. "We can't. You know this."

She nodded. "The girls."

This time it was Caleb who cupped her cheek. He stroked a finger over her lips.

"I can't hurt them," Caleb breathed. "Been too beat up by grownups, and it's not fair. I can't, even though, God, I want you. It's too soon. We can't make them hope—"

They couldn't when there was nothing official between them but this wicked heat and longing. Physical desire wasn't enough to hurt the two little people she'd come to care about so much.

It still burned. "I know."

She cupped her hand over his, holding his palm against her cheek. "You're a good man, Caleb Stone. You deserve to be happy too. Just in case no one's ever told you that."

The very corners of his lips curled. "I'll keep that in mind."

"Good."

They stared at each other, sharing air, and even though she craved *more*...it was enough. They were two adults making an adult decision to do the right thing.

They finished decorating the tree, the Christmas carols

playing in the background shockingly joyous considering the rock in her belly.

Sometimes doing the right thing sucked.

18

Caleb paused before stepping outside, the twinkling lights of the Christmas tree drawing him forward as surely as they had when he'd been a little tyke.

He stood in the silence, the living room filled with a candlelight glow from another line of lights crossing the mantle. Shiny silver ribbon twinkled, and he glanced back toward the tree.

A third look—he wasn't sure how he'd spotted them because even though they were noticeable, they weren't *that* big.

There were new ornaments hanging on the tree. Right there at little girl height where Sasha and Emma would be sure to see them. Silver ribbon in tight, precise bows that declared Tamara's handiwork as loudly as if she'd signed her name.

He didn't know how the hell she'd done it, but she had. In the time between their soul-stealing-kiss-filled evening and this morning, Tamara had found baby pictures and made new ornaments with their names in block letters, stars and stripes and glitter and all the shimmering doodads a little girl could possibly want. It didn't matter that they were babies, and barely recognizable from any other newborn, it was clear *this* one was Emma, *this* one was Sasha. Pinks and purples, blues and silver.

Caleb felt his throat tighten again.

He wandered in a bit of a haze as he did his chores, the familiar feel of the animals bumping shoulders with him as he added feed to their pails a nice, mindless task.

The whirlwind of emotions in his gut was far too big to think on straight. He had to kind of come at it sideways. Maybe sneak up on it.

He'd told Tamara last night that they couldn't get involved. And that was true—and an affair was out of the question because the last thing he needed was the girls falling in love with Tamara and her breaking their hearts.

Your heart couldn't take it too well either, his brain pointed out.

But what if she was to be more? What if she was willing to become a permanent mom to the girls?

What if he was ready to risk his heart?

He patted Stormy on the side of the neck. "What'd you think?"

Stormy dipped his head and blew a snort of air.

Caleb smiled. "Yeah. Me too."

"I thought that was Josiah's job, talking with the animals," Walker drawled, resting his arms on top of the gate. "But I guess as long as he doesn't talk back, I won't get too worried."

Caleb glanced at his brother. "Don't you have work to do?"

Walker shook his head. "It's Christmas morning, bro. Just the normal tasks, and I'm nearly done. I promised Tamara I'd come to the house and help with cooking dinner."

"Don't bother. I'll help her."

Walker stepped aside as Caleb brushed past him, returning buckets to the shelf where they were stored.

"Do you know?" Walker asked out of the blue.

Caleb twisted. "Know what?"

A little of Walker's belligerence faded. "You *do* know. That's why you're such a miserable son of a bitch these days."

Caleb debated telling his brother to mind his own business. God, his brothers were like the old, crusty ranchers hanging out on the front porch of the mercantile, i.e., the worst type of gossips. "Why'd you come home?"

Walker blinked in surprise. "Oh, no you don't. This isn't about me—"

"Why isn't it? Didn't expect to see you until a few days before the holiday, if then, and for you to be back out the first minute you could. Instead, I heard you might be sticking around until the spring." Caleb eyed Walker closer. "What happened?"

Walker folded his arms as he leaned against the rough wood slats of the barn. "You've never got much to say except when you decide it's time to grill one of us. I figure that's kind of special. You know, that you break out the words, and all."

Caleb waited.

"You're such a bastard," Walker complained.

Huh. He hadn't been sure until that moment, but it was obvious something *had* happened.

"What's wrong?" Caleb asked softer. "You've always got a home here. And if there's anything I can do to help, it's yours."

Walker dipped his head. "I know. And hey, I came back, didn't I? I know how much you care, in spite of you not talking up a storm."

"But you're not going to tell me anything more..."

"You ready to admit your secrets, bro?"

They stared sheepishly at each other. Stalemate. Nothing to admit until he'd figured out the next step, preferably with Tamara.

Silence surrounded Caleb on the walk to the house, the icy winter air slicing into his lungs, sharp and painful. At the same time, the world sparkled. Crisp and shiny, the freshly fallen snow painted the landscape clean.

Stepping into the kitchen was like walking into a hug, the house filled with all sorts of delicious scents and the low murmur of voices.

An excited squeal accompanied Emma's rush in his direction. She stopped a foot away to take a cautious sniff before throwing her arms around him. "It's Christmas."

He caught her in his arms and threw her skyward, joy kicking hard through him as laughter spilled from her lips. "How did that happen? I could have sworn it was summer. What's Santa doing coming in the middle of summer?"

Sasha was there, catching hold of his other side and squeezing tightly. "Merry Christmas, Daddy."

He reached down and lifted her as well, their squeals of delight making the warmth of the room all but disappear because this warmed him even more, inside and out. "Merry Christmas, pumpkin. Are there really presents under the tree?"

Two heads nodded. They squirmed to be set free, and he put them down, pausing to remove his boots as he gazed into the living room. "That's a fine-looking tree," he said to Tamara, who sat all bundled up under a blanket on the couch, a cup in her hand and laughter in her eyes.

"It's amazing," she replied. "One minute it wasn't there, then *poof*. The next it was."

Emma paused at Tamara's knee for two seconds before climbing into her lap as if she belonged there. But it wasn't until she cupped a hand to Tamara's ear that Caleb's throat threatened to close off for good.

Tamara's gaze met his as Emma whispered something, a sweet smile directed at him before she turned her attention to his daughter and nodded vigorously. "I'm sure Santa found the things you made. You should check the packages and see if any of them have your daddy's name on them."

Caleb stood there for one more moment before his feet carried him down the hall, vanishing into his room without a word.

He leaned his hands on the door and fought for control. This was what it was supposed to be when you had a family. This was what Christmas morning *should* be like—and the sheer wrongness of the past threatened to choke him.

He took a few deep breaths, attempting to push away the old. Wendy wasn't part of the girls' lives anymore. She hadn't been for a couple of years, and she couldn't come in and hurt them.

Tamara had shown him he had that right.

He changed from his work clothes, a real mixture of pleasure and pain swirling in his gut. This was going to be the best Christmas ever for the girls, but he still...

Why did he feel as if there were an aching, empty hole inside?

The modestly noisy house grew louder as the morning progressed and as the rest of the family arrived, the back door opening again and again as his brothers joined them.

Dustin wore a Santa hat, the paper bag in his hand that held presents taken eagerly by Emma to be placed under the tree. Sasha hauled him off to help set the table for the upcoming meal, and secrets in the form of low whispers bounced back and forth between the two of them as they worked, the lanky young man and his energetic niece.

Walker hung his cowboy hat on one of the hooks by the door before coming forward with small, twisted bits of tin foil he placed at each person's spot at the table.

Luke marched in right when they were getting ready to sit down to dinner, his arms full of packages. Penny wasn't with him.

Tamara eyed him. "Where's your fiancée?"

Luke blinked, looking up from where he'd been hugging the girls. "Penny? Oh, she said to pass on her apologies, but she couldn't make it. She'll try to come tonight, but there was something her dad needed her to do, so she couldn't leave until later."

He shrugged.

Caleb wondered if Luke really didn't mind, or if his brother was putting on a show and hiding his disappointment.

Tamara pushed past Caleb, muttering under her breath. "I hate that woman. Twit. Mean, nasty twit."

Caleb's lips quivered, but he managed to keep from outright laughing. "That's not a very Christmassy-like sentiment," he murmured back.

"She doesn't engender very many charitable thoughts on my part, but I kind of figured she'd do this." She turned, brushing accidentally against him, giving his arm a squeeze before stabbing a number on her phone. He waited with great curiosity until she barked an order at someone. "I win. Get your ass up here."

He raised a brow, but Tamara put her phone away and patted her pocket with a smug smile. "I do so like being right."

Caleb wondered if he should give the room a warning of some kind, but then it wasn't him she was pulling a fast one on, and he wasn't about to rescue his brother.

When Kelli slipped in the door five minutes later, offering Tamara the evil eye, Caleb couldn't help it. He outright grinned, especially when Luke paused in the middle of what he was doing. His eyes went wide before his lazy, half-hooded look returned.

It seemed the friendly feud between the two of them continued.

"Okay, everybody to the table," Tamara ordered, and the next few minutes were filled with the noise of moving chairs and overfilled platters being laid on the table.

An amazing spread of food greeted them. Caleb picked up the first serving spoon, and that's when he noticed half the stack of plates waited beside Tamara. She worked at his side, scooping up half of everything before the plates were handed around the circle, and slowly everyone was served.

As traditional, Ashton had joined them, and he sat there with a huge grin on his face that only got wider as the meal progressed.

They ate until Caleb couldn't think of eating another mouthful. At which point, Sasha proudly brought out a pie *she* had made, and they all had to eat a little more.

Luke made the coffee, and as they finished the last of the goodies, Ashton delivered his present, which was to open his fiddle case and play a few songs for them.

The responding applause that followed was the cue for Dustin to turn into a giant elf and start passing out presents from under the tree. The volume in the room rose, and wrapping paper flew, and through it all Caleb forced himself to keep from staring at Tamara between discovering what had caused the squeals of excitement from his children.

They ended with the little twist of metallic foil that Walker put in front of each plate.

Caleb lifted the small black device hidden inside. "Something for the computer?"

Sasha rolled her eyes. "*Daddy*. It's a USB. It means Uncle Walker gave us pictures or something. You plug it into your computer, and you can download them."

Caleb nodded at the serious expressions on Emma's and Sasha's faces. "Good thing I've got you guys to help me with that." He turned to his brother. "Rodeo pictures?"

Walker was occupied straightening his utensils. "Something like that."

Caleb wrapped his fingers around it and nodded. "Thank you."

Emma slipped to Walker's side and gave him a big hug, and he held her tight for a moment, eyes closed, contentment on his face.

Games were brought out, and more music played. The afternoon drifted into evening. Everyone who wanted to eat again loaded a plate with leftovers and heated it in the microwave, Dustin going back for thirds.

They took turns heading out in pairs to finish chores, returning to the warmth of the house as if they couldn't bear to let the holiday be over.

Twenty minutes past their bedtime, two little girls were falling asleep in the corner of the couch, but their eyes were bright with happiness and Caleb wasn't willing to send them from the room yet. So they sat, curled up together, staring at the Christmas lights and the family who were still visiting.

Luke, Kelli and Ashton were talking up a storm, the older man settled on the ledge before the fire as Kelli sat on the floor, hands waving animatedly. Dustin fooled around cautiously on Ashton's fiddle while Walker teased him.

Caleb drifted around to where Tamara sat playing with the puzzle Dustin had given her, settling on the arm of her chair.

"Thanks." He wanted to say so much more. Like thanks for poking his stupid ass and making him a better father. Thanks for taking care of his family and making sure they were all as happy as possible.

He couldn't get the words out.

She put the puzzle aside, tilting her head as she gazed up. "It's been a good day."

"Tomorrow, your family."

"And yours," she pointed out.

They and the girls were headed north to Rocky Mountain House for the annual Boxing Day Coleman clan gathering, which included his sister's new family and Tamara's family.

Shockingly, he was looking forward to it, which wasn't like him. The idea of a crowd, with so many strangers, usually would put his back up and make his protective instincts go into overdrive. Take his little girls into that situation? Never...before now.

Because while it would be loud and noisy and full of people, he was fairly certain they would care and tease and *love* his girls and make them feel welcome.

This trusting business was addictive in a way. It seemed every time he'd opened up a little he'd been rewarded—

He wondered if he should plan on ducking soon, because nothing went this well, for this long, without coming back and kicking him in the teeth.

But that hollow, empty place inside him had filled up over the past hours, and he knew the reason why.

More specifically, he knew the reason *who*, and she was watching him closely. Her face smooth and content, but a question in her eyes.

He broke eye contact, hoping his feelings weren't written too clearly on his face. He nodded politely, then rose and joined Walker and Dustin who were trying to convince Ashton to play some more fiddle.

Maybe...

Maybe Tamara was right about something else. Maybe it was time for him to do something that would make *him* happy. He didn't need to know what came a year down the road.

Tomorrow would be a good enough start.

19

$\mathcal{J}$t was the first time Caleb remembered having more secrets the day after Christmas than before.

"Will there be any other little girls like Emma and me? The twins aren't as old as us, but they're nice." Sasha bounced forward and leaned up on the back of his seat. "Can we go to the barn? I want to see the kittens. Do they have goats?"

"Is your seatbelt done up?" Tamara interrupted.

Sasha didn't break stride, but she did slide her hips back a few inches. Caleb heard the click as she redid her seatbelt. "Can we go tobogganing? Do we have to do chores while we're there? If we do, and there's chickens, I can help with the chickens so Emma won't have to. Right, Emma? What would you like to help with if we have to do chores?"

Caleb peeked in the rearview mirror so he could watch as Emma spoke quietly to Sasha before turning and tapping Tamara on the shoulder.

Tamara twisted in her seat. "Yes, sweetie? Do you have a chore you want to help with? Although I don't think you have to worry, because we're going for a party. We won't be there long enough to help with chores."

Caleb glanced off the road for a moment as a whisper drifted from Emma, too faint for him to hear.

"Nope, you don't have to talk to anybody if you don't want. Sometimes my sister Karen goes whole days without saying a word, but that's more because she's trying to be a pain in the butt."

"Tamara!" Shock rang in Sasha's nine-year-old voice. "That's not nice."

Tamara looked genuinely surprised. "Pain in the butt? The words, or the sentiment? I love my sister, but sometimes that's what she is." Tamara turned to Caleb in appeal. "Tell me I can say 'pain in the butt.'"

"I seem to have heard it three times in the last minute, so I don't think you have any trouble saying it."

Giggles erupted from the back seat.

Tamara winked before rotating to the back again. "Remember, Auntie Dare lives with my family now, so I'm sure she has talked about what amazing little girls you two are, but if anybody forgets their manners, or if you need a break, come and find me, or Daddy, or Auntie Dare. And hey, you get to see your new cousin Joey again. He's going to be a lot bigger than the last time."

"He won't be able to walk," Sasha informed her as if that were the end of that discussion. "*I* want to play with the twins."

Tamara turned back, a deep sigh of satisfaction escaping before she turned her smile on Caleb. "I'm glad you agreed to making the trip. It's a long way to go for one day, but it'll be good to see everyone. I know Dare will appreciate it, as well."

Before he could stop himself he grabbed her hand where it lay resting on the console between them. "Figured it was about the best Christmas present we could give you. The boys are doing my chores, so there's no rush to get back."

He squeezed her fingers then forced himself to let go, gripping the steering wheel and staring ahead as if it was the first time he'd seen this stretch of highway instead of the millionth.

Caleb could feel her looking at him, but it was too soon to reveal his cards. He stayed focused until Tamara gave up, distracted by something else.

"Hey, I brought something along." She shook it in the air. "Wait until you hear this."

It was the USB that Walker had given him, and she slipped it into the dash of the truck and fiddled with the buttons as he watched with amusement. "You're kidding me. I didn't know this truck could do that."

"Yeah, well, I didn't know your brother could do *this*."

She hit play then turned up the volume. They were in the middle of a country-and-western song, familiar words with a simple guitar playing in the background instead of a full band, but the tune was catchy, and the performance solid, and he tapped his fingers in time with the rhythm. "Not bad. I hope that's not pirated."

"*Daddy*. That's Uncle Walker," Sasha chided him.

Caleb listened in shock, but after a few more beats it was clear his daughter was telling the truth. "Okay, that's a puzzler. I knew he could sing, but that's not half bad."

"That's better than not half bad. You never told me Walker was a singer."

"He isn't. I mean..." He gestured to the radio and the music pouring from the speakers. "Okay, he *is*, but he's never done anything more than help get us through singing Happy Birthday without breaking people's eardrums."

Tamara grinned. "Well then, I think it's a perfectly marvelous Christmas present."

"Me too," Sasha piped up. "Maybe I can get Uncle Walker and Ashton to play at my birthday next year."

Caleb glanced at Tamara. "That's a long way away. You're already planning your party?"

"Kelli says it's important to plan ahead and not just go off half-cocked. Kelli says a lack of planning on someone else's part is no reason for her to get all bent out of whack." Her confused expression was clear in the rearview mirror. "Daddy, what's bent out of whack mean?"

Thank God that was the expression she wanted to know more about. "It means Kelli should remember little people have good hearing."

Tamara snickered, covering it up with a cough.

He was so tempted to reach over and catch hold of her hand again it was brutal.

He still had no idea what was going to happen in the next twenty-four hours, but if things went the way he hoped, they'd both be getting a very sweet post-Christmas present.

IT WAS good to see everyone in the family again, the entire group of them gathered at the Moonshine Coleman's.

Her uncle and aunt welcomed them in, but like any Boxing Day gathering, there were more people around than just family,

After making sure the girls were introduced to the other kids their age, Tamara found herself being kidnapped by her sisters, tucked in the corner where she could see the girls, but she and Lisa and Karen could talk openly without being overheard.

"You're wearing a goofy smile," Lisa pointed out. "Still having a good time in Heart Falls?"

Karen made a rude noise. "That's a needless question. Let's stick to the basics we need real answers to. What's going on? You look as if you've got secrets, and that's not allowed. Tell us now, or we'll torture them out of you."

Hand to God, Tamara was going to have reason to shoot them at some point.

Thankfully, she could answer somewhat honestly, because nothing *was* going on. Not really. "Nothing other than I'm being an excellent nanny."

Karen and Lisa exchanged glances before looking back and leaning in closer. "Define excellent."

"No, first define *nanny*," Karen demanded. "Does your job description involve extensive one-on-one time with anyone over the age of ten?"

Tamara waved them off. "You guys are terrible. Nothing's...happened."

Her confession came out with just enough hesitation she was a goner. Her sisters pounced like birds of prey on a helpless field mouse. Wanting to know who and what and especially when.

Except a second after starting, Karen pulled up sharply. "We're teasing you, but it's because we love you. Something's not okay."

Tamara hesitated. These were her sisters. If she couldn't talk to them about the most important thing happening in her life, she was in a bad way.

"I don't know what's going on," she confessed. "Wait, I do know. Caleb and I have a serious case of the hots for each other, but it would be all kinds of wrong to act on it. The girls don't need more chaos in their lives, so even though there's an awful lot of chemistry between us, we're going to do the right thing and ignore it for now."

She said it firmly, meaning every word, but the closer she came to that final statement, the harder it was to speak, until she stopped talking because her throat was closed, and tears were rushing upward.

To her horror, a sob escaped her lips, and she twisted her chair so that no one could see her make a fool of herself.

Karen leaned away as if they were talking about something inconsequential. Lisa turned her chair as well, blocking her from the other side, an arm draped casually over her shoulders as she hugged her tight.

Tamara dragged for air, fighting to keep quiet. "I'm sorry. I don't know why this is happening."

"Maybe because this hot, chemically induced passion between the two of you is something more?"

Tamara took a tissue from her pocket and wiped her eyes, "I've only known the man since October. Hardly enough time for anything more than lust to develop."

"You officially met him in July," Lisa pointed out, "which means you've been daydreaming about him for well over six months. Face it, sis, maybe this is a case of when it's right, it's right."

"Love at first sight? That doesn't happen in real life."

Karen leaned forward in her chair and let out a heavy sigh. "Yeah, course. You're right, nobody has *ever* had her heart broken by someone she only knew for a short time."

Lisa and Tamara both stared at her in shock.

Karen offered a wan smile. "In case it makes you feel any better—the only reason I would share such an ego-destroying, soul-sucking truth."

Lisa glanced between the two of them. "Okay, we need to hold a Whiskeyteers retreat so I can get the truth out of both of you, but"—she held up a finger—"that will have to wait until after this holiday season because at the moment Tamara has bigger fish to fry than satisfying our curiosity. And I can get the details from Karen when we're alone."

"You can try," Karen scoffed.

Lisa put her hands on Tamara's shoulders. "How about I tell

you something that should make you feel a little better about your unrequited love."

Tamara hissed for her to be quiet. "You think you'd have learned how to use an inside voice by this stage of your life."

Lisa motioned for them to lean in closer. "When your boss contacted me last night to find out the details for the Coleman Boxing Day event, he also arranged for the girls to stay and visit for a couple of days."

All the strange talk of chores and sleeping arrangements fell into place. "Oh. *That's* what they were talking about. That's great. The girls have been missing Dare, so if we stick around for a while—"

"No." Lisa shook her head. "*Listen.* The girls are sticking around for a couple of days, but you and Caleb are still going back tonight."

Shock rolled through her. "Why?"

Lisa blew a raspberry. "Oh, because he loves doing chores, and he's forgotten how to make coffee for himself in the two and a half months you've been living with them. I don't know why, he didn't tell me specifically, but he *did* set it up so that the girls are staying here, and you and he are going to be back at Heart Falls *without* two little chaperones."

After a careful swipe at her eyes to make sure she no longer looked weepy, Tamara twisted to be able to gaze into the room. Only half of the clan were around, the other half visible outside the window playing in the snowy wonderland, or seated around the giant bonfire pit her cousins had made.

Caleb was inside talking with his sister Dare and her cousin Jesse.

Their eyes met across the room...

Nothing.

It wasn't as if it was a magical moment. His eyes didn't light up with passionate flames. He didn't wink, or offer any insight as to why he might have gone out of his way to change plans without telling her.

"I actually think you might be right on that one," she muttered. "That he wants me along to cook and clean for him. Wouldn't that be the kicker? I get my hopes up, and then get to enjoy an empty house to masturbate in for two days."

Lisa snickered.

Karen looked a little scandalized. "God, I can't believe you just said that."

"What, masturbate?" Tamara looked at her older sister in shock. "You're such a prude, but I'll forgive you, because broken hearts suck the big one."

"Eloquent as always."

"No matter how painful, truth is beautiful." Tamara closed her eyes for a moment, considering this new twist. It was wonderful and terrifying at the same time.

What *did* she want?

She peeked across the room again, examining Caleb carefully. Broad shoulders under the neat, jean shirt that he'd worn, arms folded over his chest as he listened to Jesse and her Uncle Mike debate.

The three men were poster-perfect examples of the strength and masculine beauty found in the ranching community. Jesse's dark good looks with a firm jawline and mischief shining in his eyes. Uncle Mike's hair was shot with silver, but the family resemblance between them was so strong it was like looking at before and after photos of the same man.

And there in the middle was Caleb, not quite as young, not nearly so old, but the years of responsibility had given him a look of maturity and solid dependability that she admired in a man.

Dependable, but sexy as hell. No denying it.

But did she want him for a fling, or for something far more enduring?

Screw it—she wasn't about to lie to herself. She knew what she wanted.

The question was what was *he* thinking? Was this just an opportunity, if Lisa was right, to burn off the sexual tension driving them crazy?

Or did he want more?

She opened her eyes and smiled at her sisters. "Well, either way I'm bound to be feeling pretty content over the next couple of days. Don't phone me, don't text me, and for God's sake, Lisa, do not pick this week to take advantage of my *the door is always open* comment. Because if you show up when I'm in the middle of something entertaining? You're sleeping with the goats."

Lisa dipped her head. "I'll agree to all your terms, except one. We expect you to send at least one text, because if I'm wrong—" She made a face. "Okay, that's not possible. I'm never wrong, so forget I mentioned it. Text us anyway."

Karen smacked her in the arm. "Such a brat."

"You lurves me, you do."

Tamara did love them both. "Why is this stuff so hard? This relationship stuff, I mean."

Two pairs of shining eyes met hers. "So we'll know it's worth it in the end?" Lisa suggested.

"So we have a reason to eat ice cream, even in the middle of winter," was Karen's suggestion.

Tamara stared across the room at the man she was hoping to shove into a more than boss-and-nanny situation before the night was over. She'd always jumped in with two feet before.

Maybe the water would be cold, but hopefully the ride after would be worth it.

20

*L*isa handed her a brightly coloured package about the size of a bottle of whiskey, but far lighter. "Don't open it until you're in the car on the way home," she ordered, slipping her arms around Tamara and hugging her. "You deserve to be happy," she told her fiercely.

"Thanks, little sis. When you find out what bee's up Karen's butt, let me know, 'kay? We Whiskey Creek mice have got to stick together."

Lisa rolled her eyes before offering a kiss and backing away. She eyed the room until she spotted Emma, swooping in and lifting her up. "My turn for cuddles."

They said their goodbyes to Sasha and Emma who were buzzing with excitement to have a sleepover with extended family. Goodnight kisses and hugs and waves followed, then they were back outside. It was nine p.m. and a long drive was ahead of them.

A large question hovered.

Caleb held the door for her and she climbed in, feeling a little unreal. Of all the times she wished she had the courage to jump to a conclusion, she just couldn't.

What if he actually wanted to go back and have some time in the house quiet-like, without the girls?

They were barely out of town, heading south when Caleb cleared his throat awkwardly. "Sorry I didn't warn you ahead of time."

"I'm surprised the girls kept it quiet as long as they did. Now I understand all the questions about chores better."

She watched his profile, her blood beginning to race as he swallowed, his throat moving.

"I've been thinking. I've been thinking hard, and I don't want to put any pressure on you, but you know that issue we had on Christmas Eve?"

Issue? "Can you clarify what you mean? Because I remember a whole bunch of things going down on Christmas Eve."

He cleared his throat again. "I think both you and I want the same thing when it comes to protecting the girls." He reached across and caught hold of her fingers, and this time her heart rate tripled. "But you and I both have something else we want really bad. I thought we could meet some of those needs without complicating things for the girls."

Oh boy. "You want to fool around?"

His fingers squeezed tight. "Fool around. That sounds like something we did back in high school, and I don't mean for us to stop at kissing, or petting."

Oh boy again.

It made sense, because this thing between them was so huge and combustible, she didn't think they could deal with it by sneaking around corners and hoping for the best. But she wasn't looking just to rub out some excitement. "Caleb, I meant it. I don't want to hurt the girls, I've come to care for them, and if you and me giving into this—"

"Violent urge to fuck?" he interjected.

A flush of heat struck straight between her legs. "Yeah, that would be one way to put it. I don't want to do something that's going to make you want to fire me. The girls don't deserve that."

She didn't deserve that, but they'd stick to the girls for the moment.

Caleb stroked his thumb over the back of her hand. "I have no intention of firing you. But we're not ready to go from where we are to where we want to be in one day, and I can't hold back much longer from showing you exactly how much I want you."

A lovely rush of endorphins washed through her system. Tamara considered it better than any high she'd reached before. "So we're going home to let this thing between us progress to its natural conclusion."

He glanced over, and what she'd hoped to see earlier, all that fire and need and passion, scalded her as if she were kindling, and with one *whoosh* she went up in flames.

"Okay by me," Tamara responded.

And then incredibly, they sat there. Holding hands in the car as he drove down the highway. Tamara wiggled in her seat as she debated the proper response. Because, yes, it would be a little crass to simply stop the truck, pull over to the side of the road and go for it.

Then again, that wasn't the worst idea she'd ever heard.

Distraction. She needed a distraction.

Her eye fell on the vibrantly wrapped present Lisa had given her, and she tore the paper away, discovering, as she'd expected, a box that would usually hold a bottle of Jameson Whiskey.

Only when she popped open the top and removed the festive tissue paper, what poured into her lap were dozens of packages of condoms. Brightly coloured, flavoured, ribbed—*large*.

She shoved the wrappers back into the box as quickly as she could, latex crinkling under her fingers.

It seemed she now had not only motive but the means.

"Caleb?"

He grunted in response. If she didn't know better she'd assume he was doing something boring like looking over a tractor magazine or planning how much hay to stack in the south field.

But a quick glance to her left showed the truth. His fingers on the wheel were white, his grip so tight she could practically hear the leather scream in protest. Maybe his legendary control wasn't quite as unshakable as he wished.

Oh, she certainly hoped it wasn't.

"Could you pull over, please?"

He frowned. "You need a pit stop already?"

She shook her head happily. Then she waggled one of Lisa's Christmas presents in the air where he could see it. "I think we should start that little adventure a little sooner than waiting until we get home."

Caleb swore, snapping his head back to the front and focusing on the road as if she held a gun to his head. "Tamara. I'm not taking you in the goddamn truck."

She slid a hand up his arm, squeezing her fingers over his shoulder before sliding back down and caressing his biceps. "Why not? I have no problem giving myself to you in the truck. Or if it makes you feel better, I could take you."

The engine roared for a second as he hit the gas extra hard before growling at her. "We can wait."

But the imperturbable Caleb was fidgeting.

Tamara eased her hips forward on the seat and undid her pants.

He snapped a glance sideways. "Don't do that."

Tamara lifted her T-shirt to expose her belly then lifted her hand to her mouth and licked her fingers before sliding her hand into her pants. Curling her knuckles so they showed against the fabric of her jeans. "Just getting warmed up."

He was torn, she could tell that. Eyes on the road with just enough glances to the side to know she was driving him wild. Heck, she was driving *herself* wild, brushing fingers over her clit steadily until a soft sound of pleasure escaped her lips unbidden.

Caleb turned the truck off the main highway, bouncing down a dark side road toward a batch of trees.

Tamara let a smile sneak out, lifting her hand across and offering her fingers. "Want a taste?"

He slammed on the brakes, skidding the truck to a stop. It shimmied ninety degrees to finish parked across the dead-end road. Then he was around the vehicle, jerking open her door and releasing her seatbelt to pull her toward him. He took her lips, kissing hard and deep and fast until she was lightheaded.

Caleb reached down and stripped off her pants, pulling them down as far as her boot tops before shoving her panties away as well. He pushed her back to the seat, jerked her hips forward and covered her with his mouth.

Zero to sixty—the bit of warmup she'd had was nothing compared to the caress of his tongue over her sex. Feasting like a starving man, the five o'clock shadow on his cheeks rasped against her inner thighs. A sensual sandpaper forcing pleasure on her as he moved his tongue against her rapidly. Strong fingers dug into her ass as he lifted her against his mouth.

He'd wrung an orgasm from her in no time flat, her body shaking as he grabbed for the box on the floorboard. Caleb tore open the lid, and colourful squares went flying everywhere. He had a condom open, his cock covered. Then he stepped up on the running boards, lined up and slid in.

Slowly. Eyes fixed on her face as he pushed into her. Hard and hot and thick and oh, *yes*, it felt good.

Tamara swore, lifting her knees. She intended to grab hold of her ankles to offer him more room, but her jeans were tangled around her boot tops, so she ended up in a weird, lopsided butterfly-position as he joined their bodies, leaving her fuller than she'd ever been.

He closed his eyes, a shudder wracking his entire body as he gripped her hips and held them together.

Intimate and picture-perfect. In spite of having only briefly kissed, in spite of having all their clothes on and the awkward location for their first sexual tryst, it was perfect.

The impact of two and a half months of foreplay couldn't be discounted.

And when Caleb pulled his hips back, the perfection of it just continued. Tamara reached down and caught hold of his wrists so she could contribute. Clenching as he thrust forward, arching her back and sighing with contentment as he worked himself in and out of her.

Over and over again.

Cold air poured in the door and swirled around them as the December wind shifted over the Rocky Mountains. A glacier-kissed, ice-scented breeze that would normally have sent her running for shelter, but she was hot. Scorching, burning hot as he stared down, his ironclad grip controlling her hips.

Pleasure rose again, never quiet after her first orgasm, and she let go of his hand to strum her fingers over her clit, helping matters along. Stronger, higher—

But not quite there before he tightened from head to toe, arching against her and pulsing helplessly as he came. Release taking him and shaking him, and she couldn't even be disappointed that she hadn't gone two for two.

It still felt so damn good, and unless she was mistaken, this was only round one.

His head dipped forward, chest quivering as he breathed uneasily. "Damn."

Tamara sighed happily. "That pretty much sums it up."

He looked at her from under his brows, a small, satisfied smile curling his lips. He didn't say anything else, just leaned in and pressed his mouth to hers with a soft, tender kiss. Cold air swirled around them, his cock hard enough to be felt inside her tingling sex, and she couldn't imagine anything better.

Except knowing this was just the beginning.

He wasn't about to apologize.

If it'd been any other woman, at any other time, Caleb would have been appalled at his lack of control. But as he put them back on the highway and headed for home, Tamara was damn near gloating in the seat next to him.

Considering how good *he* felt, this wasn't a time for apologies.

He almost wondered if he was dreaming, though, because she'd agreed far more easily to his proposition than expected. It wasn't as if he only wanted this for today—only for now. He still needed to take that final step and make their relationship more official. Getting there made the distance between two points seem a hell of a lot longer than it should be.

It was like the spot out at Silver Stone where the river stood in the way, and even though the horse sheds he'd been told to go check were less than a five-minute walk apart, because of that river it was an hour unless he wanted to get wet.

Unless he wanted to face the rapids that could twirl him around and possibly send him reeling.

Tamara isn't Wendy.

Tamara was forthright, all energy and boldness as she reached for his hand, linking her fingers with his and offering a smile full of satisfaction. He felt himself smiling in return.

"I can do better than that," he informed her. "I feel like a greenhorn, trying to seduce you in the back alley of some nightclub."

"Caleb Stone. Is this something you've done a lot of? Seducing innocent young things behind taverns?"

He shook his head. "Honestly? I never was much of one for hitting the bars. Luke, Walker, and I used to go on occasion, and after Josiah moved to the area he and I went. But I mostly stopped after..."

She stroked her fingers between his, caressing. "Tell me to go to hell if you want, but do you have anybody you talk to about Wendy?"

His good mood faded slightly. "I try not to think about her."

"Which makes sense, and I get it. I'm a lot happier when I don't think back to everything that brought about me being fired, but there are times and situations it would be much easier to— I don't know. I guess I just want you to know you can talk about her with me. I'm not going to judge you for making a mistake, *if* you made any, and I'm not saying you did." She gave his hand a squeeze then adjusted position. Slipping off her boots and bringing her feet up on the seat beside her as she faced him.

"Why'd you get fired?" It was off topic, and yeah, a protective move. But he wanted to know how she'd respond.

Turns out, with utter honesty. "The reason on paper is I ignored the patient/doctor confidentiality clause when I told my friend that her mom had terminal cancer. The real reason is I pissed off a man in a position of power by refusing to worship his cock."

Caleb jerked the water bottle from his mouth, coughing as he attempted to get rid of the mouthful he had just taken. Thank God he hadn't spewed it all over the inside of the windshield.

"Was that a little too blunt? I went out with one of the doctors a few times, but it ended up he wasn't as much fun as he thought he was. And I couldn't resist smart-mouthing him back when it became clear he thought he had the right to push me around."

Caleb wiped his lips dry before glancing at her. "You? Smartass comments?"

"Shocking, right?"

He was silent for a moment. That was a pretty big thing she'd done wrong. "Was it worth it? Not the part about being a smartass, but telling your friend."

Tamara nodded. "She'd already lost her dad to cancer. It was this long, drawn-out illness that was hell on the entire family, which is why her mom was keeping her diagnosis a secret. But I know Allison. I know she would've been even more devastated to have been living hours away instead of spending those final days with someone she loved."

It was silent in the cab for a few moments, just the wheels on the pavement and the air rushing past as they drove in the darkness.

"Even knowing I would get fired, I'd do it again." Tamara spoke softly, staring out the front windshield. There was not much out there except white lines at the side of the road, and a dotted yellow passing lane flickering by like a heartbeat. Pale red taillights winking far in the distance.

As quiet as it was, the cab seemed to be filled with life and energy and powerful emotion. It was all because of *her*—Tamara.

Maybe that was why Caleb found himself telling her things he hadn't expected to. "Wendy didn't like going to the bar. I think maybe there were too many people, which meant she couldn't stand out in the crowd. I didn't mind that she liked it when I took her out for lunch while we were dating. Ginny, Dare, and Dustin were in school then, so I didn't have to wrangle babysitters or coordinate someone to cook meals at home. Wendy and I dated for three months before we got married."

Tamara whistled softly. "That's a bit of a whirlwind."

He sighed heavily. "She got pregnant."

"Oh."

Maybe this confession thing was good for the soul. "Part of the reason I wasn't too thrilled when my sister ended up pregnant. I knew it could end badly."

Tamara shook her head. "I don't think you have to worry about your sister. Jesse and Dare are both putting one hundred percent into their relationship. Did you want your marriage to work?"

"Of course. I was dating her in the first place because I thought we'd be good together." More the fool him.

"And from what I know of you, you were working to try and make that happen. I don't think her getting pregnant should have been the kiss of death on your relationship if she wanted it to work. That's what was missing between you and Wendy, at least from where I'm sitting. You gave and gave, and she didn't."

She hadn't. Caleb wasn't going to argue with that fact.

This wasn't where he had expected their discussion to go, and yet it felt right. Then, Tamara being Tamara, she dove right back into the conversation and through the other side. "You haven't had sex since she left, have you?"

Not much use in lying. "Explains why I was so fast off the handle."

Tamara snickered. "Any session of fooling around that ends with me coming at least once is a win. Don't sell yourself short. I had fun."

"Me too."

Then damn if she didn't do it again. "How much sex did you have before that?"

"*Tamara.*"

"What? I'm trying to prepare myself for the next forty-eight hours."

He fought to keep from smiling. He considered her question and it was easy. "Not much."

"Define not much—?"

"What the hell do you want? What difference does it make?" He'd never even told Josiah this. "Emma turned seven late September. Add nine months. You're the one doing math for me."

He had to admit the stream of curses that confession induced was satisfying.

She reached across and grabbed hold of his hand, linking their fingers firmly. "Well then. It's a good thing I've been taking my vitamins."

There really wasn't any answer to that one.

Then she stopped with the embarrassingly blunt questions. He worried that the remainder of the three-hour trip would turn into something awkward, or worse, a constant temptation to pull over and take her again.

Instead she decided to get his opinion on a whole number of household things they needed to catch up on, hauling a small notebook from her purse and going through a detailed list. Activities for the girls, questions about the ranch and the financial side of things. Heck, she had Ashton's birthday party on the list.

The entire time they held hands. He hadn't expected that simple act to feel so huge. So intimate.

An hour later Tamara closed the book with a satisfied snap. "Consider that a business meeting well accomplished. And the party planned."

"Kelli will be glad."

Tamara laughed as she squeezed his fingers then let go for a moment so she could put her notebook away. "What's her story? Sounds as if she's been working at Silver Stone for a long time."

He nodded. "She showed up one spring when we were shorthanded. I thought Luke had hired her, he thought Ashton had, and Ashton thought I'd put her on payroll. None of us had, but she was there, up on horseback and doing a full day's work, so we let her continue."

"That's a little weird, isn't it? I mean, not so much the female ranch hand as the fact she had to be barely out of high school."

Caleb glanced at her, but Tamara didn't look concerned, more intrigued and curious. "Don't tell her, but I did a police search on her. It came up negative. I figured she had her reasons, and Ashton decided he wanted to mother hen her, so we let it go. Never had a reason to regret it."

"I like her," Tamara admitted. "Reminds me of my sister Lisa. There's not much they wouldn't do on a dare, but you know when they got your back, it's all out."

"She's a part of Silver Stone as much as any of us."

Silence fell. Tamara leaned forward and turned on the music, Walker's voice filling the cab.

Caleb felt a little embarrassed he hadn't known something this big and important about his brother. And yet, as the story about Kelli's arrival at Silver Stone reminded him, there were a lot of times he hadn't quite known what was going on.

And he'd been far too oblivious when it came to the damage Wendy had done in his little girls' lives.

Tamara is not Wendy. He reminded himself of this fact, but it was tough to still the doubts. What if he made another mistake? How much damage could be done this time?

But glancing beside him, he was struck by the honesty in her eyes. Blunt spoken, living life at high-volume, choosing to do what was best for a friend in spite of the devastating damage it did to her own life—those were not the acts of a woman with an ulterior motive.

He glanced at his watch. Nearly midnight. It should be late enough their arrival at the house might not be noticed. Because whatever else needed to be decided, Caleb Stone hadn't had enough of her yet.

Tamara seemed to be on board with his thoughts as he pulled

into the parking space nearest the front door. He turned off the lights quickly and left them in the dark.

Sheer mischief shone back as he glanced at her. "Are we hiding?" she asked.

"We have a limited amount of time." He was out of the truck, pulling her after him. "I don't want to waste it."

She took him by the hand and raced up the walkway. They slipped in the front door, and he caught her by the shoulders, pushing her back against the nearest wall so he could lay a finger over her lips.

They stood in the darkness, listening.

Wonderful, amazing silence answered.

Two cool hands pressed against his face as Tamara aimed his gaze at her. "We have a limited amount of time," she repeated his words. "And I don't want to waste a minute of it."

He expected her to slip up on her tiptoes and kiss him, so he just about fell over when she did the opposite. Sliding her back down the wall, hands braced across his chest, then lower, lower. Until she was on her knees and her fingers were tangled in his belt, eyes flashing at him from behind her red-framed glasses.

He swore, the faint glow from the outdoor yard light shining through the front window to land on her face as she grinned up, rapidly undoing his belt buckle. Unsnapping and unzipping before she used two hands and a firm grip on his jeans to pull everything off his hips which left his rising erection in full view.

Caleb braced an elbow on the wall. "Hell, yes."

She didn't answer, just slipped her fingers around him and stroked. A slow-motion tease that she added her mouth to, licking in a circle around the sensitive head, getting him wet.

Nothing but sensation. Definitely no thought. Pleasure crawled up his spine as she sucked deep, taking half his length. Pulled back, tongue flicking at the base of the head. Pressed forward, her fingers digging into his butt cheeks as she encouraged him to rock toward her a little farther each time.

He threaded his fingers through her hair, curling the strands around his fist. Careful to control the depth and thrust, and floored by how mind-bogglingly good it felt.

She tightened her grip and pushed him back enough he popped free.

She tilted her head. "Ready for a challenge?"

Caleb chuckled. Only Tamara would think of adding a game to sex.

Then she blew his mind, releasing his ass and reaching up to tug at his wrist. "No hands," she ordered.

He pulled his fingers away slowly, the threads of her hair sliding like silk over his knuckles. He placed his second elbow on the wall on level with the first, palms above them to form a triangle to give him something to lean on as he stared down.

Tamara turned back, and after resting the head of his cock on her open bottom lip, placed her palms on either side of her hips against the wall.

If anything, Caleb got harder. It was all up to him now, rocking forward and watching his cock slip into her mouth. She tightened her lips, sucking hard as he dragged back, and that sense of impending explosion grew tenfold.

He tried to keep it slow. Tried to keep from rutting forward like some out-of-control sex fiend, but she'd closed her eyes and was making the most delicious noises. Encouraging him to go harder, deeper. Pressure increased rapidly until he was seconds away from disaster.

"*Tamara—*"

She must've understood his question because she opened her eyes, and even stretched around his cock, it was clear her lips were curled in a smile. When she sucked extra hard on the next thrust, Caleb lost it. He stilled, deep in her mouth. The rhythmic motions of her swallowing stripped every last bit of control from him.

It was a good thing he had both hands on the wall or else he would've tipped right over. His legs shook so violently the house could've been in a full-on earthquake.

He finally regained enough brainpower to pull back his hips, his cock coming free with a pop. Tamara smiled as she rose to her feet, arms tangling around his neck. She kissed him, tentative at first as if she wasn't sure how he'd take that idea, but to hell with that.

He pressed them together, pinning her to the wall as he kissed her hungrily. Pants still hanging, his ass out, and wave after wave of happy endorphins flooding his system.

The best part? He had no intention of letting her go any farther than his bed for a good long time.

A light turned on behind them, and the floorboards squeaked at the end of the hallway.

21

Tamara and Caleb snapped their heads to the side just in time to see Dustin round the corner, baseball bat raised threateningly.

The young man spotted them, his eyes widened, and he pivoted on the spot to give them his back. "Jeez, what the hell?"

Caleb grabbed at his pants and jerked them back into place. Tamara's heart leapt, somewhere between surprise and amusement.

"What're you doing here?" Caleb demanded.

"It was too noisy in the bunkhouse so I decided to sleep in my old room downstairs. I heard these strange noises, and I didn't expect you guys back until tomorrow." He glanced over his shoulder. "Is it safe to look yet?"

Tamara put a hand over her mouth to keep from laughing out loud. Poor kid.

Caleb didn't seem to be as entertained about the whole thing. "Good night, Dustin."

"I'll go back to the bunkhouse," he said.

"You do that."

"Dustin," Tamara interrupted before the kid could escape. She waited until he looked down the hallway, and even in the dim light the bright red colour splashed over his cheeks was clear. "We don't have to tell you not to say anything about this, right?"

He nodded quickly. A hint of his usual youthful attitude reappeared along with a cocky smile. "Knew you liked him."

This time she was the one who pointed down the hallway. "Go."

"Going." Dustin vanished.

Tamara and Caleb stood there in the hallway until the sound of the kitchen door closing echoed through the once again quiet house.

She turned to Caleb who stood inches away from her, his expression wary. "Well. That was unexpected," she said.

He dragged a hand through his hair. "Complicates things."

She shook her head, sliding her hands around his waist so she could nestle their bodies together. "Not really. This is still time for us, and we don't have to make any commitments about what we're doing. I'm okay with that. For the next two days we just go on how we began."

"This isn't a fling."

"We don't need to decide everything right now," Tamara repeated.

Caleb took a deep breath. "You don't think Dustin'll say anything?"

If she knew Dustin, he'd probably have plenty to say, but it wouldn't be to anybody but her or Caleb. "Talk to him tomorrow. He's old enough to know how to keep his mouth shut."

Her sexy cowboy still looked concerned, but he cupped her face in his hands and leaned in to kiss her, and the gentle pressure of his lips against hers was enough to wash away any worries of their escapade spreading too soon.

It was a whole different sensation to stand in the middle of a familiar place, pressed against his warm body and kissing in such a slow and leisurely way. They'd done the fast coupling in the car, and the blow job moments earlier had been hot and wild.

This was intimate in a way that touched her heart differently. Her pulse wasn't racing although it was strong. She wasn't squirming with sexual wildfire, but the need for the man she was pressed against was no less intense for all that it was quiet. Soft and slow and still sending her senses reeling.

He pulled back from her lips, pressing kisses to her temple then along her jaw and behind her ear. When he bit her neck her entire body shook, massive goose bumps rising. She moaned in approval.

"I want to see you naked," he whispered.

She caught his hands and backed toward her bedroom, keeping their bodies in contact as they shuffled. "Me too."

He grinned. "You want to see me naked, or you want me to see you naked?"

"Both. Right now, desperately."

She reached behind her and pushed open the door, and something in his eyes flared for a second with pain.

Oh dear. It seemed Emma might not be the only one with hang-ups about this room.

She caught her fingers around his belt and tugged their bodies together. "There's more room in here, and a far bigger mattress. But if it's going to drive you crazy—"

Caleb shook his head, answering part of her question by crowding after her and forcing her into the room. He closed the door behind them.

She moved to the bedside and clicked on the light.

A soft laugh escaped him. "I don't know why that should surprise me."

"What? That I want to have sex with you on the biggest bed possible?"

He pointed behind her. "That you're turning on the light so I can see you better."

Amusement bubbled up. "Yeah, I don't do the shy-and-retiring maiden very well."

"Good." He stepped forward until they were facing each other, four feet apart. They'd kicked off their boots in the front hallway, and they both stood there in stocking feet.

He started at the bottom and took a slow, thorough examination as his gaze drifted up her body. When he reached her face, laughter rumbled up from deep in his chest. "Keeping your glasses on?"

Instinctively Tamara's hand rose to adjust them into a better position. Today she'd worn a pair of delicate red frames that matched her holiday blouse. "I can't see without them, remember? And I have no intention of missing any of the show."

Caleb moved in on her, tapping his finger on her nose briefly. "I thought guys were the ones who got turned on visually."

"Girls like looking too."

He stroked a finger down the buttons on her shirt. "You watch sexy things, Tamara?"

"You mean like porn? All the time." She eased herself against him. "You look shocked. Did I scandalize you?"

He undid her shirt, gaze fixed on his fingers as the buttons slipped through the buttonholes and the fabric edged apart. "A little, but I like it. Feel as if I should watch you while you're at it. Maybe I'll learn a thing or two about what you like."

"Well, we could do that. Or you could ask me. Or better yet, we can just try it all and see what fits."

She already knew some things that fit nicely, thank you very much. And as much fun as it was to have him peeling her shirt off her shoulders, what she wanted was to watch.

Tamara pressed a hand to his chest and pushed him back half a step.

She undid her pants and let them fall to the floor, stepping out of the fabric puddle so she stood in underwear and bra more than an arm's reach away.

When he would've reached for her she held up a hand. "Not so fast. Your turn. Lose the shirt. And the rest of it."

Caleb didn't bother to unbutton anything. He pulled his shirt from his jeans and lifted it over his head, arms crossing as he stripped the fabric away. Abdomen muscles flexing as he moved, his happy trail wiggling as it disappeared enticingly under his belt line.

His strong forearms were covered with a dusting of hair, biceps bulging as he folded his arms over his sturdy chest. "Since we're taking turns."

"You still have your pants on," Tamara protested.

"Only two articles of clothing left," he pointed out. "Oh, sorry. Socks means three."

"We can't forget the socks." She reached behind her and undid her bra, wiggling her shoulders to let the fabric fall to her hands so she could throw it on the nearest chair.

Caleb's gaze locked on her chest, and she took a deep breath, arching her back to see the fire flare.

He didn't look away as he dropped his jeans, kicking them aside so he stood in boxer briefs, his erection a thick ridge clearly visible in sharp contrast to the tight fabric.

She couldn't resist closing the distance between them. She stroked the very tip of her fingers over his hipbones before slipping a hand under the elastic of his waistband and grasping his cock.

Caleb's eyelids fluttered shut. "I thought we were looking first and touching second?"

He braced his legs wide as she pumped, enjoying the weight in her hand too much to stop. "Oops?"

She got in a couple more strokes before he wrapped a hand

around her wrist and extracted himself from her grasp. He picked her up and placed her on the bed, stepping back as she wiggled upright.

A moment later he'd lost the briefs as well, and she curled her arms around her legs and looked with admiration on her living Adonis statue. Trim hips, with deep V-cut muscles rising up from his groin. His oblique muscles were visible, the solid ridges of his pectorals slightly out of balance as if at some point he'd broken ribs. Every shadow, every dip highlighted the work of art the land had turned his body into. Hard physical labour and sheer determination had left him without an inch of extra fat.

A heavy shadow coloured his chin and cheeks, his eyes watching with an intensity that lit her internal pilot light.

Finally, she dropped her gaze. Fully erect, and beautifully proportioned. She could write a medical paper on the perfection of his equipment, but since the days of medical paperwork were behind her, she would just appreciate it for the wonderful gift it was. At least the way he used it.

"You done looking yet?"

He didn't give her time to answer. Crawling forward on the bed, rearing up on his knees, he stared down intently.

Tamara reached for her panties, intending to wiggle out of them when he shook his head. "My job."

The evening was far from over. She lay back against the pillows and waited.

CALEB HAD no intention of moving quickly. It had taken far too long to get to this point, and in spite of having to deal with the complication of Dustin discovering he and Tamara were having a—

He didn't know what to call this other than mind-blowingly fantastic.

Here she lay, naked except for a scrap of fabric over her sex, and those ridiculous fuzzy socks she loved, and he wasn't going to worry about the semantics of what to call the event. He was going to make sure they both had a damn good time.

Even after the truck sex and that dirty-as-hell blow job, they'd barely begun. This was the first time he'd gotten to see the soft swells of her breasts, nipples tightening as he watched.

Caleb adjusted position to lie beside her, and for a moment he was frozen with indecision. Where should he start?

She laid a hand on his cheek and that seemed as good a beginning as any as he brought their lips together for another kiss. They'd had violent, startling kisses, and sweet slow kisses, but this was the first time they'd kissed with their bodies hip to hip, pressed tight, nearly naked. Her soft breasts with those tight nips teased his chest as he leaned against her. Tongues dipping and retreating as they tasted each other over and over.

Tamara slid her fingers into his hair as they continued, heat rising at a modest pace.

Caleb slipped a hand over her hip and up until his hand covered the swell of her breast. He rotated his palm in a slow, teasing circle, letting her nipple drag against him. One side, then the other, and when he could finally bear to take his lips from hers, he cupped his hand and plumped up her breast so when he shifted position he could suck her nipple into his mouth and tease the tip with his tongue.

Tamara's fingernails scratched his scalp, harder now as he sucked more intensely. She shivered as he gently put his teeth to her.

He had no idea how long had passed as he moved from side to side, taking his fill of her breasts before skimming a hand over her ribs, following with his tongue. Moving down her body an inch at a time, licking and sucking and biting.

He stopped at her belly button, flicking his tongue into the dip before sliding over to a hipbone. Now, finally, he tucked his fingers into the edges of her panties and lowered them enough so he could tease the sensitive spot where her leg joined her torso.

Tamara attempted to bend one knee, but he pushed it aside, widening her legs to a V as he settled between them. Her panties still covered her sex and he caught the front between thumb and forefinger, using his other hand to reach below and wrap a finger around the gusset. Squeezing the material into a thin strip of fabric that he dragged back and forth over her sex.

A low, breathless moan escaped her as the material rubbed her clit, slipping between the lips of her sex.

She was wet, so very wet, and he couldn't resist pushing the fabric aside and sliding a finger into her depths.

"Caleb."

"Still looking," he told her.

Her low pants of excitement were wracked with a complaining tone as he added a second finger and continued to work them slowly in and out.

"*Caleb...*"

He tore off her panties, tossing them to the floor. He lifted her knees and pressed her legs to either side until she was wide open, her pussy glistening with moisture.

"Hold them there," he ordered.

Tamara caught her knees and stared down at him, glasses perched on the end of her nose as she offered a rosy-cheeked smile. "You are a very thorough looker," she teased.

He didn't answer, just rose up so he could peel off one furry sock then press a kiss to the arch of her foot.

She giggled, the entire bed shaking as her laughter grew. He ignored her, although he had a smile on his face as he sucked her toes into his mouth one by one. Next came more kisses, from her ankle up the backside of her leg until he could torment the sensitive skin on the back of her knee with his tongue.

The giggling stopped at that point, turning into moans of ecstasy.

He repeated everything on the opposite side, and laughter returned as he peeled off her second sock.

"Caleb Stone. Do you have a foot fetish?" she demanded.

He gripped her ankle more firmly then teased his tongue between her toes. Tamara's eyes widened, pleasure streaking across her face.

He was having too much fun to stop. This time he didn't hesitate for more than a second at the back of her knee before continuing all the way along her inner thigh, scraping his whisker-roughened cheek against her soft skin. Pressing her knees farther toward her head so her hips rocked off the bed.

Open and ready for when he dropped to his elbows and licked delicately.

"*Oh...*"

Caleb took his time, tasting and teasing. Listening to the sounds she made in response to each one of his actions as he learned what she liked and what she loved.

And every time he glanced up she was still watching, gaze on his mouth, drifting over his features. Eyes fluttering shut as her body tensed under him, closing on her peak.

He pulled away before she could climax, swallowing her soft moan of protest with a kiss before he rolled away, digging in his jeans for one of the condoms he'd stashed.

He was back on the bed in seconds, pushing her back when she would have sat up to join him.

When he lifted the wrapper to his mouth to rip it open, though, Tamara stole the condom from his fingers. "None of that. No teeth near condoms unless you're doing it the right way."

Her words were confusing enough to make him hesitate. He found himself being levered to the bed, her firm grasp around his shaft as good as a nose ring on a bull. "The right way?"

Tamara removed the condom then placed it on the head of his cock, and the next second she'd leaned forward and was using her lips to roll it down his length. Slow repetitious movements that threatened to send him flying over the edge far too quickly.

"Fuck."

She pulled back and wiped her mouth. "Strawberry. My favourite."

Caleb laughed, pulling her into his arms and catching hold of her ass. He lifted her over him, but she rolled to her side. Moving together to line up, he slid deep, her leg draped over his hip giving him perfect angle to be surrounded with white-hot pleasure.

There was too much to feel. Too much to enjoy. Tamara scratched his back, sliding a hand over his ass as he pumped against her. He got a breast in his fingers, kneading the heavy weight before pinning the tip of her nipple against his fingers with his thumb and rolling.

Another kiss, another caress. And through it all, the motion of their bodies rocking against each other, ancient and perfect and far too raw to resist.

Tamara arched against him as a throaty cry escaped. Her sex clamped down, and he swore, fighting off his release for another thrust. And another, long enough to drag out her pleasure until she gasped every time he drove forward.

He lost all finesse, rolling her to her back, locking his elbow around her knee to pull her farther open so he could drive deep for his last thrusts.

Release started somewhere near his toes and went all the way up, shooting through his system as if he were being electrocuted, power surging until the top of his head was ready to come off and stars formed in front of his eyes.

They clung to each other, breathing heavily. He didn't want to leave, but he took care of the condom quickly before returning and pulling her back into his arms.

She curled against him, and he realized that sometime in the last ten seconds she'd finally removed her glasses. "You don't need to see anymore?" he teased.

Tamara shook her head, a gentle motion against his chest. Her arms draped over him, their legs tangled. "Need sleep."

It was late enough that it made sense. No postcoital serious discussion, no questions about where they went from there.

He rolled far enough to turn out the light before coming back to cradle her. Staring around the room that had once been his wife's.

No. Before that it had been *their* room. The place where he and Wendy had started their married life, before everything had gone to hell.

Before that, once upon a time, it had been his parents. A place where love had lived.

It was just a room. It was the people in it who mattered.

A soft snore escaped Tamara, and Caleb found himself smiling. The sleep of the innocent, in the best sense of the word. Tamara had no agenda. No reason to withhold or barter her affections. Just honest pleasure and connection between the two of them.

He fell asleep wondering if it was possible to hit the reset button and actually start over.

Waking less than four hours later at his regular time, he was groggy enough to wonder what the hell was going on before he remembered he was in bed with Tamara.

Sometime during the night they'd rolled and were now spooned together. Tamara's backside against his groin, his hand crossing her body and cupping her breast.

Getting up to deal with chores was the purest form of hell

he'd ever experienced. Forcing him away from a warm, soft woman and into the cold outdoors was just cruel.

The animals didn't give a damn how mean it was. Hell, he swore his horse was laughing evilly when he went to saddle her up.

Caleb should've known he couldn't go the entire morning without being accosted by his younger brother. Dustin, who usually survived early-morning shifts by consuming massive amounts of cola, was waiting for him by the feed stores. He attempted to look casual but something was on his mind.

Maybe the kid would be too embarrassed to say anything if Caleb didn't bring it up first. "Morning."

"What are you and Tamara doing?"

So much for avoiding the issue.

Caleb glanced around the barn before motioning his brother to join him. He leaned against the solid wood wall and debated what to say.

He was tempted to basically say nothing, but the concern on Dustin's face was real, and all those old instincts of trying his best to teach his brother what he needed for life—hell, Caleb had screwed up pretty big on that when it came to setting an example with his first marriage. Saying nothing wasn't an option.

So he went with the truth. "I don't know."

Dustin hadn't expected that answer. "Oh."

They stared at each other for a full minute before Caleb carried on. "We didn't expect to bump into you yesterday. We're still figuring out what we want, so it's important you don't say anything to anyone."

His brother shook his head. "I won't, but Caleb..." Dustin lifted his eyes, and instead of a teasing young kid there was someone teetering on the edge of adulthood, concern darkening his features. "I like Tamara. And I want you to be happy, and if there's some reason you're staying apart because you don't think getting married again is a good idea, well, then I think you need to know, I think this is different. She's not like Wendy."

"She's not," Caleb agreed.

"And you're not the same as you were before," Dustin continued in a rush.

Okay, that was a little more confusing. "What's that mean?"

Dustin shrugged. "I mean, you're in a different place than when you and Wendy got together. I know you've got Emma and Sasha, but all the rest of us—we're grown up now. You don't need to take care of us."

"You're still my family. And we still need Silver Stone to run well and support us."

"Right, but you've got all of us to help you with everything. So if being with Tamara makes you happy, and if she wants to be with us—" The kid's cheeks flushed nearly as red-hot as they had the night before when he'd interrupted them. "If she wants to be with *you*, then I hope you guys end up together."

In the first time in a long time, Dustin was the one who walked away from the conversation before Caleb had a chance to.

Romance advice from a nineteen-year-old. Huh. Caleb watched his kid brother vanish around the corner.

The kicker of it was—it wasn't bad advice.

22

"*How* do you want to do this?" Tamara asked. It was just past noon, two days later, and they were lying in bed with nothing but lingering heat between them.

Caleb traced a trail over her breasts, his gaze following his fingers. "I just showed you how we do it. Need me to demonstrate again?"

She shot a hand down to cover her sex before he could make it there first. "Stop or I won't be able to walk." She tilted her lips toward him and gave him a kiss. "Although, I'm not really complaining about that option."

The past couple of days had been a glorious haze of sexual satisfaction. They'd started each day tangled together, then he'd drop in for lunch, which had turned into a quick romp. Followed by shower sex before dinner.

Sitting in front of the fire in the evening, their glances would become longer and longer, until they were shutting up the place an hour before usual, slipping off to her bedroom to start again.

Tamara figured the man had over seven years of celibacy to

make up for. She wasn't going to deny him. So self-sacrificing of her, to be willing to have sex at the drop of a hat.

In her imagination, her sisters' eye rolls were audible. *Self-sacrificing, ha!*

It had been worth it because Caleb wore the expression of a well-satisfied man. "What's your question?"

"What do you want to tell the girls?" They'd ignored the conversation until now, as agreed, but it couldn't be put off any longer. "They'll be here in a couple hours."

He didn't hesitate. "We tell them we're getting married, and that you're—"

"Caleb Stone." Utter shock hit and instinct kicked in. She smacked a hand down on his shoulder. "Number one, that is *not* what we're going to do, and number two, you didn't ask me."

A frown folded his features. "I could have sworn I did."

Tamara thought back. "Unless *oh my God, oh my God, hell yeah* is cowboy for *Tamara, will you marry me?* you seem to have missed that detail."

He shrugged, the slight motion shifting his broad shoulders against the tangled sheets. "Marry me."

Okay, great in bed, sexy and dependable, and not a romantic bone in his body. Tamara raised a brow and ignored the little fist bump of happiness inside that he'd at least popped the question.

Once he'd been prodded. Hmmm.

She stuck to her guns. "Nice try, but no. Considering you've gone to your knees before, I'm not accepting that."

For a second his eyes clouded, but she refused to let his past remain a forbidden topic between them. "I get that you have bad memories, but you need to think big picture here, dude."

"I like the view from where we are just fine," he grumbled.

Tamara sat up sharply to glare at him. While she'd been willing to let the past few days be all about the physical, that wasn't enough to base a marriage on. And she was fairly certain she wasn't the only one in the relationship who actually cared.

Getting him to admit he had feelings for her might be the biggest battle.

Her on the other hand? No problem expressing her feelings, at least regarding the annoyance rushing her. Yes, he'd asked her to marry him, and an honest thrill was running through her system, but...

But...

It wasn't enough, and it wasn't fair to either of them to not fight for *everything*.

Hence her annoyance rising to the top and escaping. "You not being much of a talker might be a good thing, because you're doing a fine job putting your foot in your mouth."

His face registered confusion. "What? Do you want a ring? Because we can get one by tomorrow. Maybe later today."

"A ring would be part of it, but it's not the main thing." She folded her arms over her chest. Either he was being deliberately obtuse or the man honestly didn't have a clue. Tamara examined his face, but it was unreadable again. He'd closed off and shut down, and *hell no* to both of those.

It was one thing for her to be stupid in love with the man, but was it too much to ask that he feel the same about her? No, of course not.

He probably *was* in love with her but too stubborn to admit it yet.

Fine. She'd take this back to where she knew they were in one hundred percent agreement. The girls.

"I don't think it's a great idea to drop a bomb like that. They like me plenty at the moment, but I'm their nanny. If you simply announce we're together, they might get all scared that mothers are different than nannies, and they need to know that I'm still *me*, and not the title behind my name. That things aren't going to go back to how they were with Wendy."

He nodded, shifting back on the bed. "Ideas?"

"We go slow." For his sake as well. Maybe a bit of time would be enough for him to figure out what he'd missed in that lame-ass excuse for a proposal. "Give it another month or so. Switch things up around Valentine's Day."

Hint, hint.

He nodded, but she could tell he wasn't happy with the idea.

"We can sneak away sometimes to be together," she suggested.

"I thought you wanted to keep this quiet. No way that's happening if we're caught sneaking around."

"It's all I've got," she said.

He kissed her, hard. Demanding a response, and before he left her bed she was once again a wet noodle, sated and happy.

But he left the room as well, taking his clothes with him, and she stared at the closed door and wondered how long it was going to take to break through those final barriers. Wendy had hurt the girls, but she'd done a number on Caleb as well. It might take a while for them to finish the healing process.

Tamara did the next thing. She got up and made cookies. A triple batch, so she'd have extra to send home with whoever dropped off the girls. Then she retreated into the office to finish updating the books using the information she'd gotten from Caleb during the ride home.

Dealing with the financial side of things was a distraction of a whole different sort. Caleb's comment when he'd asked her to take over the task came back to her—that he'd probably hire a bookkeeper only to find out there wasn't enough money to keep them on.

After an hour with the paperwork, she had to agree. Silver Stone was going to have to batten down the hatches. Nothing terrible, at least not yet, but when she compared this year's bills summary with previous ones, expenses were up and income down just enough to make keeping in the black uncomfortable.

A knock on the door to the office brought her gaze up to meet Walker's. She waved him in. "What's up?"

He strolled in, glancing around the room. "Wow, you cleaned up the hurricane damage."

"It wasn't quite that bad, but yeah. There's a floor. Who knew?"

He turned a grin on her. "Hey, Caleb forgot his phone. Wanted you to know when the girls arrive, bring them to the barns. He'll be working with Josiah."

"Sounds good." She eyed him. "I enjoyed your Christmas present, by the way. You're good."

A flush hit his cheeks. "Thanks."

"You planning on doing anything more with your music? That was a demo tape, right?"

For a grown man Walker was suddenly fidgeting like a kid. "Sort of. Just a decent recording a friend made. I don't know— getting into the music industry is pretty time consuming, and so's rodeoing. It's probably not a good idea to try and do it all. I've got Silver Stone to help take care of, as well."

"No reason you can't make an attempt. The ranch will be here. You know your brothers wouldn't want you to give up on a dream because you felt obligated to hang around."

He dipped his chin. "Don't know if it is my dream, or something I fell into. Still figuring that part out. What's important, what's just fun. What my goals are long term. You know, the tough decisions."

Yeah, she could appreciate the difficulties more than he probably guessed. "Well, I hope you have fun while you're deciding."

"No problem there. I always have fun." He tipped his hat then left the room, and she got back to work.

But she was waiting on the front porch when one of her family's trucks pulled into the yard. Tamara admitted it—she'd missed the girls. As much as she'd enjoyed time alone with their daddy, the sensation of happiness welling in her belly as Sasha and Emma dropped from the truck and raced toward her was strong and addictive.

Lisa strolled forward, basket in hands. "Hey, is this the right place? I'm looking for the Heart Falls Zoo. I've got two monkeys for delivery."

Sasha stopped short of throwing herself into Tamara's arms, twisting to offer Lisa a *hah, hah, very funny* expression. "I am *not* a monkey."

"Lion? Tiger?" Lisa let her eyes get big and wide. "Was I transporting dinosaurs without a permit? I'm glad I didn't get stopped by the RCMP."

Tamara accepted a hug from Emma, enjoying the brief snuggle as Sasha proceeded to make claw fingers and roar at Lisa.

"Yup. Watch out, Tamara, we've got a dangerous Stompasaurus on the loose," Lisa warned.

"Too bad. I made cookies, but since dinosaurs aren't allowed in the house..."

Sasha stopped mid-roar.

Tamara held out a hand for Sasha's bag. "Did you have a nice visit with Auntie Dare?"

"It was great, only Joey has the sniffles so she didn't want to take him on a long drive, so Auntie Lisa said— I mean *Lisa* said she'd bring us home. Can we have cookies now?"

Sasha being home meant the house was no longer silent. Tamara smiled. "Yes. Drop your bags in the laundry room, grab a cookie, then we're going to the barn."

"I bet Eeny, Meany and Miney missed us," Sasha told Lisa. "You should come and say hi too."

"You have time?" Tamara asked.

"Oh, I'm not going anywhere until I help you find your phone. You must have lost it since you left Rocky." Lisa gave her a pointed look before following them into the house.

Oops. "Right. I was supposed to text you." Tamara grinned. "I was...busy."

A smile crossed Lisa's face, followed by concern, but she held her questions until the four of them were walking across the yard, Emma and Sasha leading the way, cookies in hand.

"You had a couple *enjoyable* days?" Lisa asked out of earshot of little ears.

"Yes."

"And...?"

Tamara answered softly. "He half-assed asked me to marry him."

"I knew it," Lisa gloated. "The marriage bit, not the half-ass. Let me guess, you told him you guys should wait, right?"

Seriously? "How on earth? How come you know that?"

Lisa shrugged. "Because you're you. Those two kids are amazing, and while I know you're in love with the guy, you want it all. Him in love with you, *them* in love with you—it'll happen."

Hope swelled. "You don't think I'm wrong for not just accepting and being done?"

"Hell, no. I'm proud of you." Lisa stopped and gave her a hug. "You've got a heart the size of Alberta, sweetie, but you use a lot of it making other people happy. You don't always do what would make *you* happy. He'll get there, you'll see. You'll both be better off knowing this is more than lust or convenience."

Tamara squeezed her. "How'd you get so smart?"

"I'd tell you I learned from my big sisters, but actually, I sent away for an extra-large box of smarts from Amazon. Delivered right to the door, very convenient."

"Brat," Tamara teased.

"Always." Lisa whistled at the girls who were crawling on the goat pen and making horrifying noises. "Hey, no dinosaurs around the goats."

Laughter rose. Tamara felt a little better at her sister's assurances that she hadn't just thrown away her future. Because Lisa was right.

Those little girls were in her heart as hard as their daddy. She wanted it all.

Now if that future would just hurry up and arrive.

FOR THE UMPTEENTH time that afternoon, Caleb found himself staring into space. And again, he forced himself to get back to the task at hand, helping Josiah check and file the horses' teeth.

He'd been as shocked as Tamara at his proposal. Nearly fallen over when the words came from his mouth.

Maybe deep inside he'd been hoping to sneak it past her. If she'd agreed, he'd have been done, and the only thing that would change going forward would be where she spent her nights.

Only she was right—changing their relationship wasn't going to be as simple as that.

He wanted her physically. He wanted her for his girls. It was still frightening to admit he wanted her for anything more, but now that he'd stewed about it for most of the afternoon, he'd figured it out. That was exactly what she was hinting at.

She wanted him to say *I love you*. And he didn't know if he could yet.

Waiting was the only solution.

Josiah's voice cut through his thoughts. "Of course, you could breed watermelons."

Caleb blinked at that. Nope, made as little sense the second time as the first. "*What?*"

His friend slapped a hand on his shoulder. "I told you three times we're ready to move to the next horse, and you didn't budge. You're wool gathering, which makes me suspicious."

No way was he admitting to anything. "Of what?"

Josiah eyed him closely. "You miss the girls."

"Yup." That would do as a distraction. Caleb would admit to anything else right then to avoid confessing he cared for Tamara more than he'd expected.

That he might be falling in love.

"Must have been weird, not having them around the place for the first time ever."

"Quieter."

"Surprised you didn't give me a shout. I would have come over, helped to pass the time. It was quiet for me at the shop."

Caleb felt bad for a second. Very briefly, though, considering what he'd been doing instead of visiting with Josiah and playing cards. "Next time."

"Hello." Tamara's call interrupted them. "I have two small people with me who have a ton of energy to burn after sitting in a truck for too long. Anyone in here want them?"

Caleb didn't have to pretend anything as he stepped from the pen to greet his daughters.

An instant later they were both in his arms, squeezing him tight as they planted kisses on his cheeks. "We fed the goats, Daddy. Tamara said she did our chores while we were gone. Did you eat all the candy canes? Hi, Josiah."

The whirlwind that was Sasha dropped to the ground and ran back to Tamara's side, but she reached behind her for another woman's hand.

She tugged Tamara's sister into view, pulling her forward. "Lisa brought us home. Lisa, this is Josiah. He's our godfather. Kelli says he's too pretty to spend his days talking to animals."

Josiah let out a guffaw, turning it quickly into a cough as Caleb gave his daughter a stern look.

Only Lisa was grinning as she held out a hand. "I don't know. Maybe bright blue eyes and killer smiles make the horses happy. Hello, Mr. Coffee Shop."

"Hello, Woman With Opinions About Breeding Etiquette. Nice to officially meet you."

Caleb glanced at Tamara who was trying to keep a straight face and not succeeding. "Do you know why my best friend has lost his mind?"

She blinked innocently. "Josiah? Oh, he's fine. He got a raw dose of my sister a while back, and she's a touch sharp on the unprepared palate."

"Some people like their food with a bite," Lisa quipped.

"I like sharp things," Josiah said at the same time, and the two of them laughed as if they'd just done something hysterically funny.

Caleb looked to Tamara for further explanation, but she just shrugged.

Emma slipped her fingers in his hand and tugged to get his attention.

"Yes, button?" he asked, leaning closer.

"I missed you."

His heartbeat was back. "Missed you too."

She curled an arm around his hips and held on. She was too big to suck her thumb, but he could tell she was needing a little extra cuddle time. He scooped her up, nodding to Josiah who was chatting with Lisa. "I'm calling it a day. You mind?"

"No problem," Josiah assured him. "Dentistry can wait until tomorrow."

"You want a hand?" Lisa offered.

Josiah blinked. "You want to help me float the uneven teeth in Caleb's horses?"

She shrugged. "Why not? I just spent three hours driving, and I'm sticking around for a while. This will let me stretch my legs."

"Up to you, I guess. And Caleb. What'd you think?"

Emma had laid her head against Caleb's shoulder and was humming softly, and he was more focused on her and making sure that he didn't do something incredibly stupid like walk over to Tamara and haul her into his arms for a kiss.

Two days of unlimited physical contact was going to be a hard habit to break.

He met Lisa's gaze. "Your choice. If it'll help you relax, go for it."

Tamara added over his shoulder. "Why don't you both join us for supper when you're done?"

"Works for me," Lisa said brightly.

So it was him and Tamara with the girls, walking back to the house. Sasha chattered nonstop, and Emma tossed in the occasional near-silent comment.

Tamara walked at his side, not saying anything. She opened the door to the house and quickly went about getting dinner together. The girls pulled him off to the side, and while he loved hearing about their trip, it seemed strange to not have Tamara joining in.

When she put Josiah in the chair next to him at dinner, positioning herself on the other side of Sasha again, it seemed a little as if she were punishing him. Creating a physical barrier to match the emotional one still between them.

Boss and nanny instead of lovers.

It might be necessary, but he didn't like it one bit. And that in itself was the beginning of an answer, he supposed.

23

The new year arrived, and school started again, this time with the whole rash of activities to get the girls and herself out of the house.

Tamara was bundling them up one Saturday afternoon when Caleb showed up on the porch, pulling to a stop in surprise as he met three fully snow-suited individuals.

"I guess my idea of coming in to play a game isn't going to work," he said.

"We're going tobogganing," Emma announced unexpectedly, racing back into the mudroom to grab a toque and pull it firmly on her head.

"Come with us, Daddy," Sasha begged.

Emma nodded and two little faces stared up at him pleadingly.

Tamara was a goner as well. Only she managed to offer a friendly smile instead of one that said too clearly how she felt. "We found the perfect spot last week, and now that the creek is frozen, we don't have to worry about doing another splashdown."

His gaze drifted over her face as he nodded. "I was going to take the rest of the afternoon off. I'd love to join you, then maybe I can take my favourite girls out for supper."

Emma and Sasha bounced with excitement as they wholeheartedly agreed. Warmth like the heat from a summer day enveloped Tamara from the toes up. He'd kept eye contact as he said *his favourite girls*, and now his gaze dropped to her lips, pupils dilating as she licked them, not because she was trying to drive him crazy but because being around the man made every bit of her react.

But this moment wasn't sexual, it was *more*. As he switched to a different jacket and grabbed a thick pair of mitts, Tamara prepared for an afternoon of heartaching bliss.

They climbed into his truck to have room for four, but Caleb insisted she take the wheel. "You know where we're headed."

A collection of vehicles had gathered to the side of their destination, and Caleb reached into the back of the truck and pulled out the sleds he'd transferred from her vehicle to his. One was old-fashioned, long with a gentle curl at the front. The other, a sit-upon with a steering wheel, like a mini ATV without an engine.

Which was when Tamara realized she hadn't thought this out, because as they marched up the hill, children running around them, the toboggan arrangement had been perfect for three people. Not so much for four.

Sasha jumped up and down as she pointed to where she wanted her sled positioned. "Push me, Daddy," she ordered after settling into the seat.

"You need a push? It's a pretty steep hill," he warned.

Sasha rolled her eyes. "I like to go fast."

Caleb glanced at Tamara, his lips twitching. "That's kind of what I'm afraid of."

Tamara snickered, lining up the other sled and sitting down so Emma could crawl in front of her. With a squeal, Sasha was off, Caleb sending her on the way with a gentle push before standing to watch her steer her way down the slope.

Then he turned toward them. "You two ready for a push?"

Emma shook her head, then sweetly made a request. "Ride with us."

Tamara's heart was in her throat. Since Christmas Emma had taken to speaking out loud around her far more often, and every time it happened she felt as if she was privileged to be trusted.

Only as Caleb moved to fulfill his daughter's request, Tamara was about to be enveloped in his arms.

"Scoot," Caleb said, patting her familiarly on the butt.

Tamara glanced around, but none of the families racing up and down the hill were watching them with anything more than a moment's interest. She shuffled forward, tucking her feet into the front of the sled and curling around Emma so Caleb had room behind them. He settled, his legs tucked under her knees.

There might have been a million layers of fabric between them, but Tamara didn't care. Caleb got their forward momentum going, then reached around her waist and grabbed hold, locking their bodies together to guide the sled.

They made it safely past where Sasha stood, arms raised high in a victory salute. For a split second after they came to a stop Tamara leaned back against Caleb, pressing as close as she dared. His chin was tucked over her shoulder, the scruff on his cheek brushing hers as his warm breath created a cloud in the cold wintry air.

A small moment of intimate pleasure in the midst of an innocent childish activity.

Emma was up like a jack-in-the-box, giggles escaping as she attempted to help Tamara to her feet. The little girl tugged her forward, but it was Caleb's hand on her butt that sent her vertical, his palm lingering for the briefest of seconds. With a smile in his eyes, he grabbed the sled rope, striding over to Sasha to help pull hers up the hill as well.

There were other families playing, childish laughter and squeals of delight ringing out, and the longer it went on, the more Tamara knew this was what she wanted with all her heart.

Now if one irritatingly stubborn man would get his act together and *say* something, they could move toward making this a full-time reality.

The perfect afternoon of tobogganing was followed by a quick dinner out at a local diner—quick because both the girls were falling asleep at the table.

She and Caleb continued to work with each other, sharing evenings. His brothers began to drop in a lot more often, though, and she wondered if Caleb had actively encouraged them to show up as chaperones. Most nights she was the one to say good night before the living room was empty.

She tried to tell herself going slow was a positive thing, but she missed him in her bed.

Funny—they'd only had two days to themselves, but she wanted the man desperately. She could only imagine what it was doing to him to know she was just down the hall and yet out of reach.

But while she waited, she worked.

The whole puzzle of how to help Silver Stone became her new quiet obsession. She talked to everyone she could, being careful not to reveal why she was asking.

Ashton gave her a slow nod when she mentioned the feed orders seemed steeper than in the past. "Floods a few years back were rough, but we'll get back on track. A man's got to work with the land, not against her. She'll take care of us. She always does."

She called Josiah out to do a checkup on Stormy, which was kind of overkill considering how well all the horses were treated at Silver Stone, but gave her a chance to ask him about trends in ranching and what he'd observed recently.

Thankfully, Caleb's best friend had stopped flirting with her. He was a lot more talkative than Caleb, and before Stormy was checked head to toe, Tamara knew enough to start her own ranch in the area. She also knew enough about the current state of the economy to know she'd be crazy to think about it.

"Things are tight everywhere," he finished bluntly, patting Stormy on the withers before rejoining Tamara outside of the stall. "All it'll take, though, is one good break and it'll all turn around."

What he didn't say was one bad break could just as easily be the end, which was what Tamara desperately didn't want to happen. Silver Stone was Caleb's home. It was home for Emma and Sasha, and all the others who'd become incredibly important to her.

Karen gave her the first real push toward a seed of an idea. They were texting one morning, Tamara bundled up in her warmest coat, with a toque on her head and a quilt wrapped around her, hiding her phone under the massive pile to keep her fingers from freezing between messages.

Karen: *guess what's arriving today*

Tamara: *a herd of elephants?*

Karen: *smaller, and far more woolly*

It couldn't be something as simple as sheep because they already had a number of flocks on the Coleman land.

Tamara: *long-haired rabbits?*

Karen: *you get cookies for being close. Alpacas*

Tamara: *get out!*

Karen: *seriously*

Tamara: *please videotape yourself the first time you ride one, and post it on YouTube*

Karen: *ha! Don't tempt me. No, this is Hope's fault. She*

convinced the family Alpaca yarn can be a good moneymaker, so we're going to try

It made sense. The Colemans had enough land and enough workers to add to the operation.

Tamara: *maybe I need to get you to send some to Silver Stone*

Karen: *hell, no. It was bad enough we brought goats to the property. The horses are too valuable to mess up bringing in other animals. The only diversification Silver Stone should try is mineral rights*

Did Karen know something she didn't?

Tamara: *Diamonds? Rubies?*

Karen: *black gold*

Sudden disappointment hit.

Tamara: *I think they'd know if they had oil on their land*

Karen: *they've never tested. I asked Ashton when I was there, and he said they'd never had the time or inclination to worry about it after Caleb's parents passed on*

The conversation drifted to other things after that, but Tamara was intrigued by the idea.

She did a little Google research later that day, digging into what testing involved, but she found a lot of dead ends and not very clear information.

In the end, she decided before she said anything to Caleb, she should have possible solutions for him. She sent an email to Karen asking if she had any contacts in the industry. Then the kitchen door slammed, and the sound of Sasha complaining loudly and Emma crying dragged her from her chair to find out what the girls were fighting about.

Thankfully it was something solved easily with a couple quiet apologies followed by milk and cookies. Tamara's quest to help improve Silver Stone's future was tucked aside in the daily routine of dealing with the girls and not accidentally blurting out to Caleb that she loved him.

THERE WERE few things that Caleb detested. Cruelty, laziness—he hated to think of it as a diss list of his ex-wife's personality traits, but the one thing he'd never had to personally deal with before in his life was jealousy.

He worked hard, and he was good at what he did, so when they were out roping and one of his brothers managed to pull faster or drive harder, he could pretty much say he felt a sense of pride in that as well. It wasn't him accomplishing the task, but it was family, and that was just as good.

So this strange beast in his belly that wanted to rip and tear and shred was mighty uncomfortable.

Caleb glanced at the delivery truck still parked outside the house, and finally couldn't take it anymore. He abandoned his chores and strode across the yard, slowing to step softer on the deck so he didn't appear to be a madman rushing into the house.

As he'd approached he'd caught a clear glimpse in the window of Tamara laughing, the blond-haired young man who'd brought out the filing cabinet she'd ordered leaning on his dolly as he flashed her a smile, admiration in his eyes.

Caleb's feet marched him forward. He was through the door an instant later. The two of them glanced toward him, Tamara with a welcoming smile, the young man grabbing hold of his equipment and subtly backing away from Tamara.

Yeah, Caleb's expression might hold a little more heat than was polite, but damn it all—

"Need some help?" His tone was almost civilized.

Okay, maybe not.

"We're done." The kid hauled himself toward the door, but more importantly away from Tamara who was now regarding Caleb with one brow raised.

He opened the door before the kid could even put his shoes

on, and now Tamara had her arms folded and she gave him the evil eye.

She turned to send the boy off with a kind word. "Thanks for your help. I'll make sure I stop by the store once I've talked to the girls about the bookshelf."

The young man didn't do more than offer a quick smile before taking off, swerving away from Caleb as if to stay out of reach.

Caleb pushed the door shut with a solid click before turning back to Tamara.

Her lips twitched.

"What?"

She took a deep breath and let it out, her amusement showing through. "He's just a kid. And he was being helpful. Did you need to mark your territory that hard?"

He crowded toward her. "Nobody knows you're mine, so excuse me if I find it a little frustrating."

"You don't think I'm entertaining kids barely out of high school right here in the house, do you? Because if you do you think that, we have a problem."

"I'm not worried about you, but I know what it's like to be that age and in the presence of a woman sexy enough to give me dirty dreams."

Her eyes brightened. "Oh. I'm the type of woman who inspires dirty dreams? I like this."

Caleb's control wavered. "You know damn well you inspire more than dirty dreams. I'm so fucking hard all the time around you it's amazing I can walk. I know I said no fooling around, but it's fucking killing me."

Tamara looked around the room before deliberately glancing at her watch then back at him.

"The girls aren't home for another couple hours." She stepped closer, drifting her hands up the front of his body to pop open the first button on his coat. "I won't tell anyone."

God, he shouldn't do this, but there was no way he could stop. He crowded against her, ignoring the faint voice of reason that suggested he at least take her to her room before stripping her naked.

Screw reason. He wanted her here. Now. Branding her and marking her thoroughly so that every time she looked around this room she'd remember *them*.

He grabbed the bottom of her T-shirt and ripped it over her head, reaching behind for her bra hooks. His fingers fumbled for a second before he had it loose. She helped, shrugging the straps off her shoulders, soft fabric falling to the ground.

Her lush womanly curves were bared before him, a spark of mischief in her eyes. Caleb picked her up around the thighs, a squeal of surprise bursting from her as she caught his shoulders for balance, peering at him through cheerful yellow-framed glasses.

The extra height put her breasts level with his face, and he licked one nipple before taking the other into his mouth, sucking in pulses as he stumbled blindly the rest of the way to the living room.

Her fingernails dug in as a hearty moan escaped her lips. She slid her fingers higher, threading them into his hair so she could pull him tighter to her breasts.

He wanted to drop her on the sofa, strip her down and drive into her. He wanted to take his time, and tease every inch of her skin. Somehow he couldn't do either of those, because she was gripping him tight, pulling and tugging where she wanted him, and suddenly he knew the one thing he needed.

Control. Over her, since it appeared he didn't have a damn bit over himself anymore.

He settled her hips on the back of the couch then caught her wrists in his fingers, jerking them away from himself then slowly pressing her arms behind her back. The move thrust her chest forward, and pleasure grew inside him as she squirmed in his grip.

"Sit still," he ordered, adjusting her until he could clasp both wrists in one hand, leaving his other hand free to cup one full breast in his palm. He squeezed, then again, massaging the heavy weight as he stroked his thumb over her nipple. The nip tightened up, pressing against him.

Her moan of approval grew louder, and her head fell back as she pressed into him harder.

Still trying to take control.

Caleb tugged her wrists again. He placed his other hand against her lower back and arched her so she was precariously balanced. Fully exposed as he leaned closer and stared into her flushed face. "*Sit still* means I'm in charge. Don't move."

Her eyes widened for a second, and a flash of heat reflected back—not anger, lust.

That was all it took for him to keep going. Lowering his head to work one nipple then the other, sucking and biting until her breasts were rosy red from the brush of scruff on his cheek and the pressure of his lips.

"Oh God, Caleb. *More*," she begged.

Just because he agreed didn't mean she'd get what she asked for. Not right away.

He leaned her back farther until her shoulders rested on the seat, her hips still raised on the padded armrest. He placed a hand on her belly to keep her trapped with her hands underneath her. "Stay like that, and I might let you come."

He got a deliriously delicious growl back in response.

He ripped her jeans open then stripped her. Hands under her ass, he adjusted until her butt hung slightly off the edge of the armrest. One foot rested beside her hips, the other leg he placed over the back of the couch, spreading her wide. She was exposed to his gaze now, moisture clinging to her curls.

Slowly, ever so slowly, he slipped a finger through her curls to open her. "I get hard, but you get damn wet, don't you, darlin'?"

"Yes." She sucked in a gasp as he dropped to the floor and placed his mouth over her and drove his tongue deep. "Oh *yes*."

The taste of her did nothing to cool the flames, but the noises she made were enough to allow him to slow slightly. He needed to hear her trembling on the edge, as desperate for him as he was for her. Teasing now, flicking his tongue against her clit, circling again and again until she squirmed, hips thrusting against the firm grip he used to pin her in place. When he sucked her clit into his mouth, strumming rapidly with his tongue, her ass cheeks tightened, hovering on the edge of an orgasm.

He slowed, enjoying the sound of her cursing as he rose a little higher to gaze into her flushed face.

"Open your mouth," he ordered. Eyes glassy with a haze of passion, she obeyed. He slid his fingers past her lips and over her tongue, pumping them in and out as if he were fucking her mouth.

Another moan escaped her, her chest rising and falling rapidly. The pulse at the base of her throat throbbed, matching everything in him.

He pulled his fingers back and took control of her nipple, leaving it wet after pinching lightly.

Another time past her lips, their eyes locked as he painted her other nipple with more moisture, the peaks standing upright, eager for his touch.

The third time he trailed his hand down her body until he finished between her legs, her wet heat beckoning him in. Just the tips, around, then dip. Around, and a little farther. Around, and to the first knuckle.

Tamara arched against him, trying to move, but he kept her

pinned in place, teasing over and over until his fingers were buried in her, the soft pads brushing the inside of her sex.

He hit the right spot and her eyes widened. "Oh my..."

It was too good to stop. Caleb bent over and added his tongue to the party and Tamara bucked as if she was going for an eight-second, full-score ride. Deliciously dirty noises escaped right before her sex tightened around him like a trap, her orgasm grabbing hold and tearing her over the edge violently.

Caleb had his pants to the floor and his cock covered seconds later, dropping to the couch and dragging her into his lap.

Tamara grabbed his shoulders and as he guided her hips over him she reached down and helped aim.

He loved teamwork.

He loved it even more when she straightened and there was no reason for him to go slow. He jerked her down, deep and fast, setting off another set of rollers, her sex wet and tight around him.

That's when he locked her in place and enjoyed the ride, her body squeezing the hell out of his cock as she writhed and moaned and came hard. Her torso shook wildly, and every time she stilled the slightest bit he pressed deeper, retriggering her pleasure.

"Caleb. Oh my God, stop, *stop*..."

He paused, as difficult as it was, but she was clutching his hands, riding him now. Driving him into her core even harder.

"Tamara? Yes or no?" he demanded.

"*Yessssssssss*..."

Thank God. He fisted her hips tight, thrusting up like a piston. The pressure of her body around him sent him whirling as she took everything, and gave back just as much. Pleasure and aching need and desire for even more. Her body was his, her hands on his shoulders clutching as if she didn't want to let go.

Ever.

He broke, the soft touch of Tamara caressing her fingers over his face a sweet tender contrast to the extreme rush of pleasure sliding along his spine and exploding from him.

He was still shaking, and she was kissing him. Stroking her fingers through his hair, touching her lips to his, to his temples. Caressing him as if she couldn't get enough.

Touching him as if she loved him.

And in that moment, Caleb dared to dream. Maybe he was ready for a new forever to begin.

24

The cold snap was over. A Chinook had blown in and wrapped Heart Falls with the illusion of springtime. Melting puddles were everywhere, dry grass poking up through holes in the snow, and the musty scent of changing seasons shoving memories at Caleb like a toppling haystack.

His parents had passed away in February, nearly eleven years ago now, and yet as he walked to where they were buried, he felt a little as if it were yesterday.

Didn't matter all that had happened in the ensuing years—his marriage, his children, his brothers and sisters growing from youth to adulthood—it was as if none of that existed, and he was still that headstrong yet innocent man who'd been tossed into responsibility so far over his head there'd been moments he'd found it hard to breathe.

Caleb slid off Lacey's back, stepping to the plain headstones on the hillside, He knelt to clear away the dried remains of the flowers one of his siblings had left the last time they'd been there.

His family teased that he was a man of few words, but in this place it seemed he could speak and speak and never come to the end of it. Hell, sometimes he'd come out to the graveside and shout, torn and ripped up inside when he felt he'd failed in everything that he had to do.

Maybe it was easier because they never spoke back, and yet he knew as surely as if they were alive, his parents were still guiding him.

"I love her," he admitted. "I think you'd have liked her. Tamara's smart, and she's funny, and the way she sees what needs to be done with Sasha and Emma makes me love her even more."

He laughed, staring over the fields and mountain ranges. Big Sky Lake sparkled in the center where the water was still free-flowing, the wind stirring up the surface and sending darts of light toward him as if there were fireworks shooting into the sky.

"Pretty stupid, though, that I'm up here telling you instead of marching back into the house and telling her. Maybe I just needed a little practice," he explained. "I remember you used to tell each other *I love you* all the time. Luke, Walker and me, we used to make all those rude noises when we caught you, but secretly, we thought it was pretty damn cool. I liked seeing it too. You didn't just say the words, you showed it—"

And as if his parents had given him a pointed look, Caleb felt chastised as hard as if they'd spoken.

"Ah hell. You're right. I hate to tell you both, but your oldest son is a bit of an idiot at times." He got to his feet, slapping his gloves against his leg. "But he's still learning. Hopefully that will be enough."

It was time to stop procrastinating. He might be a fool, but he'd been watching closely over the last while, and his girls had to be at least halfway in love with Tamara by now. They'd have time to finish falling in love—

At the end of the road leading around the back of Little Sky Lake, a truck was parked, and a man was walking the hills. It wasn't an area any of the Silver Stone crew needed to be, and Caleb was distracted enough to need to go and find out more.

It took a while to get down from the hillside. He returned Lacey to the barn then drove the back roads until he finally ended up pulling his truck in beside the stranger.

The man was coming down to meet him, heavy canvas bag looped over his shoulder, a set of binoculars in his hand.

"Can I help you with something?" Caleb asked.

The man held forward a hand. "Finn Marlette. You one of the hands here at Silver Stone?"

"Owner. Caleb Stone."

The other man lit up. "Nice to meet you. I didn't expect to see you until later."

Caleb thought for a moment. Unless Ashton had forgotten to tell him something, there was some kind of mix-up. "Sorry, why are you here?"

"I'm doing some preliminary map work. We wouldn't be able to get in and do any testing until the spring, but I was in the area, and I thought I may as well take a look."

Nope. Caleb still didn't have a clue. "What kind of testing?"

Finn's tanned face crinkled in amusement. "Funny how often this happens. The owner's always the last to know. Viability for oil production. It's likely you'll be pleasantly surprised. I know your closest neighbours don't have wells, but you've got an intriguing—"

"You want to put an oil well on our land?"

Finn shook his head. "*You* want to lease out your rights so my company can put an oil well on your land, if there's anything to produce. I'm the man who figures out if the investment is viable."

While the idea of striking oil somewhere on the Silver Stone land had potential merit—he wasn't ignorant, he knew what kind of money that might involve—Caleb needed the conversation to rewind a whole hell of a lot. "I didn't hire you."

"No one hired me, at least not yet. I promised I'd do the preliminary checks as a favour to an old friend."

The only person that Caleb knew even remotely tangled up with oil was Penny Talisman's dad, but the idea of her coming up with something like this seemed way out of character. "Give me a name."

"Karen Coleman."

The warmth of the Chinook vanished in an instant, and an icy cold blast cut through him. Karen, which meant Tamara. Which meant the woman had arranged for someone to come onto their land without informing him.

He didn't trust himself to say anything to Finn at that moment, simply tipping his chin then offering a curt farewell. "Don't set up anything else until I tell you."

Caleb stewed the entire drive back to the ranch house, frustration and anger rising far hotter than he expected. When Tamara wasn't in the house for him to ask what the hell was going on, it made him that much angrier.

"Anyone seen Tamara?" he demanded after marching into the barn.

Kelli and Walker looked up from where they were repairing a show saddle. "She went for a ride," Kelli said.

"Which way she'd go?" Caleb was already moving to saddle his horse.

"Not sure, but most of the time she heads toward the falls." Walker this time.

"How the hell do you know that?" Caleb demanded, his volume rising above anything he would normally use. "Why the hell does everybody else know what's going on, and I'm the last to learn?"

He ignored the expressions of shock on their faces and finished saddling his horse. He mounted and headed toward the falls while his temper to continue to boil.

He spotted her horse before anything else. Stormy wandered lazily as he pawed at the thinnest patches in the snow to get at the grass underneath.

Tamara reclined on the rocks where they'd first met, the black surface soaking up the sun's heat and keeping the surface snow free. Caleb abandoned his horse and marched toward her.

He must've made a noise because she sat up from where she'd been relaxing, offering him a smile that faded the closer he got. "What's wrong?"

"We raise horses, dammit. We run a damn community-supported agriculture program, and we're stewards of the environment. I'm not against progress, but I expect to be asked before I let anyone climb all over Silver Stone who might simply rip her up and tear her apart."

Her expression went from concern to confusion. "Caleb. I have no idea what you're talking about."

"That man wandering my land. Eyeing it to figure out where he can poke holes into the ground and suck it dry. You don't think I can make enough money to care for my family? You don't think I can make enough money to care for *you*?"

He turned away from her, dragging a hand through his hair, whirling back before she could get any words out. "Okay, maybe it's a good idea to see if there's oil on the land, but you didn't *ask*. That's not how we do things around here, and if you and I are going to be together, then you have got to not go around me."

Her jaw was no longer hanging open. She'd closed her mouth and was eyeing him, head tilted to the side. Absolutely silent as she listened intently.

Which was good, because he was just building up a full head of steam. "This relationship is *not* going to be like the one I had with Wendy where we ignored each other then went and did whatever the hell we wanted. You and me, we're going to *talk* about things, and together we'll make the decisions. Together we'll decide what's right for our girls, and how to raise our future kids, the ones you and I will have. We're going to argue, and fight, and talk it out until we make the best damn decision, and we're going to do it all *together*. Do you hear me?"

She'd have to be deaf to not hear him, he was all but roaring by this point.

Tamara was still silent, but the corners of her mouth had curled up. The longer he shouted at her, the wider her grin became, and now he didn't know if he wanted to kiss her or pick her up and shake her.

"What the hell is so goddamn funny?"

She stepped forward, placed a hand on top of his clenched fist then eased up on her tiptoes.

And kissed him.

TAMARA WASN'T certain how he was going to react, but there was no way she could continue without being in his arms.

Caleb seemed to agree because he reached down and caught her, clutching her as they kissed, and kissed, and kissed. Soft and sweet moving to passionate and needy before slowing again until he put her feet back on the ground and they eased apart, foreheads pressed together as he stared into her eyes.

The specifics of what they were fighting about didn't matter, she was just so damn happy he was *fighting* because it meant he'd changed.

When Wendy left, he'd shut down. Or, maybe it had even been before then he'd learned to walk away from any situation that was going to hurt or be an emotional challenge to him directly.

Now all his passion and fire had burst free, and she could

work with that. He wasn't holding back anymore, so they could finally, *finally* move on.

"You want to tell me again, from the start what's got you all riled up? Please?" she asked as sweetly as she could.

He held her, bodies close. Speaking softer as if embarrassed by his earlier explosion. "There's a man on my land who says Karen Coleman sent him to do an assessment for oil."

A flash of anger rolled through Tamara. "Well, that's annoying. Considering I didn't ask her to. I asked her if she *knew* someone, I didn't give her permission to start the ball rolling." She cupped a hand against Caleb's cheek, stroking her fingers over his ear. "I wanted to come to you with an idea, not an ultimatum."

He looked horrified. "I shouted at you for no reason?"

She kissed him quickly, pulling back with a sincere smile. "Oh, I am so glad you shouted."

He paused then shook his head. "Nope. Now I'm back to having no idea what the hell is going on."

He might not yet, but he would soon. And Tamara was beyond the point of no return. She was tired of waiting, and now that he'd crawled out from the shell he'd retreated into, she pretty much figured they could make up the rest of it as they went along. She wanted him.

No, she wanted it all. Him, the girls, more kids. "You know how I like to interfere?"

"You gave that up."

"Yeah, bullshit on that." She pulled a face. "The good thing is, since I'm so meddlesome and all, it means I can do this." Tamara curled her hands around his neck, holding him trapped.

"You plan on throttling me?"

"Maybe. Not today, but maybe tomorrow. Or the day after that. Because, you know what you need, Caleb Stone? You need me. You need me in your life, causing you grief and making you crazy, and since I'm such a kind and giving person, I'm totally going to sacrifice myself and say yes."

His lips twisted. "I don't recall asking you any questions recently."

"Other than how my hearing is?"

He actually flushed.

"Never mind that. Yes, I heard you, and now I'm on a different topic. Keep up," she teased.

He cupped her chin in his hand. "I'll try."

"We're both forward-thinking individuals. In fact, you're going to get to brag a little in the future, Caleb Stone, because you know what?"

It was the craziest thing, but it was right. She dropped to one knee in front of him, holding his hand in hers.

He raised a brow, gentle smirk twisting his lips as his anger dissipated and his curiosity rose. "Forward thinking is good and fine, but you got any idea what the first thought that hits a man's mind is when a woman drops to her knees?"

She mock punched him in the gut before wrapping her fingers around his belt buckle. "Later. I'm being romantic. Hush."

"Ahh. I'll take notes."

God, she loved his dry sense of humour. And his bossy demanding ways. She loved everything about him, and it was time he knew it.

"Caleb, you're the second-stubbornest ass I've ever met." She made a face. "I see the most stubborn every time I look in the mirror."

"Not going to argue."

She'd get everything she wanted in the end, even if the route there was a little twisted. "I love you. I know you love me too, even though you're not ready to say it. I'm willing to wait until you realize you do, but in the meantime, you're right. We're going to be together, you and me. We're going to be a family, because I love those little girls of yours with everything in me. Which is really convenient because I'm hellishly in love with their daddy as well."

He was smiling now, face full of sunshine. All his frustration and anger gone. "Very convenient."

She let all the emotion inside her shine out best she could. "You going to marry me, Caleb Stone?"

He sighed, long and heartfelt. Utter happiness in the tone. "Yeah."

Tamara laughed. "I love you. Direct and to the point."

"You want it done up fancier? *Hell*, yeah." He hauled her to her feet and kissed the tip of her nose. "Better?"

"Perfect."

He tucked his fingers underneath her chin and lifted her face so he could brush their lips together. A brief, gentle caress. Slowly growing in passion until she realized he was fiddling with the button of her jeans.

She caught his wrists in her hands. "Really?"

"I just got engaged. I think a celebration is in order."

His logic was hard to debate, but there was another matter. "You carrying a condom?"

That pulled him up short for a moment, but then, to her utter shock, his face twisted into what could only be called a cheeky grin. "You know my little lecture earlier about talking everything out?"

Lecture. Okay, she'd go with that, but she snickered. "Yeah?"

"New topic for discussion." He took a deep breath. "I kind of mentioned kids—and I don't even know if you want any, other than the girls."

Holy cow, the man went from not talking to hitting up huge issues in a few words. "You asking if I want to have your babies? Because the answer is yes."

He closed the distance between them again, hand settling on

her hips. "You mind maybe getting started on them sooner than later?"

Not at all how she expected her afternoon off to go. "Why not? I have a couple hours to kill."

Caleb laughed, picking her up and bringing their lips together again. Tamara wrapped her legs around his hips and held on tight as he lowered them to the rock face.

The winter sun was barely strong enough to heat the skin he exposed, but the black rocks held lingering warmth. The Chinook wind caressed them with soft, heated fingers, and the sharp scent of grass and snow filled her senses as Caleb pulled off one of her boots and helped her out of a single leg of her jeans. He tugged himself free and brought her over him, quick, but perfect.

He touched her intimately, teasing and stroking as he kissed her, keeping her in the sunshine and protecting her from the hard surface under their knees until she was squirming with need.

Then he lowered her slowly, joining them. Raw and needy and nothing fancy, just them and the land. Silver Stone watching like a sentinel as they made love, the roar of the falls in her ears.

Or was that the pounding of her heart?

She rocked over him as he kissed her, tongue teasing, teeth nipping at her bottom lip. Kisses pressed over her face as he cupped her head and held on tight.

Held on as if he was never letting go.

The wind blowing past caressed them, warmth like the touch of a gentle lover, and as she came, Tamara looked into the eyes of the man she loved.

It didn't matter that he hadn't said it yet, not in words. He'd said it over and over again with his body, by his actions. And when he breathed out her name, Tamara kissed him fiercely.

The distant roar of the falls a blessing on their new beginning.

25

Caleb guided her back to the horses, slightly shocked at how well everything had gone.

She'd proposed? Hell if he'd let her take it back, though. She was his, and there was nowhere to go from here but forward.

He lifted her to Stormy's back then mounted his own horse, riding side by side along the path back to the house. She didn't seem to want to talk and he didn't mind a moment of silence.

He was thinking plenty about what he needed to say in a few minutes.

He sent off a quick text to Luke, asking him to be there when the girls got off the bus. The world had pivoted in one moment, and the changes weren't done yet.

Caleb plotted and planned and debated as they took care of their horses, quietly working. Glancing at each other often, exchanging meaningful looks. Tamara wore a smile as wide as his.

Caleb would've said Tamara was the best thing that ever happened to him, except that'd be a lie. He had two little girls he loved beyond reason, and a family that was a part of him right down to the tips of his boots.

She wasn't better than that, but she was what made everything else complete. She was the love that wrapped his world into a firm, steady bundle, the binder twine securing the broken pieces of his heart.

Seems as if he could think it, he should be able to say it.

He waited for her to finish washing up then grabbed hold, walking hand-in-hand back to the house.

"You ready for this?" she asked as they stepped on the porch.

He opened the door for her, looking her over from top to bottom as he let every bit of his love show best he could. "Are you?"

Emma and Sasha were seated at the island. Luke stood by the counter, hand in the cookie jar, guilt twisting his smile as Caleb eyed the handful he already held.

"Didn't know when you'd be back," he explained, "and everybody's hungry."

Everybody?

Tamara leaned around him to peek into the living room. Sure enough, his other two brothers were there as well, Walker relaxing in the easy chair, Dustin with his feet up on the coffee table.

Caleb hesitated for a moment before figuring what the hell. It looked as if he was going to have an audience, but he'd put this off for long enough.

Tamara wouldn't mind.

"Everyone in the living room," he ordered.

His family moved, questions on all their faces. Dustin's gaze stuck on where Caleb had caught hold of Tamara's fingers and refused to let go.

Emma and Sasha perched on the edge of the coffee table, staring at them in confusion.

He shook a finger at the audience and told them sternly, "Sit for a minute and just listen."

Then he turned to Tamara and took both her hands in his. He looked her in the eye and ignored the fact they had five additional gawking witnesses.

"I know you said you didn't expect me to say it yet, but I've been working my way up to this for a while, so I don't see why I should hold off any longer. I don't have anything to give you except my heart. It's been a little bashed up and bruised, but I think it still works all right. I'm ready to trust you with it."

Tamara tilted her head, eyes brightening with moisture.

He hurried to carry on before she could speak.

"I fell in love with you that very first moment, when you stepped in front of me, so bold and so brave, and so right. And then you came out here and stepped into our family"—he waved a hand toward the living room, all the while keeping his gaze fixed on hers—"and you just kept being you. Thoughtful and caring and everything we needed, but this isn't about them. It's about *us*. I've fallen in love with you, Tamara Coleman, and while I hope everybody else feels like I do about you joining our family, I don't want to wait anymore to tell you something important. I love you."

Her eyes sparkled, her grip on his fingers tightening. Was it possible he'd actually rendered her speechless?

"Daddy?" Sasha spoke quietly.

He tore his gaze off the woman he loved to answer his daughter. "Yes, pumpkin?"

"Are you and Tamara getting married?"

Tamara answered before he could. "I asked him if it would be okay, because I'd like to be his wife. And I'd like to be your and Emma's mommy, so it would kind of all work well if we got married."

Emma spoke. Quiet but clear above the other low voices in the room. "You...you want to be our mommy?"

Caleb's throat was closing up. Tamara gave his hand a

squeeze before letting go and lowering herself to kneel at eye level with his little girls. "With everything in me. I would love to be your mommy."

Emma threw herself at Tamara, Sasha following a second later, and Caleb caught them before they hit the ground. The four of them in a heap like a pile of puppies.

Like a family.

A sound broke through the laughing and crying. It was clapping, rising from Luke and Walker who both wore unabashed grins. Dustin wiped at his eyes and tried not to look like it before he joined in as well.

Caleb wrapped his arms around his precious family and held on tight. He wasn't ever letting go.

IT HAD TAKEN a while to settle everyone down, but after the handshakes and hugs and the kisses and questions were over, they'd finally got everybody to the table and figured out something to eat.

Tamara kept catching herself on the verge of tears, happy ones, and took a moment to slip away to send an email to her sisters.

Have decided to stay permanently in Heart Falls. Asked Caleb to marry me; he said yes. Seems I've got a new home and two little girls without having to go through labour. Karen, remind me to kiss you when I see you next. Lisa, when are you coming to visit?

They both responded almost instantly.

So happy for you, although I'm not sure what I did. Call me when you can talk— Karen.

I'm working on it, the visit part. And you asked him to get married? Just double-checking, because I've got fifty bucks riding on it. Love you, love to the girls, and to the big grumpy cowboy, although I bet he's not so grumpy anymore. <3 <3 Lisa

Laughter bubbled up. Of course Lisa had money bet somewhere, but Tamara didn't need to know the details.

What she needed was to enjoy the cuddles she was getting from both Sasha and Emma, arranged on the couch so they could curl up beside her. That left Caleb sitting kitty corner to them, but the contented smile on his face made it clear he was happy to watch from a bit of a distance.

Sasha of course decided to try to prolong bedtime by saving her questions for then. Lying in bed she reeled them off rapid-fire. "Do Emma and I get to be flower girls? Are you going to get married here at Silver Stone? Are you going—?"

"We haven't figured it all out, yet," Tamara warned her. "But you will definitely be in the wedding. You're part of the family, aren't you?"

Sasha seemed happy enough with that answer. She lay back on her pillow and examined Tamara with that Caleb-like gaze. "You're going to stay."

Not a question. Not a demand. Satisfied and content, as if she'd decided the trial period was over, and Tamara had passed.

Tamara was very glad.

Sasha blew a kiss at Caleb who stood in the doorway then rolled over. All her protests and complaints gone—at least for now.

Emma had a little more to say about the subject. She insisted both Caleb and Tamara accompany her to her bedside to tuck her in. All her boldness in speaking out loud had evaporated, but it was clear she had something on her mind.

"What is it, button? Caleb asked softly. "You want to tell me?"

She leaned in close and whispered in his ear, his eyes darkening as he glanced at Tamara who had settled herself in the chair next to the teeny bed. "Emma wants to know if she can call you Mama."

It was nearly impossible to swallow past the giant knot in her throat. "I would like that very much."

Emma didn't seem to be done. She patted Caleb's hand, then spoke louder. "That makes you my Papa."

Tamara bit her tongue. Maybe they'd read the Berenstain Bears too many times lately.

But Caleb just laughed. "That sounds fine with me."

He gave her a kiss then slid back on the bed so Tamara could come in and finish pulling up the sheets. Emma tucked her stuffed monkey under her arm and pressed a kiss to his forehead before lying back and offering her lips to Tamara.

Tamara kissed her, caught in place as little arms tangled around her neck and squeezed fiercely.

"I love you," Emma said clearly.

"I love you too," Tamara managed before her ability to speak vanished. She snuck from the bed and out of the room, letting Caleb finish the task before she completely lost control.

He met her in the hallway and pulled her into his arms, holding her close as he let her regain her equilibrium. Then he tugged her back to the living room, pulling her to the floor in front of the fireplace. Cradling her.

They were quiet for a long while, but they didn't need words. Tamara's brain was full, and her soul content.

Eventually they moved a bit farther apart, got drinks, and sat down to figure out what came next.

They spent a couple of hours talking, laughter and kisses

mixed in with all the words. Tamara figured she still put in three-quarters of the total conversation, but she didn't mind.

Caleb didn't need to talk his head off to get his point across.

And when they rose to get ready for bed, Caleb was by her side, following her through the door into the master bedroom.

She raised a brow.

He tried to look gruff, but it came out kind of sheepish. "I'm not waiting. We'll make it official, but until then, you're mine. That includes sleeping in the same bed, and I don't care who knows it."

"Good answer," Tamara teased, although she noticed he made sure to turn and lock the door.

He took her to bed, stripping them both before slipping off her glasses and putting them on the nightstand in spite of her protests.

He turned off all the lights, and they made love in the dark, hands caressing, lips touching, all their other senses primed. Tamara's heart overflowed with happiness, and she didn't need to see to know he was smiling as he brought them both to heaven.

She didn't need to see to know he was smiling as he kissed her then cradled her in his arms all night. She was smiling too. Ear to ear, to be truthful.

So thankful she'd found a way into her rancher's heart.

EPILOGUE

*W*alker leaned back in his chair and watched the sun set behind the mountains, gold and yellow reflecting off Big Sky Lake to form a mosaic of blue and shimmering lights.

So. Big brother Caleb had the guts to try again.

Considering *Walker* was supposed to be the brave one in the family, it was—humbling. Maybe he needed to be braver and try again as well. He had a golden opportunity waiting for him, and here he was, letting it drift away.

What he dreamed about was a home and happiness like Caleb and Tamara were building, but the only woman Walker had ever wanted was gone.

If he did come back to Silver Stone full time, he'd be no more help than any other worker. Maybe out there he could do something big. Make some serious money, and make a difference. Be there for his family in a way that would change their lives instead of being a burden on them.

Walker worried at the idea all night before finally giving in.

He threw his guitar in the back of the truck along wi
and went to say farewell to his family.

One more shot.

One more try.

He had to take it.

~

New York Times Bestselling Author Vivian Arend invites you to Heart Falls. These contemporary ranchers live in a tiny town in south central Alberta, rucked into the rolling foothills. Enjoy the ride as they each find their happily-ever-afters.

~

The Stones of Heart Falls
A Rancher's Heart
A Rancher's Song
A Rancher's Bride

~

ABOUT THE AUTHOR

With over 2 million books sold, Vivian Arend is a New York Times and USA Today bestselling author of over 50 contemporary and paranormal romance books, including the Six Pack Ranch and Granite Lake Wolves.

Her books are all standalone reads with no cliffhangers. They're humorous yet emotional, with sexy-times and happily-ever-afters. Vivian pretty much thinks she's got the best job in the world, and she's looking forward to giving readers more HEAs. She lives in B.C. Canada with her husband of many years and a fluffy attack Shih-tzu named Luna who ignores everyone except when treats are deployed

Printed in Great Britain
by Amazon